The New Mrs D

By Heather Hill

The New Mrs D
Heather Hill

Published by:
Fledgling Press Ltd,
7 Lennox St.,
Edinburgh,
EH4 1QB

www.fledglingpress.co.uk

ISBN 9781905916986

Printed and bound by: MBM Print SCS Ltd, Glasgow

www.hell4heather.com
Cover design: D16.co.uk

MIX
Paper from
responsible sources
FSC® C117931

'There is a word in the Greek language for which there is no English equivalent. It is 'meraki' and it means 'doing something with soul, creativity or love – when you put something of yourself into what you are doing'.
– *Translating the Untranslatable*, NPR Books.

About The Author

Heather Hill - comedy writer and mum of five (not the band) lives in Scotland and is one of a rare kind: the rare kind being one of the 0.5% of females that is ever-so-slightly colour blind. She is known to have been prevented from leaving the house with blue eyebrows on at least one occasion.

You can visit Heather's blog and send her a message at www. hell4heather.com – she loves to hear from readers, especially if you put 'cake' in the subject line. Or catch her on Twitter, where she is still found sharing photos of her breakfast. Follow Heather – and her breakfast – @hell4heather

Acknowledgements

I owe a huge debt of gratitude to Paul Johnson, the first person to kick me over the starting post by dotting my t's and correcting my 'eyes'. Also to him, I am grateful for a short, true story about how funny Greek bread can be. Thank you, my friend.

To Professor Lionel Wilson, Emeritus Professor of Earth & Planetary Sciences at Lancaster Environment Centre, Professor Willy Aspinall, School of Earth Sciences, Bristol University and Dr Wendy Stovall, U.S. Geological Survey, California, thank you for your collective thoughts, expertise and hilarious anecdotes on the subject of volcanoes.

To Nick Elliott, thank you for offering to tell me how to blow up a small country, a village, a house or an oven . . . and how to escape on a moped afterwards.

To literary agent, Hannah Ferguson, who first believed in me and Mrs D. Thank you for your unfailing optimism, advice and encouragement.

To Flora Napier of Blueprint Editing, Edinburgh. You gave me confidence and a much needed kick up the bum. I couldn't have done it without you.

To Glasgow artist, Dennis Bannister, who let me sit in on his painting class in the name of research, all for the price of a bottle of gin.

To the first person to read the original, scrappy draft – my lovely niece Laura Fenwick. Even after three reads, she still came back for more.
To my brother, Barry Smith, thank you for so many things; but most of all, for your chequebook.

To my extraordinarily supportive author pals, Fleur Ferris, Amanda Prowse and Mark Leggatt – I don't know where I'd be without any of you. You made me laugh, cry and get off the floor when I thought I was sinking. Because YOU know what it's like.

To my brilliant husband, Stephen, who has worked extra shifts for two years, starved, saved, laughed and cried with me in order to see my writing dream come true. You are my life and my rock; thank God for you. And thank you for my new whisky addiction.

And to five young people who drove me to do it, my children Becki, Ryan, Liam, Kyle and Luci, who make me proud every day. I hope I manage to do the same for you.

Love you all X

For David Dando
This is all your fault; and I will always
love you for it.
Shine on you crazy diamond.
TOY x

Preface

'I remember clearly and will never forget the golden moment when I revealed my truth. Out through the locked up and suppressed little voice hidden deep down within, I allowed myself to say, "I always feel as if I need to give people what they want."

It was almost as if lightning struck and the clouds parted at the same time. I sat there comfortably in the chair of my therapist's office, and with a deep breath I knew that "it" was over. I did not know what "it" was or the amount of work and change that would follow, but I knew that I was ready and willing.

I grew up co-dependent. From the influence of an alcoholic and narcissistic father to the string of narcissistic relationships formed afterward, my identity evolved through who I was to others and what I had given to them.

A relationship with a narcissist defines your existence as not your own but as a part of theirs. Others saw me as shy and nice, but I did not realise that I was lost and without balance.

I wanted others to be their authentic selves, truthful and free, but I could not do that for myself so I continued giving up and giving in. Not all was bad—life is beautiful in each form—but I knew I would need to learn something different, as I always dealt with fears and anxieties.

So I have learned something different. I had to dig down to reveal my true, authentic, beautiful self.'

— Anna Puchalski

Chapter One

Bearded lady, 41, slightly used, with
squishy, puffball belly subtly disguised by
low-lying nipples, seeks man with GSOH, porn
allergies and willingness to share razor.

As I finished the last pistachio and gazed over the blue
Aegean Sea, a promise of marital happiness glinted
back at me in the form of that annoying bastard – the
romantic evening sunset.

'Oh sod off!' I told it. It didn't.

Neither did the couple on the next balcony. They continued
to suck face with even noisier gusto than I could muster
while stripping a Magnum ice lolly of its crackly shell.
Ooh, Magnums. Before I ate one, usually after one of my
frequent moments of relationship misery, I would
separate the chocolate from the creamy vanilla
inside. A marriage made in heaven, destroyed in my
hands. Funny that.

A dark figure on waterskis appeared, ripping across
(and ruining) the previously smooth, 'let's stand close and
drink this all in together darling' Aegean stillness.

'Good!' I thought, my mind a delicious, wine-fuelled haze.

Then, 'I wonder if he's single?'

If he could read my thoughts from afar I'm pretty sure waterski guy, who I had already decided was a Hollywood-smiling, Gerard Butler looky-likey, would say, 'Actually, I'm on my incredibly romantic honeymoon having the time of my life, just like you.'

Sighing, I picked up my faux lonely-hearts ad scrawl and added:

Enjoys expensive dining funded by proceeds of
very recently pawned jewellery.

So, Devastation, we meet again. And I can't *wait* for you to meet my mother, who is about to find out the £8,000 she spent on my wedding had maybe not been her best investment. All thanks to the love of my life, David Dando.

Mrs Bernice Annabel Dando. Christ. Why hadn't I spotted beforehand the hidden warning in my new initials? Mrs B. A. D. Idea. We had been just four days into our honeymoon when I'd picked up my new husband's mobile and snuck off into the bathroom as he slept, hoping to search for the taverna a tour rep had told me was the most romantic spot on the island. But instead of the eatery I was hoping to come across, I found an internet history full of video 'eat me outeries' which David had almost certainly cum across.

I'd only half-glanced as the first page flashed up, my eyes distracted by the reflection of the newly-wed vixen in the mirror. 'It's now; it's time,' I had told myself. 'Today, I'm going to knock his damn socks off.' I'd squirted my neck with David's favourite perfume (the one I hated), pushed my boobs back into the cups of my nightie and winked at my reflection.

It had been four days since we were married, yet in all that time he just hadn't quite been able to get in the mood.

'It's just all the stress from the wedding, Binnie. It'll be alright after I've chilled out and released some tension for a day or two.'

I'd flattened my bed-head hair and admired myself in my new, semi see-through nightie; all the while playing out a sexy, early morning seduction in my mind as David lay snoring in the next room. I'd whispered a husky, 'Hello, Mrs D,' and blown myself a kiss before my gaze fell back down to the screen. Which was where I met the naked, stretched out, legs akimbo torso of 'Josephine – the Nymphotast'. I'd blinked and stumbled backwards, stunned and disbelieving. Not again; not now! It was as though the phone had delivered a short, sharp electric shock. Scrolling the web page up and up, because surely this must be some mistake, I'd felt a familiar pain. Only this time I had an overwhelming rush of anxiety too. I'd just got married. I'd just said, 'till death do us part' to this man in front of everyone! The phone had clattered off the floor tiles as my legs gave way, sending me sliding down to a broken heap beside it. Somewhere in the dizzy distance, there had been a dull *thud, thud, thud*. Someone calling my name.

'Binnie, are you okay? What happened in there? Let me in!'

I'd lain there staring into space, my stomach threatening to throw an early morning cup of hotel room coffee back out. I'd heard heavy, rasping breaths. Mine. As my heart had hammered, I'd turned my head to one side and caught my reflection again in the floor to ceiling mirror. The seductive temptress had vanished, and all that remained was a pathetic, love-starved blob in a pink nightie. The woman that nobody wanted.

He'd found his tension release on our honeymoon alright, it just hadn't been with me. But then, why should I be surprised? I'd already discovered – countless times during our six-year relationship – that he'd been viewing porn when he could have been making love to me.

As I'd sat on the cold, hard, bathroom floor, my heart was bursting, yet the tears just wouldn't come. I'd willed myself to cry, but inside I felt cold, like somehow I had known this was coming. I *had* to know; he'd done it all before. Of course, *this* is what he'd been doing. This explained what he'd been getting up to each morning while I strolled to the local shop for our day-old English-language newspaper. On our bloody honeymoon! He'd joked about my leaving him in the room for a while so he could have a shit in private . . . But he'd just wanted to *be* a shit in private.

Stupid, gullible me.

Now, as it turned out, ours had been a marriage of convenience. He'd conveniently forgotten to tell me that, despite all his pre-nuptial promises, he hadn't in fact given up populating his internet browser with a video library of his many and varied kinks. And *I* had conveniently forgotten that, as a somewhat weathered 40-something mother-of-two who no longer wore her tits up to her chin, I was unlikely to keep him interested in me 'till death did us part' anyway. Life begins at 40DD. Period.

But he'd made me believe he could change. There had been a year of nothing to worry about. A whole year! No internet history filth stumbled upon, no finding him creeping into bed, spent, at 2am and no elongated showers after another repeat episode of *Baywatch*.

Yet in all that time he had continued to 'suffer' from impotence, though only with me it now transpired. With 'Slutty Josephine, the Nymphotast' I imagined he'd been a veritable Colossus complete with accompanying fireworks. The scrunched up, crusty contents of the wastepaper basket in our honeymoon suite said it all. Yesterday, those tissues were testimony to a bout of hay fever brought on by Greece's glorious flora and fauna. Today they were evidence of my new husband's betrayal.

After what seemed like an hour of him swearing he was going to 'find out who had been doing all this rubbish on his phone' he'd finally given in and admitted guilt.

'I was watching it for us, Binnie,' came the excuse after this latest find. 'It was just a means to perk myself up a bit.'

With the benefit of embarrassing hindsight I realise my screamed reply had most likely been heard by Suck-Face couple next door.

'*Thanks* David. Thanks for explaining that you have to ogle some perfectly sculpted 20-year-old before you can face having sex with me! Only, you're forgetting one teeny, tiny detail.' (I even did that awful wiggly thing with my pinkie finger, just to emphasise the point.) 'We haven't actually had any sex, remember?'

That had made him wince. Even I couldn't believe I'd been so cruel. I was hurting, I was angry, yet, unbeknown to him, deep down I was lost.

He'd spent the next hour trying to convince me how sexy I was to him, just like before. I felt almost inexplicably numb.

'You promised to love me in sickness and in health,' he had cried. 'Well, this is my sickness! The only thing that gets me off is porn. It's just . . .' At this point his face had screwed up and he'd been unable to meet my gaze as he delivered a final blow to my heart. 'I love you, Binnie, I do. This is not about you. This is just something guys *do*.'

He'd reached for my hand, but I pulled away.

'Something guys *do*?' I'd said.

'Well . . . come on, Binnie. It isn't personal. It's not like I'm messing about with a real woman.'

'You're not?' I held up his phone again, revealing Josephine in all her banana-toting glory. 'So this is an object to you, not a person?'

He fidgeted and lowered his eyes. 'Well, yes, for want of a better way to put it. She's real to someone but to me, sure, she's an object to get off on.'

I stared at him in disbelief. 'David, where is the man I love?'

'I'm right here for you, where I've always been. This is nothing. It means nothing.'

'YOU HAVEN'T BEEN HERE FOR ME,' I yelled, throwing the phone at him. 'You've been getting off with HER!'

Six years of bottled up fury and anguish were unleashed from a place inside me I hadn't known existed before that moment. I'd told him he was, quite literally, a jerk-off. Then, I'd told him to something-else off before heaving his suitcase at him. There would be no forgive and forget, unlike every time before. Maybe he was right; this was just something men do. Yet, I just knew I couldn't stand it anymore. If that meant being alone for the rest of my life, so be it.

'Get out, David. I just can't look at you right now. You've made me sick inside.'

'But Binnie, this is our honeymoon! We're supposed to do this together. You're my wife and I can't be without you! We can work on this, I know we can.' He fell onto his knees and pulled me towards him again, hugging my waist and sobbing, 'Please, *please* don't do this.'

I pushed him away, still unable to cry.

'GET OUT!'

It hurt to watch him beg. I'd felt a strange mixture of anger and guilt. Maybe it was my fault for letting myself go. Maybe I was being an insecure prude. But as I had fallen back onto the honeymoon bed, where only yesterday the maid had left a cascade of red rose petals arranged in the shape of a heart, I'd held my head in my hands and at last the tears had come. Suddenly, like some out of body experience a person might have in between life and death, I saw myself as a bystander might: a sad, love-drunk woman believing all her partner's lies. It made sense to feel that way because right at that moment I *did* feel dead – dead inside. The New Mrs D, with the same old Mr D. I'd been feeling sorry for him and making up excuses in my mind for his terrible behaviour for too, too long. I had allowed him to do this to me. I'd made it all happen. I'd married a man who saw me as undesirable.

'But . . . what about . . . us?' David had stammered, his eyes full of tears.

'I don't know, honestly I don't.'

'Will you just . . . what about our envelopes? Can we at least open the envelopes?'

Again outside of myself, I'd watched a smiling me from the past: an excited wife-to-be writing my secret honeymoon wish before pushing it into an envelope. Sadly for David, it hadn't been, 'please turn out to be an arsing liar.'

'Oh, David,' I said. 'It's all so irrelevant now. Please, just go.'

'But when will I see you?'

Looking into his doleful, hazel brown eyes − the same ones I'd fallen for long ago in happier times − had made my heart ache all the more. 'Soon,' I'd told him. 'For now, I just want to be by myself.'

I'd stood up, pointed to the door and at last, he had left.

Screwing up the empty pistachio bag and tossing it into the waste paper basket with the tissues, I picked up David's still sealed envelope containing his honeymoon wish and turned it over in my hands before flinging it back in to my suitcase. I just needed to be without him right now. Staring out into space, still in the lacy nightie I'd been planning to seduce him in, I reflected on this latest reason for breaking yet more promises.

'It was just a means to perk me up a bit.'

Attempting to perk David up a bit had been all I'd thought about these last few years. Just as my own libido reached its peak, I'd found a man in a permanent trough. But there wasn't a wild, wanton thing I hadn't been willing to try to get him in the mood and prove to both him, and myself, that I was no prude.

I'd stripped naked in the garden and, despite feeling like a pot-bellied pig, rolled in mud (like the mud wrestling women I'd found in his computer history) − 'Oh, er, isn't it a little bit cold for this, Binnie?' I'd dressed like a prostitute, donning a short skirt, no knickers, fishnets and high heels while waiting for him to come home. 'What on earth? I mean . . . Wow, you look hot! Just give me a few minutes, I've been bursting for the bog all afternoon.' As he trundled off to the bathroom with a copy of the day's paper, I had waited but, suffice to say, he hadn't been able to rise to the occasion anyway. All that if-you-can't-beat-'em-join-'em effort, only to feel like a very uncomfortable frump in she-wolf's clothing. Then there was the terrified look on his face every time he found me all dressed up and raring to go. I was always left feeling demanding and silly, when all I wanted was a chance for a normal sex life. Nothing outrageous. No seven nights a week and twice daily. Just *some* sex.

Tossing the envelope he'd begged me to open back into my suitcase, I gave an almighty sigh, and the waistband of my bikini pants rolled below my belly for the third time that day. With no-one here to care, I had stopped sucking in. I argued with fashion designers in my head. 'Why the hell can't you make pants your average size 16 woman can sit down in?'

My tears had long since subsided and from my broken self, a bitter, cynical woman I hardly recognised had emerged. It was she who had raided the mini bar before starting on the snacks, leaving her stomach swollen with a confusing concoction of emotions, four mini bottles of wine and a bag of pistachios. That's why my pants wouldn't stay up.

Sex with David had usually been a disappointment – almost non-existent, actually – so, why the hell had I married him?

I did it for love.

I did it for love.

That has to be the most devastating phrase in the English language for any woman. Along with 'there's no wine left', and 'click here for Josephine's cum shots'.

Every time I'd caught him using porn in the past, I'd

dithered over whether this was his problem or mine. Was this a good enough reason to quit on my relationship? My first husband, Michael, had loved me for all of two years before moving on to someone more exciting and yes, this time I wanted to prove I could 'do' marriage. There was no sex, sure, but David had a problem and I thought we had been making it better together. David was broken and I had thought I was going to be his saviour – the wife-in-shining-armour to fix him.

'Do you, David, take this woman to be your lawfully wedded wife? Do you promise to love, honour and cherish her daily until about ten thirty at night when BabeStation starts?'

Some people believe there is a silent witness to your life inside of you. This, they say, is the part of you that makes you able to recall what you dreamed about when your brain was asleep. It is the tiny, almost imperceptible voice in your head that tells you not to do something when you are about to make a huge and dangerous mistake. Well, mine is broken.

I shook my head in self-deprecation and peered up again to seek out Gerard Butler, who was now bobbing around in the water, having fallen off his skis. As the speedboat turned back and began to circle him, I watched as he flailed around, up to his neck in the rippling and heaving of its wake, struggling for breath, knowing exactly how he felt.

David and I had gone through hospital tests where he'd been given a clean bill of sexual health, and months of therapy, only to reach the conclusion he had dulled his senses with porn and we decided together that the only answer was complete abstention from it. He'd agreed, led me home and just plain pretended to quit. For my part in this whole mess, I had believed him.

Why, why, *why* did I agree to marry him?

Sooner or later, I would have to go home, face up to what had happened and hear this question from everyone else. But, to admit my second marriage had begun to fail in its first week, all because of what many would consider 'harmless porn browsing' would take a lot of courage.

If I decided to call it a day, what would I say to my friends and family? 'He left me' or 'I threw him out'. Which explanation would make me look less like the bad person? Of course, I shouldn't care less, yet I hated the idea of being judged. I had already asked myself all the questions people were going to have for me.

'You dumped your husband just for looking at porn? That's what men do!'

'How insecure is *she*?'

'Why didn't you just watch it with him?'

It was going to be hard telling people that porn was my sole reason for giving up on David. They didn't know what I now suspected to be true: that any chance we had of a normal sex life had been wiped out by his 'me time' for six years. Who would go through with a wedding knowing all of this? How could I have been so foolish?

Idiot. It didn't matter what anyone else thought of me at this moment, no-one could hate me more than I hated myself.

It was safe to assume, from the fact that no-one back home had guessed anything was wrong, that David had gone into hiding so no-one would suspect there was a problem. He'd probably taken a flight back to England and was now holed up in some hotel room to avoid being seen, with a laptop and a phone, wondering which one he fancied the most tonight.

I felt fat and dowdy – the opposite of the ideal, sexy

woman men cannot seem to resist. My body was old, old, old.

Damn him. And damn Josephine the Nymphotast, with her beach ball tits and Barbie doll waist, who somehow experiences scream-out-loud pleasure three seconds before Shaved-Arsed, Utility Repairman enters her. (What the bloody hell was a 'Nymphotast' anyway?) Damn the 'call me and cum' Freeview television babes with their youthful, perfect bodies, who wiggle half-naked on our screens, post watershed, trying to shake free of their own arse cheeks. The same ones I'd caught David watching while I'd been waiting, willing and ready for him in our bed! Because sex sells! Pah! And men are buying as their wives carry on in ignorant bliss. Well, not this wife. Not anymore. If only hindsight was less 'hind' and more 'sight'. Only now could I see how gullible I had been. Only now − after our wedding!

Damn him and damn my self-propelled roll-down bikini pants. (I pulled them back up again.) I had other choices. Who knew? And I choose to hold myself right now. I choose to stop feeling scared, gullible, stupid and afraid of being alone, even though, okay, technically I was on my own and in a foreign land. Is it ever too late to decide to get it right for once? Sod David Dando and sod his lies. I'm staying right here in Greece. I am strong, independent and . . . and . . . something else! *I wonder if they have any more of this wine?* Moreover, I am going ahead with every one of the fun-filled activities he and I had planned for the next ten days. (Except the scary scuba diving thingy. Bloody *Jaws* had ruined any enjoyment I'd ever had of swimming in the sea.)

What was I saying? Ah yes, I am *strong*. I am *fierce*. I am *woman*.

Who the hell needs a husband anyway? Even on your honeymoon.

Chapter Two

Please Binnie, I need to speak to you. The
sex is a problem, I know. But I've changed
for you just as I promised. I do desire you.
I do!

After blocking David's number on my mobile after
this fourteenth text had woken me up, a new message
notification appeared on the home screen. I clicked it open
and immediately wished I hadn't. It was from Smother.

You'd think after having spent so much money
on your daughter's big day, she'd at least
contact you to say how her honeymoon is
going.

I felt myself shudder − not really knowing why − and
deleted it. How I needed a mother right now, the kind I
could call and cry to, admitting the wedding had been a
terrible mistake and all of the reasons why. But I didn't
have one of those. I had a unique and rare kind of mum,
the last person I wanted to go to in a crisis. The kind who
enjoyed a drama − and none more so than one of mine.

I clicked the television on, hoping to find any non-romantic or funny programme to take my mind off things, and settled for the three and three-quarter hours epic that is *Ben Hur*. Sorry, Smother, the guilt will have to go on hold for a while. Just for once, I need to look no further than taking care of me.

As Judah Ben Hur fought off the desire to start a mass slave rebellion, I rubbed my soggy, swollen eyes and pondered the more ambiguous question of what dress to wear for a solo expedition to the honeymoon hotel restaurant and how to get the 'tears of my doom' swelling round my eyes to go down. Marching into the bathroom, I splashed water on my face before drying it with a towel that smelled of David. Then sunk to my knees and cried my heart out, right there on the floor.

In the background, the television was still blaring.

'Your eyes are full of hate, 41. That's good. Hate keeps a man alive, it gives him strength.'

Pulling myself up I looked at my eyes in the bathroom mirror, still bloodshot from bawling. All I could do to get through this evening was to stop thinking about how much I loved David and keep reminding myself how angry I was.

'Are you going to jump in the pool with that bloody sarong on?'

I straightened my shoulders and flushed crimson. It was the first morning of our honeymoon and I was sitting on the edge of my sunbed next to the busy hotel pool, with a towel around my shoulders and the sarong hiding my midriff from view. I could feel people around us watching me.

'Come on, woman,' David carried on, waving me into

the water beside him. 'Just get up off your fat arse and get in. Nobody's looking at you, you daft moo.'

I recoiled at the word 'fat' and bit my lip, my eyes welling up. It was our honeymoon and he'd called me 'fat'. I was The New Mrs Fat. 'Telephone call for Mrs Fat.' 'Hey, how's married life, Mrs Fat?' 'Has anyone seen Mrs Fat today?'

'Oh, don't upset yourself,' he laughed. 'I'm only joking, you know that. Come on, my beautiful, new wife. Get in.'

A nimble young woman strode past between us, in nothing but a tiny pair of sea green bikini briefs and a pair of flip flops. I watched as David followed her with his eyes, doubting whether he could tell me the colour of her bikini briefs. I felt a familiar lump in my throat. *It's normal, it's normal. We're married, not dead.*

'I think I'll just go get another cocktail,' I told him. 'Back in a mo.'

It was half past eight by the time I picked myself up to get ready and pulled on a forgiving, floaty dress I'd treated myself to on the first day of the holiday. Squaring up to my reflection in the mirror, I said aloud, 'Not bad at all, Mrs Robinson,' before telling myself 'That bastard isn't having my fidelity a moment longer – any more than I had his.' I was impervious; Ben Hur . . . in a little black dress.

With my blonde, wavy locks dried and three coats of blotch-camouflaging make-up applied, I swallowed my angst and made for the lift, speeding up past Suck-Face couple's door. God help me if I bumped into them and they saw it was me who had been doing all of the shouting and screaming during The David Eviction.

Feeling reprieved at getting past room 718 without incident and, seeing its doors about to close, I dived into the lift. Which is where I joined Mr and Mrs Holdy-Hands. That was all I needed now, to witness someone else's marital bliss in an enclosed space. Just great!

'Hi,' I said, almost unable to bear the stab of pain their happy togetherness brought me. As they both nodded a reply, I shook it off, repeating in my head, *'I am strong' 'I am confident' 'I look amazing in my beautiful, new dress.'* I had to get through this one night. All I had to do to begin was put one foot in front of the other.

Stepping out to the moonlit, open-air restaurant, I breathed in, brushed my fringe from my eyes and strode into the middle of the busy restaurant to find a seat. It was then I realised I was surrounded. There was a reason David and I had chosen to stay here and not with the rest of the adventure tour group we'd booked with. This was a romantic, honeymoon hotel.

Everywhere couples were gazing into each other's eyes, clinking glasses and toasting their successful, loving relationships, almost as if they knew mine was in the toilet. *Could this evening get any harder, God?*

Yes, it could.

Just as I was beginning to refocus on finding a table, a man moved a chair for his wife just in front of me, kissing her shoulder as she passed him to sit down. I turned in another direction, swallowing hard as I took in the scene before me – this hotel was a lovers' paradise. Everyone was still going about their normal, happy lives and most likely looking forward to having rampant, holiday sex tonight – even with each other! This place had no tables for one, or an uneven three. I was all alone, in honeymoon central.

Just three nights earlier, David had looked into my eyes across one of these very candlelit tables, telling me how much he couldn't wait to get me back to our room. We were ecstatic newly-weds, giggling like teenagers as we rushed away early, having guzzled a bottle of champagne. And later, out on the balcony of our honeymoon suite, in the warm night air and under the romantic, Greek moonlight . . . I'd beat him twice at gin rummy. It was all I could do to keep my mind off all the sex we weren't having.

'Waitress?'

The Shoulder-Kisser was waving my way. I moved back, turning to let whoever he was calling past. There was no-one behind me.

'Hello? Waitress?' he shouted again, snapping his fingers.

'Excuse me?' I laughed, pointing to my chest in a 'surely you don't mean me' way. Even though he wasn't smiling, I threw him a quizzical smile and turned away – only to see a woman in an identical dress to mine weaving in and out of tables with a tray full of drinks. I looked around and spotted another identically-dressed woman. And another. Finally, a waitress brushed past to take the man's order, but not before stopping to give me a sympathetic smile.

Maybe it was a congratulatory one. 'Well done, Binnie,' it said. 'Your sexy, new dress is hotel waiting staff standard issue.'

Suddenly my head hurt again. What was I thinking, coming down here all by myself without David? What had I done?

I can't do this. I can't. I can't.

Face flushed and heart racing, I grabbed hold of the waitress's shoulder as she was rushing away to collect the man's order and whispered, 'Is it possible to get wine . . . er . . . lots of wine – and dinner – sent to my room?

Chapter Three

```
One   of   the   local   dishes   is   called
Stifado.   Tried   not   to   stare   at   him
too   much   whilst   at   dinner   with   Mr   D.
```

I posted my 'everything-is-normal' Facebook status, attached a picture of some nameless Greek hunk I could do with meeting right now, and sighed. By the looks of the newly pebble-dashed toilet in my hotel room, Mrs D had drunk this tiny island dry last night. Any thought of Greek beef stew made me feel like rushing back in for another round of vomiting. The absence of Mr D was something to be left out of my updates for now, so my family back home would believe everything was rosy, if only for Sally and Beth's sake.

Despite my daughters' approval of David, they had been unenthusiastic and, I sensed, a little embarrassed at the prospect of my getting married again.

'Why bother at your age, Mum?'

It was all I could do to stop imagining the Grim Reaper at the end of my bed with a 'Get It While You Can' sign.

If this was all going tits up, telling them both the whole disastrous story of my sex life wasn't an option. They just couldn't bear to consider my sexuality in any way, shape or form. My thoughts wandered to a recent conversation with my own mother, just before the wedding, and I understood.

'Binnie, can I please come to yours for a bath today? This walk-in shower is fine but I have terrible trouble with some weird swellings on my bits. The only thing that soothes me is a nice, long soak.'

I took her off the speakerphone so she couldn't hear David's screams in the background.

'Nooooooo! Goddddddddddd! Pleeeeeeeeeeeeeeease!'

The final realisation that now, to my kids, I was my mother, had happened on the day of the wedding, whilst dashing naked from the bathroom to my bedroom and bumping into them somewhere in between.

Laughing, Sal had said, 'Never mind, Mum. I've seen worse, you know.'

To which Beth quipped, 'HOW exactly have you seen worse?'

That wonderful, quirky, Bethsome humour; I loved her for it.

As nausea overtook me, I stripped for my shower and glanced in the mirror at thick, dimpled thighs that couldn't possibly have belonged to the former fastest 800 metre runner in my high school athletics team. David had seen me cry myself to sleep many times, wracked with feelings of inadequacy over my body after finding him ogling someone else's. This morning I felt so sick, I knew it was time to stop abusing my body. It wasn't going to help me feel better.

With most of our problems seeming so far away in

the past, our wedding day had been the happiest day of my life. Within an hour of the ceremony, I had changed my Facebook username to 'Mrs David Dando', as if Facebook updates were all I lived to do, as necessary to life as breathing in and out. Why didn't I just write:

```
I'm not saying I take my phone everywhere,
but can I just ask one quick question? Do
I take this man to be my lawfully wedded
husband?
```

Although I was desperate to free myself from all the negative emotions swimming around in my head, I cursed my protruding belly as I showered. This hated body that belongs to the only one of two sisters who hadn't got a belly button ring – in the knowledge that every time she sat down the damn thing would have disappeared, sucked into a ductile cave whilst simultaneously acting as a 'Give Way' sign for her knicker elastic. If only it were possible to scrub off all the lumpy parts that made David not want me. How could I make all these thoughts stop?

Tears flowed freely under the spray and I washed them away and hugged myself. 'Bernice,' I said, 'it's time to love yourself better.' I held myself for a long time, feeling the dull, gnawing ache in my belly from yesterday's excesses and finally sighed, before jumping out to get on with the day.

I can do this. I can!

I wrapped myself in a fluffy white towel and walked back into the bedroom, pausing to pick up my faux lonely hearts ad and toss it into the bin. I picked up the pen once more to make a new list. A list of commandments – from me to me. I needed something to work towards, to get me through the rest of the holiday and onwards for life. And I needed it now.

The 'Five Daily Steps to a New Bernice' Plan
1. Thou shalt do one thing a day that scares the crap out of you.
2. Thou shalt never again indulge in negative self-talk.
3. Thou shalt cease looking in magnified mirrors for evidence of beard. Please refer to previous point.
4. Thou shalt not neglect thy pelvic floor. Ten minutes a day AND NO LESS!
5. Thou shalt remember that God is all around . . . And she doesn't like swearing.

I heaved a heavy sigh and vowed not to let David sway me from my new path of righteousness again, before typing in a sixth.

6. When life throws shit at you, grow great, big, fuck off roses.

There goes the fifth commandment.

The girls – my wonderful, supportive girls – frequently told me I wasn't as big as I thought.

No, 'Hey Mum, you're not fat', but a teasing, 'Okay, you're a bit curvy but not in a needing-a-crane-to-go-out kind of way.'.

Smother would tell me I was overweight at any given opportunity and in such a way as to make me unsure whether I was being insulted or not. I thought of the last email she sent me:

Darling, I have this article for you to read and DON'T THINK I'M TELLING YOU YOU'RE FAT BECAUSE I'M NOT. It's just these new pills that I've been on have made me shed a stone in a month! You must try them!

I loved how she used capitals to emphasise the point

she was trying to make, knowing full well my brain would pick out the words 'YOU'RE FAT' all by itself.

My persistent queries to my friends of, 'Do I look fat in this?' were invariably met with 'You're lovely as you are.' Didn't they know *that* answer just plays a tape in a broken woman's head that says, 'I'm acceptable, normal and not at all extraordinary?'

And, dammit, I want to be extraordinary!

On reflection, it appeared that my ideal world would contain: a man who doesn't lie and friends that occasionally will. Too much of my time had been wasted trying to work out what turns men on. Wasted − thanks to six years of living with someone who had no desire for me.

How would I ever break another failed marriage to my daughters? They themselves were just starting out in the world of relationships and needed me to be a motherly fountain of good advice. How could I face telling them I'd failed again? And as for my own mother? It just wasn't worth contemplating.

'Mum, there's something I have to tell you.'

My mother stood aside to let me in her front door and frowned, brushing my hair down with her hand. 'Jeez,' she complained. 'You look like you've been dragged through a hedge backwards. Where are the children?'

'They're at school, Mum, it's Thursday. Look, something has happened . . .'

'Have you been crying? Oh Christ, what have you and Michael been rowing about now? You do give that poor man a hard time.'

She bent down to straighten the front door mat which I had dislodged from its uniform state in my haste to get in out of the rain. I stood shivering behind her, drenched and with no coat on, having bolted over from my house, waiting to be hugged, or at least offered a towel.

'Mum,' I said, through chattering teeth. 'I need to talk to you. I found this catalogue in the loft and inside there were these letters and anyway it turns out that . . .'

'Ooh, talking of catalogues,' she interrupted, straightening up again and peering through the narrow glass window of her now closed front door. 'I need to go and speak to Jenny across the road. Do you know she owes me three week's catalogue money? Damn cheek. Like I can afford to pay her debts! Why don't you go in the kitchen and make us a cup of tea? I'll be back in a jiffy.'

Reaching over to the coat hook for her jacket, she took off into the street I'd just come in from without looking back. As the door slammed shut behind her, I told it:

'Michael's been having an affair.'

After testing the hotel's less than efficient plumbing system with at least one bottle of the previous night's wine, I washed my face, brushed my teeth and stared bleary-eyed at the person in the mirror, wondering who the hell she was. Jeez, I had to cut back on the booze. But, however terrible I felt right now, I was determined to get on with the holiday programme. I had to.

David and I had planned a special honeymoon of firsts, choosing an adventure excursion company recommended by a lifelong friend of his, who had moved out to a tiny, not so commercial Greek island to work for them. A bachelor at forty-eight, several years ago Chris had begun spending six months in Greece teaching painting to tourists and six months back home in Nottinghamshire, where he had an art gallery. As David and I had sifted through the brochure, full of pictures of things neither of us had ever done before we'd agreed to have our very first class learning to paint with Chris. We'd both been looking forward to seeing him, especially because his being in Greece at this time of year meant he had missed the wedding.

The rest of our planned experiences were nothing too insane, just a series of mini-adventures and experiences for us to pick from. We had cut out the ones that appealed, then folded and thrown them into a fez. The same one I'd sported while wearing a pair of see-through knickers and not a lot else to perform the Zorba dance on the day the honeymoon travel tickets had arrived. Classy. Really, really classy.

'Oh, you can kiss me on a Monday, a Monday, a Monday is very, very, good!' I belted out.

'I can't kiss you on any day if you're in Turkey – where they actually wear the fez – and I'm in Greece.'

'Oh,' I sulked. 'How am I to know the fez has nothing to do with Greece? Call the Geographical Hats Society!'

'You plonker,' he'd laughed, knocking it off my head, but (sigh) leaving my knickers on.

Then we played the honeymoon raffle, taking turns to draw out a full itinerary of adventures for our trip. It was all my idea, another of life's new adventures. Maybe it was my approaching middle age, maybe the prospect of getting married again, but in the past few years I'd developed a desire to really find myself and cram just about as much life into whatever time I had left. Turning forty did that to you. One day you feel a world away from old age and the next you are realising that, if you're lucky, you've reached the fifty percent of your life mark. I looked back over the fifty percent behind me, and saw nothing, except the incredible experience of the birth and raising of two wonderful girls, for me to feel proud about. Not one thing. And right then I knew nothing I'd done so far in my professional life had ever seemed to fit. So, I took to the vast library of self-help books out there and began to devour everything and share it with a less-than-enamoured David. He agreed to the new experiences, but begged me to stop reading 'you either get it or you don't' paragraphs from Dr Phil aloud. This honeymoon was meant to have been to be a fun, romantic start to our life together for David and, unbeknown to him, the beginning of a secret quest I'd set myself to unpick my life's defining moments - the things that had happened along the way to change me forever. Funny that the honeymoon itself should turn out to be one of them.

'Can we at least open the envelopes?'

David's last plea popped into my head uninvited. A secret, 'let's do this together' suggestion written in private, sealed inside envelopes then exchanged with each other, to be opened on the penultimate day of the honeymoon. My envelope from David was still in my suitcase and was, not without a dab of irony, tucked under my sexy, now-redundant honeymoon negligee. No doubt, his suggestion was to watch *Debbie Does Dallas* together. Or maybe – just maybe – he had opened his heart in a way I hadn't seen him do before. But why open it now? What was the point? I couldn't – wouldn't – let myself read it. I had to focus and pull myself together for the painting lesson.

I had been facing the prospect of seeing Chris again with some trepidation, mainly because I feared looking a prat – neither myself nor David could draw for toffee;

a fact proven time and again on games nights at home when the girls had destroyed us at Pictionary. Painting lessons with David, I imagined, would be as funny as trying to guess *An American Werewolf in London* from his hysterical, child-like sketches.

'*The Muppets Take Manhattan*?'

'No, no!' (He had drawn something resembling Animal holding the US flag next to a clock tower.)

'Once Upon a Time in America with the Muppets?' Beth would always join in on our turn.

'Aaaarrrgggghhh!'

'Aaaarrrgggghhh? Is that the first letter of the first or the second word?'

Now, there was another reason for my apprehension about seeing Chris again. How could I explain appearing there, on my honeymoon, without David?

I had no idea how was he going to be with me, yet I really wanted to see a friendly face. He was now the only person I knew on the island and I felt sure David would have been way too embarrassed and proud to have turned up there. I liked Chris; and I wanted to take his art class as planned.

All I had to do now was work out how to get to his villa. For years I'd been unable to get back behind the wheel but now I wanted . . . no, I needed that independence.

'Can I help you, Mrs Dando?'

The receptionist using my new married name gave me another unwelcome jolt of pain. As newly-weds, you go to any lengths to hear and use your new name. Except when you decide to call time on your marriage four days later.

'I love you, Mrs Dando.'

And I love you, Mr Dando.

'Would you pass me the salt, please, Mrs Dando?'

Why are someone else's squirty-cream covered boobs looking at me from the browser on your mobile, Mr Dando?

'Mrs Dando?'

'Mrs Dando!'

The receptionist's voice snapped me back to the present. Right. Time for me to try something new that wasn't on the itinerary; taking to the open road, alone, for the first time in years.

'Yes,' I said. 'Can you tell me where I go to hire a moped?'

Chapter Four

Beep! Beep! Beep! Beep! Beeeeeep! This isn't
an episode of The Osbournes . . . We're
renting mopeds!

At the age of 18, I passed my driving test and wrote-off
my dad's car on the way home. I lost all confidence
and handed back my keys, deciding never to take to the
wheel again.

I'd only taken my eyes off the road for a second – to
throw my L-plates into the back – when the corner of one
of them caught in the brushed nylon roofing material and
pinged back at my head. But that wasn't when the crash
occurred . . . the crash occurred when I bent forward to
pick them up for another go. 'It could have happened to
anybody,' didn't seem to convince my dad as I handed
him the now-detached steering wheel of his prized Sierra
Cosworth.

From then on, I'd relied on others to drive me around.
Following a barrage of 'Are you stupid?' type abuse
from my furious mother when I got home, and my own

realisation that I must be the most accident prone woman on the planet, all the confidence gained in 30 weeks of driving lessons was lost forever.

'My darling Binnie, I'm going to teach you to drive if it's the last thing I do!'

With David gone there wasn't going to be anyone to drive me around or teach me to drive – I was on my own. My driving license was in my handbag 'just in case' David could talk me into hiring a moped – though I'd been convinced he'd never be able to do it. My choices were to stay round the hotel pool with a group of unadventurous, sunbathing couples, or to get out and explore the real splendour of the island alone. It was no contest. For the sake of doing everything on the adventure tour group itinerary, I was going to have to take to the open road alone. Never had I needed some freedom to explore as much as now.

The short walk from the hotel to the moped centre took me past shops where I was able to purchase supplies to aid my sickly stomach. Bye-bye sugar low – hello very large bag of mini chocolate croissants, two cartons of orange juice and a packet of mints to stop my breath vaporising all the new people I was about to meet at the painting class. I downed the first carton of orange juice greedily, but still my suffering, grief-stricken belly wasn't accepting any food callers.

'Now, remembers Mrs Dando, you drive with bike on the right. It is not like in the English.' The boy from the hire centre handed over the map he'd drawn to Chris's villa and searched my face for a glimmer of understanding as I sat astride the moped. Peering through the visor of my oversized helmet at the controls that he'd just spent an age explaining, I nodded . . . and the world went black. Pushing the helmet around until I could see again, I took the map and his pencil before grabbing the handlebars. This didn't look so hard; what had I been worried about? Front brake. Back brake. *'Why would I want one half of me to stop and not the other?'* Accelerator.

'And this button is . . . ?'

'BEEEEEEEEEEEEEP!'

'Oops! That'll be the horn,' I laughed, as several mystified faces appeared from nearby shops to see what the noise was. The boy, who looked about 12, failed to see the funny side. Judging by the look on his face in my rear view mirror, he was pretty worried.

'How on earth do people manage with the island heat in this headgear?' I asked, turning towards him, but finding I could only see half of his face as the mahoosive helmet remained facing forwards. I adjusted it again, just in time to spy him rolling his eyes.

'Don't they make these things for people with normal sized heads?' I muttered into the sweaty, foam lining.

'Mrs Dando,' the boy began, gravely, 'do you understand? Do not forget. You drive on the . . .'

'. . . right side of the road. I get it. Really, how hard can it be?'

It wasn't my voice I heard answering him so impatiently; it was my mother's.

'Come on Bernice, just pedal! How hard can it be?'

I was ten and sitting aboard my new bike, frozen to the spot. Dad was holding me, and the bicycle, upright.

'Just push off from the kerb,' Mum wailed at me. 'Go! Go!'

I gave the brakes one last squeeze, to check again if

they could stop me from having the horrible collision I was busy picturing in my head. But even as the pads tightened against the wheel, reassuring me that stopping was possible, I couldn't let go of my father as he tried to push me while attempting to release my vice-like grip on his arm. I couldn't be alone on that big, wide, busy road. Couldn't. Couldn't. *Couldn't.*

'For Christ's sake, Bernice, you're ten!'

The secondhand bike was thrown back in the garage within ten minutes, with Mother shouting, 'Never again! What a waste of money that was!'

Sniffling and crying, I hoped for some comfort and reassurance that I wasn't useless and we could try again another day, but she was staring at the bike on the floor of the garage with a look of disappointment.

'We can send it back, George,' she called after my father, ignoring me. 'I think the store might refund us if we tell them she's too scared to ride it.'

'No, Mum, I want to ride it, I do!' I cried. 'Please let me try again another day.'

'No point,' she shot back, hurrying to follow my father. 'You never just try things for me, do you? How can you let me down after I paid out all that money? Your little sister has been riding a bike since she was seven. When are you going to grow up?'

'Mrs Dando,' the boy brought me back to the present with a wave of his hand in front of my face. I'd clearly glazed over for a few seconds. 'Are you okay?' he asked.

'Fine,' I said, a little more confidently than I felt. I turned the throttle on the bike. 'Let's do this!'

'Okay. And Mrs Dando?' he continued. 'Can I have my pencil back?'

Except I didn't have the chance to respond to that last bit because I was already revving off, giving an awkward 'I'm okay' wave to the lad. Which I wasn't because I hadn't meant to move forwards at that moment. *Where did he say the brakes were?*

Even over the sound of the engine and through muffling headgear, I could hear shouts from behind and risked a swift peek over my shoulder. Seeing the boy waving at me, I waved again, but struggled to keep control of the bike which mounted the kerb, sending several stray cats scattering up trees to safety.

'Aww, come on!' I complained, revving the engine a second time. Looking back at the hire centre, I saw the boy had been joined by what looked like two huge Greek men, and all three were now running after me, gesticulating wildly. *Shit, was I about to be arrested for pencil theft?*

I turned the throttle to full and, as my head was almost torn off my shoulders with the force of sudden forward motion, I threw the pencil to the ground behind me with a shout of, 'There's your pencil!' The moped charged onwards, bumping up a cobbled side street. It seemed there was no way to stop, even if I wanted to, without crashing into something.

'Mrs Dando! MRS DANDO!'

Another rearwards glance showed that the sales boy had now jumped onto a rental moped with the beefy henchmen on another, all in pursuit. Oh God, this was it; I was about to be ambushed . . . maybe even killed! Tomorrow's island newspaper headlines flashed into my head:

BRITISH PENCIL THIEF RUBBED OUT BY
LOCAL HITMEN

Would a stolen pencil *really* warrant such an elaborate daylight operation? *Of course not, stupid woman.* Maybe I was being mugged. Was it the stash of euros in my purse that I'd flashed while paying for the moped? Oh no, wait – they surely weren't after my faux diamond-emblazoned Primark flip-flops?

In a panic, I kicked one off into the path of an elderly couple as they strolled out from a hotel car park. The shoe shot straight into the old man's portly, bare stomach with a sickening slap.

'They have the diamonds!' I called, mercilessly pointing them out to the gangsters before whizzing onwards to make my getaway.

But it was all for nothing; the roar of bikes continued behind me. I slowed to turn a corner into another side street and heard a shout.

'Stop! Mrs Dando! You stop NOW!'

What on earth could they want? I reached down with one hand, trying to take the other flip-flop off to throw back as a ransom, but dropped it instead. As I cursed myself and looked up, an ancient Greek woman on a scooter was zipping round a bend straight at me, only swerving at the last second to avoid a collision.

'What the . . . ?'

'WAAAAHHHH!!!' We screamed the last part in unison; 'Waaaahhhh', it transpired, being the international synonym for 'OH SHIIIIIT!' In an instant, her front wheel bounced off the kerb, sending both the old lady, and the basket of lemons balanced on her handlebars, flying, Frank Spencer style through the air towards a couple of teenage boys. *Christ, I'm in a Carry On film.*

'Save the lemons!' I called back, rattling onwards with no time to look behind again or wonder why my first manic thoughts were for Frank Spencer and the fruit – not the little old lady. Speeding away from the increasing chaos behind, I rounded a honking car pulling out from a driveway and yelled at its startled occupants, 'CALL THE POLICE!'

Despite the throttle being fully open it seemed the tiny engine had no more to give and the roar from the biker gang got closer. Turning round once more, I could see the two bikes were still in hot pursuit, and for the first time I noticed the boy had a very fat man riding pillion. So there were four of them! And the fourth had mad lady-killer written all over him. Heart pounding with fear, I grabbed the nearest thing to a weapon from the moped basket and began hurling ammunition overhead at the assailants. However, taking my eyes off the road to lob miniature chocolate croissants was a last, fatal mistake.

Crunch!

The moped bumped straight up a kerb, sending my stomach boinging up to my lungs and my knicker tops rolling back down below my belly again, as the bike came to a near halt. This was it, the end. I waited for my life to flash in front of me . . . but a massive, spiny bush got there first. Without testing the moped's brakes, and fuelled by an extraordinary burst of adrenaline, I dived off, sending it ploughing, un-helmed, into the bush. This was where, in a moment of TV cop-esque brilliance, I rolled over and over onto a grass bank before springing back to my feet.

'Whoa!' For a split second, Mrs David Dando was Lara Croft; crime fighting, tomb raiding stunt rider. That was until My Big Fat Greek Assassin got off his bike and made towards me and I remembered who I actually was. Bawling Binnie – with her knickers rolling down again.

'Don't kill me! Don't kill me! I'm unarmed!' I yelled, trying – and failing – to get my helmet off before throwing up my hands in surrender to the waiting gang.

'Other side, Mrs Dando! Other side!' yelled Zorba the Crook, taking a handkerchief from his pocket to wipe bits of chocolate and pastry from his fat sweaty face. Spying his accomplices coming up behind, I turned around and threw myself face down in the dirt with my hands behind my still-helmeted head.

'Okay, okay,' I whimpered, 'just *please* don't hurt me.'

There are moments that should flash through your mind when you think death is imminent; the faces of loved ones, lifelong friends, long-forgotten happy moments, childhood memories. This was my crucial moment – and I was going to die wondering if Greece had body bags big enough for me in this colossal monstrosity of a biking helmet.

The Fat Assassin flopped down beside me and prodded my shoulder. '*Oh God*,' I thought. '*He's really mad! Goodbye cruel world!*'

```
Dear Facebook, today I was so hot. Oops,
bloody mobile phone typos! I was s-h-o-t.
```

'Mrs Dando . . .'

As I lay there with my eyes screwed shut, waiting to feel a gun in my ribs, (please God let it be a gun in his pocket), hearing him huffing like a muddy, wet contestant on *Total Wipeout*, his voice took on a calmer, more sinister tone.

'I not kill you. You kill yourself.'

I froze. Oh my God, he was going to make me shoot me.

I heard him take another deep breath and cough. 'Mrs

Dando,' he said finally. 'You drive with the moped on the other side!'

'I didn't mean . . . I wasn't . . . oh!' *Ah. Right* . . . I rolled back over to face him, but again, could see nothing but blackness.   So, I wasn't going to be bumped off for stealing the island's only pencil. Or for assault with a supersized bag of mini croissants.

Twisting the monstrous headgear off and easing myself upright, I was met by four nonplussed faces caked in, well . . . cake.

'Oh,' I said, smoothing my hair in an attempt to recover some composure. 'Well, er . . . why didn't you just say so?'

Chapter Five

Discovered my superpower isn't making a cool 'KSSHHH KSHHH' noise when I walk. Unrelated: Now have 40 smartphone photos of the inside of my pocket.

Pulling over to catch my breath, drink some more juice and update Facebook, I gazed through olive groves to the distant horizon where real life, work, bills and complicated relationships awaited my return. Still a little shaken from the moped chase, I realised that for that whole brief, albeit zany window, I hadn't thought of David once. Closing my eyes, I breathed in the sweet and savoury aroma of lemons and olives and thought of myself zipping through the island's sleepy, cobbled streets on the wrong side of the road. Despite a slight prickle of embarrassment, a wry smile spread across my face. It was so wonderfully liberating taking to the road alone, I understood now. I opened my eyes, taking in the astonishing view, and made friends with the glinting Aegean once again.

There is a moment in every relaxation tape I've listened

to when Mr Making-Me-Sleepy-Voice-Man tells me to imagine my calm place to begin. That place for me was usually here in Greece, sitting with my toes dipped in the warm, almost silken waters as the scorching, summer sun nipped at my shoulders. I was already beginning to relax again . . . Until I remembered I was about to face my husband's best friend.

It seemed so long ago now that David had first introduced Chris and me, two months into our relationship, and as time passed and we saw Chris time and again, it became clear that we had a lot in common. We had the same sense of humour, came from similar backgrounds and liked all of the same things. It seemed I had passed the 'meet the best friend test' with flying colours.

Then, one night, right in the middle of a conversation we were having alone at a party, everything changed. We were both more than a little inebriated; laughing until we cried as we always did, when he stopped, touched my hand and said, 'You know, David is my oldest friend. I wouldn't want to see him hurt.'

'Hah,' I laughed. 'I'm not going to hurt him.' Noticing his serious expression, I changed my light-hearted tone to a more serious one. 'I like him a lot.'

He grasped his pint glass with both hands and stared solemnly into the beer. 'Me too,' he said.

'Are you saying I've got a rival for his affections?' I asked, only half joking.

'I'm saying let's change the subject,' he replied, looking so uncharacteristically serious that it felt almost like a reproach. I was puzzled, but put it down to the drink and did as he'd asked. After that night, we never really talked that much again. Shortly after, I'd tried to recall the conversation leading up to his unexpected sharpness

– maybe I'd said something stupid and he'd gotten the wrong end of the stick? Maybe he'd told me a secret about David that he wasn't supposed to reveal? But I couldn't remember what had occurred. When I mentioned it to David, he just shrugged it off.

'Oh, Chris is just funny sometimes,' he said.

'Are you sure you're not hiding something?' I asked.

'Apart from that time he went to prison for me, no,' he joked.

Six months later, Chris had headed out to Greece for a new life and I hadn't thought about it again until now.

There was only a short uphill drive remaining, but now the pain in my heart was beginning to dull, replaced by nervousness.

I was going to have to face Chris and his painting class alone . . . and shoeless. I imagined him quizzing me.

'Teenagers threw your flip-flops away?'

'Yup. Flipping flip-flop flingers.'

Choosing one of the smaller, less touristy islands had been David's idea; not just to meet up with Chris again, but to explore these little-known corners of the earth, filled with undiscovered treasures, coupled with a list of new experiences we'd planned like conspiring children. In truth, it was a life experience I'd planned to have 23 years earlier – right before discovering I was expecting Sal.

Michael, Sal's father, was a college mate I barely knew. At 19, without even having had time to wave goodbye to a higher education, we had chosen to 'do the right thing' and get married. By 21, when most of our friends were leaving university to dry out and get respectable jobs, I was already a mother of two with a husband. But at least I wasn't alone on that road.

It was 15 years before I really got to know the person I'd married, when a collection of love letters – stumbled upon while tidying the loft – revealed he'd had a mistress for six of those years.

Michael was now married to Caroline, but I'd never told the girls their dad and new stepmum were a perfect match – of lying, cheating, conspiring lowlifes. I'd even accepted Facebook friend requests from both of them to keep the 'happy, extended family' dream alive.

Caroline would like to add you as a friend.

Bloody fiend more like.

For me, reading the words 'Caroline likes this', with the jolly little Facebook thumbs up beside it under my holiday snaps, was tantamount to winning first prize in a glamorous grannie competition. When Sal and Mark announced their engagement and Caroline had updated her status to say 'Ooh, can hardly believe I could be a grandma soon' it burned my heart like ice.

'*My* children. *My* grandchildren,' I felt like screaming out, but swallowed the words. All that mattered to me was Sal and Beth's happiness. And *they* adored her.

Smother – who had made sure she too was friends with Caroline on Facebook – had written her congratulations to Sal, Mark *and* Caroline underneath the post. She had always maintained a friendly relationship with Caroline, although she knew why my marriage to Michael had collapsed.

'Well, she hasn't done anything to me really, has she? And she's so good with the girls. I like the way she fixed Beth's hair for her party last summer. You know you were never any good at that kind of thing. She came and did mine too, for my reading group social. That reminds me, I must send her some flowers to say thanks.'

Blinking at the memory, I recalled too, the only person who had been available to decorate a new flat before someone moved in recently. A person who had never painted a wall in her life, had very little money, but wanted to try and make everything nice for her mother; an old woman who was forced to move from the house she'd lived in for twenty years into something smaller and easier to manage. A person who had showed her mother all the newly decorated rooms, grinning from ear to ear while feeling shattered – but more than a little proud – at what she'd achieved. It took two seconds for her to feel slapped in the face.

'Well, this will do for now, Bernice. At least I'll be able to pay someone to do it properly once I'm settled in.'

Discarding the juice carton to the back of the moped basket, along with thoughts of Smother, I pressed on, even remembering at the last minute to move back to the right hand side of the road. Before long, I turned into a quiet lane that stopped before large, black iron gates with a sign that read:

Chris Paynton. Art Classes. Please ring the goat bell.

Hmm . . . did I need a goat right now? My stomach gurgled as I removed my helmet and glugged down more orange juice, praying it wouldn't be making a reappearance anytime soon. It would be a good day; I'd had many a fine moment ribbing Chris about being an artist called Paynton. Once I'd explained away the absence of my husband – his best friend – I was sure we would just fall back into the old routine. I rang the bell.

Sure he'll be pleased to see you. Because you just sent his lifelong friend packing – the person he'd asked you not to hurt. For the first time, I faltered. What was I thinking, coming here after all that had happened?

As I considered turning back, six heads, alerted by the dingly-dong of the goat bell, popped up from a leafy patio area above. *Well, I'm here now.*

'I'm looking for Chris Paynton,' I called.

'Hold on!' The voice came from just in front of me, making me jump.

'Hello?' I said, holding on to the gatepost for support as the day's heat and yesterday's wine had a foam party in my belly. Inside the gate was a small white car with an ample, khaki-shorts-clad bottom sticking out of its back door.

'Just . . . getting . . . some . . . oh, wait . . .' the bottom grumbled. Finally, Chris, owner of said ample bottom, emerged, holding a large box of brushes and cloths and clutching two large rolls of paper under each arm. What I hadn't reckoned for was how much more attractive he would look carrying a few extra Mediterranean diet pounds, newly greyed hair and a suntan.

'Bernice!' he said, walking towards me happily. All I could think of was how much his clear, blue eyes resembled the placid deepest depths of the Grecian sea. And how happy he looked. A stab of envy and a longing for his carefree life in the sun overwhelmed me. How well it suited him.

'Oh, er . . .' I smiled and smoothed my wind-blown hair back down.

Chris dropped the paper rolls on the ground, laid down the box and stood twisting the barrel on the bike-lock that was holding the gate closed. For a second he stopped as he spotted my bare feet.

'Well, you got here at last,' he said, getting back to opening the lock. 'Congratulations on your wedding! Where's the blushing groom?' He glanced behind me, then back at my feet.

My stomach lurched. 'He, erm, isn't coming,' I said.

Finding the right combination at last, the lock gave way and he opened the gate, beckoning me onto his property. He looked puzzled.

'Sorry about the locked gate – it keeps the damned goats out.' He stared a third time at my bare toes, then at the moped, as if mulling over the situation in an attempt to understand his friend's absence, while I fought an inward battle with the unexpected pain – seeing him made me think of David. 'There was no fence when I moved here,' he continued. 'And the bloody things took over and ate everything in sight.'

'I see,' I said, still holding a forced smile whilst racking my brains for an 'Oops, I kind of lost David' excuse. 'Perhaps if you got rid of the goat bell they'd stop coming round so much?'

He laughed and beckoned me in, onto the crisp, gravelly driveway. Which was when another, much more immediate pain hit me. *Owww!* The gravel was boiling hot! I hobbled in, gritting my teeth and trying my utmost to look normal.

'They don't wear shoes in England anymore then?' he asked.

'They do. Such boring, conventional people in England, don't you miss them?' Knowing my sense of humour was still intact soothed me somewhat. David hadn't taken everything.

'Conventional, yes. Sadomasochistic – maybe not so much. How's this heat on your soles?'

'Honestly?' I was now hopping from one foot to the other, trying hard to keep from crying out as they burned. 'I think I'm already onto a new layer of skin.'

'Follow me,' he said. 'I have water *and* shoes. So, where *is* David? Hung over or something?'

Helping him with the rolls of paper, I followed him up the pathway towards the group waiting on the patio. My feet hurt, but not as much as my brain, which was still scrambling for a story. Why hadn't I thought of one before I got here?

'You haven't heard from him then?' I asked.

'No. Not at all,' he said, concern in his eyes.

'Well, okay,' I said, taking a very deep breath. This was it. 'Yes we got married as planned, and it was a beautiful day. But, it's just me here today. It's just me on the entire honeymoon now, actually.'

'I don't . . . ?' he started.

I didn't want to stop for breath or questions, which I hoped wouldn't make me sound heartless. He was the first person I'd told, and it felt very, very painful speaking about it.

'Do you mind if we leave it at that just for now? I know you two are good friends so it might not be appropriate for us to discuss it. I'll let him explain, *his* way. I'd just like to take your painting class, Chris, if you'll still have me?' I could feel tears welling up in my eyes and I rubbed them away quickly. *'Just let me get through this day,'* I thought.

As he stood, looking for all the world like he was wondering what to say next, I saw sympathy behind his kind eyes and felt myself blushing. How I hated the blushing thing – the embarrassment of being a fair-skinned English Rose. It was all so *awkward*. I shouldn't have come.

'Right, understood,' he said at last. 'And yes, of course you can take my class.'

There was no time for me to wonder what he thought of me right then, I just wanted to get on with things. He stole another glance at my bare feet and winced.

'Look, I have an old pair of sandals belonging to a friend that you can borrow.'

I hadn't meant to make David being gone and my missing shoes sound connected, but it seemed I had, as if there had been a row on the way here and I'd flung my shoes at him. *'Go away, and take my shoes with you, you bastard!'* This unspoken explanation was going to have to suffice for now. It was way better than admitting I'd smacked a random old codger with a flip-flop on the way here.

As we continued up the winding path, to my enormous relief he didn't ask any more questions about David. He paused and nodded toward the imposing white washed villa, with its sea-facing balcony. 'This is my summer home, Villa Miranda,' he explained. 'Downstairs there at the front is a little apartment, but it isn't being used at the moment.'

'It's beautiful,' I said, amazed. It was also huge. 'Such a colourful array of flowers, too.'

'Yes, I planted them all myself. I'll just grab those shoes for you. They're a size six, I think. Is that okay?'

'Yes, I'm a five but they'll do fine, thank you. She won't mind will she?'

'Who?' he said.

'Your friend.'

'Oh no, she's long gone,' he answered, matter-of-factly. As he turned to fetch the shoes, I peered around the extensive villa grounds, waving a hello to the watching, smiling faces under the pergola and sighed. Despite the unwelcome reminder of David that Chris had unwittingly brought me, it was good to see him again after all these years, now all silver-haired and tanned, with his Grecian villa, all this land and so much taste and sophistication . . .

'Here we are,' he said, reappearing from the outhouse with a grotesque pair of wooden clogs. 'This is all there was. Could have sworn there were some sandals in there. I could lend you some of my shoes?' With the poker-hot floor still searing through my soles, a pair of fig leaves would have done right now. However, glancing at his feet, which were at least a size eleven, I decided against the Binnie-the-Clown look, smiled and went for Binnie-the-Clog-Dancer.

'Guess you've been to Holland recently?' I said, holding out my hands for the shoes.

'Not me, my friend,' he replied, brushing off a few cobwebs. 'And not recently.'

'Great!' I laughed. 'Loud, ugly *and* fusty shoes.'

The rest of the class were still waiting and, as I made my way over, all eyes on me, Chris introduced us.

'Everyone,' *CLOP. CLOP.* 'This is my good friend, Bernice.' *CLOP CLOP CLOP.*

'Everyone' was smiling at me, (and the clogs), yet a weird apprehension – bringing about a fresh desire to vomit – took over. *'I'm Bernice and, oops . . . this is my orange juice.'* For the first time it began to sink in that I was going to do all these new things alone. There was very little I'd done alone socially in my entire adult life and *nothing*, as it happened, that I'd done before wearing silly, wooden clogs. Perhaps a yodel would be appropriate?

As Chris turned, at last, to the task of setting up his

materials, a petite, elderly lady with grey hair held neatly in a tight bun waved a sheet of paper in my face. She reminded me of Mrs Pepperpot, a tiny character from some much-loved books of my childhood. Staring down at the clogs, which were the most uncomfortable chunks of wood I'd ever worn (out of a list of none), she said, 'We all hae stickers,' in a thick Glaswegian accent. 'How are ye spelling Bernice?' 'GRETA' was emblazoned on her own sticker.

My relief that any difficult conversations with Chris were over for now was overtaken by a moment of confusion, as it took a few seconds for my brain to decipher Greta's question. Not because of her Scottish accent, but because trains whizz through Glasgow's underground system slower than she spoke. 'Er . . . B.I.N.N.I.E.,' I spelled out. 'Most people call me Binnie.'

David called me Binnie. Up until I'd met him, I had been Bernice. Why had I forgotten that?

Beaming an enormous, toothy smile, Greta said, 'Och, that's whit we cry they fellaes that tak wir bins awa in Glesga, eh Hughie?' Chuckling at her own joke – which was just as well because it took a few seconds for me to make out what she was saying – she nudged the little old man beside her who was transfixed by my clogs. He regarded my face over tiny, round glasses before winking.

'Well, hello young lady,' he said, his twinkling, mischievous eyes giving me an appreciative once-over. 'Nice to see mair o' the talent's arrived!'

My immediate reaction to comments like this from strangers was often one of outrage. But something behind Hughie's cheeky smile made me feel at ease, like a kindly, familiar old uncle had just told me how cute I was.

'Och, awa, Hughie, ye wee flirty Wullie, ye,' Greta scolded

with a somewhat sharper nudge this time, before turning back to me. 'Ma husband's a wee bit lippy, hen. Yeh'll get used tae it.'

I did the polite laugh again, though I'd hardly grasped a single, solitary word.

'Hello, Willie,' I said, shaking his hand. 'I'm afraid I don't have much talent where painting is concerned. I don't know anything about art.'

'Well, ma name's Hughie,' he hooted, 'but if ye really want to meet the wee guy . . .'

'Ahem. Do you know Van Gogh, Bernice?' Chris cut in.

'Not personally . . .'

'Well, may I introduce you, as I do to all my new students,' he said, pointing to a slate plaque hanging off a nail on one of the pergola beams. Chalked upon it were the words:

If you hear a voice within you say 'you cannot paint' then by all means paint and that voice will be silenced.

I smiled at him and we gazed at each other for a moment. His eyes held a deep thoughtfulness – no doubt he was worried for David – and I was filled with a terrible remorse, like it was my actual fault. In a flash Hughie broke into the moment, slapping the 'BINNIE' badge straight onto my chest, giving it a good rub for super adherence.

'Aye, weel,' he said. 'Van Gogh heard a wee voice say "cut aff yer ear," an' then the whole lot o' they wee voices were silenced.'

I couldn't help but laugh.

Across the table from Greta and Hughie were a couple

of attractive, Nordic blondes who looked so alike they could have been brother and sister. Chris introduced them as Edvard and Ginger and they both nodded a hello but neither spoke, going back to a copy of the brochure they had spread out in front of them – presumably checking the day's itinerary. I, on the other hand, had completely forgotten what we would be doing. 'Painting stuff' just about covered it for me.

The last in the group – an older, cheerful-looking woman with dark plum-coloured hair beckoned me to sit beside her. She wore a bright blue, flowery scarf with an orange vest top and offered a hand in greeting.

'Hey there,' she said in an American accent. 'I'm Linda. How d'ya do, Binnie?'

I shook her hand just as a dark-haired, voluptuous beauty brought a tray of glasses and placed one in front of me.

'And this is my right-hand woman, Mita,' Chris said.

Mita smiled, regarding me with deep, mahogany eyes before lifting a jug from the table and pouring ice and water into my glass.

'Hi,' I said.

'Hello,' she answered with a nod.

'Can ah get some mair o' that watter too?' said Hughie, as he held his glass, grinning like a loved-up teenager. I guessed he would be very thirsty today. Just like me, Mita seemed unperturbed by his attentions. Hughie, I decided, was very much a harmless geezer. A little bold, a little comical and more than a bit brazen, but harmless.

'Okay class,' Chris began, smiling at me. 'We'll start with a little easy sketching and I'll explain a bit about perspective.' The smile was a small gesture but made me feel at ease. Maybe our friendship could continue where it left off in spite of everything. As Mita passed out artists' pads and pencils, Chris held up a picture that reminded me of a psychiatrist's ink-spot test. 'What do you see?' he asked.

Oh hell! This was where I'd reveal that everything reminds me of a page from the Kama Sutra and get hauled off to a clinic for sex addicts. *'Is this painting by positions, as opposed to numbers, sir?'*

'I think me an' Greta did that one back in 1973!' Hughie piped up. So, warped minds across the generations think alike. Last month I became Smother, now I was Hughie.

The morning was spent sketching the ink spot and a series of inanimate objects, while at the same time, everyone chatted and got to know each other, with some prompting from Chris. He nodded to me first, 'Why don't you tell the class a bit about yourself, Bernice?'

'Well, I'm a little hung over after throwing my new husband out of our honeymoon suite last night and downing two bottles of wine . . .'

'Actually, there isn't a lot to tell,' I said. 'Do you mind if Linda goes first?'

Linda, it transpired, was already a practised artist as she had taken up painting two years ago after retiring from her job as a school principle.

'I turned sixty, had the chance of early retirement so decided to go find myself,' she explained.

'I'd love to do that,' I said with a sigh. 'I hate my job.'

'Well darlin', take it from an old pro. Don't wait 'til you're my age to start doing what you love instead of working any old raggedy job you hate. I wish I hadn't wasted so much time.'

'Oh, it pays the bills,' I sighed, 'but a part of me wishes

I had so much money I could just quit. That's wrong though, isn't it? There's so much need in the world.'

'There's nothing wrong in wishing you were rich,' said Chris. 'Don't beat yourself up on that one. I always think of all the good I could do for others if I had loads of cash.'

I paused to consider his words; it was the first time I'd looked at it like that. Whenever I allowed myself to wish for a better life, it felt selfish. People in the world were starving; it wasn't fair to consider myself anything other than one of the lucky ones. But I knew he was right, I would love to have enough to share — to make other lives easier, not just my own. I considered my childlike scribbles of the morning for a second, and announced, 'Well, if I'm going to dare to make my fortune it won't be my art that does it.'

Linda laughed. 'It's not bad. This sort of stuff can go for millions of pounds to some art collectors.' I liked her very much.

Edvard spoke for himself and Ginger. 'I am an architect and my wife is an accountant.'

'Ah, figures,' said Linda. The joke was lost on everyone except me. I threw her a wry smile.

'What about you, Greta? And Hughie?' asked Chris. The couple answered at the same time.

'Retired,' said Greta.

'Playboy,' said Hughie.

'He's retired an' he *reads Playboy*,' Greta added.

As we all laughed, Chris knelt down and studied my drawing. Taking my pencil from me, he began sketching some more lines over mine. His face was so close to mine it felt a little awkward, like those moments when the optician is peering into your eye with an ophthalmoscope and you're scared to breathe in case you blow in his ear.

'I know, it's rubbish,' I began.

'It came from your mind to the paper,' he said, still concentrating on the drawing. 'That creative process is beauty in itself. It's all about personal interpretation.'

'*Meraki*,' said Mita, who now sat watching us from a nearby sunbed.

'Yes indeed, *meraki*,' Chris replied.

'I love making art,' said Linda. 'Having the freedom of creativity to express yourself is really somethin' else. But you gotta help me get these lines right, Chris.'

And with that he had gone from me to her.

In half an hour, we were all through with sketching and had moved to watercolour painting on easels in the lower gardens. Linda chose an intricate spray of oleanders to paint, while I picked an olive branch.

'Funny that I should paint something my husband would love to have from me right now,' I mused to myself. No-one, except Linda, heard, and she stopped painting to look at me. I explained, 'Since we're going to see more of each other, you may as well know, I came here with a husband.' I felt a familiar sting behind my eyes. *Don't, don't, DON'T!*

She put down her brush and came over to stand beside me. 'And he's gone home?' she asked.

'Yes.' I held in my tears and wondered why on earth I'd spilled the beans so early. I didn't even know Linda.

'Oh my darlin', that's terrible! He cheat on ya with some bimbo?'

'I haven't decided yet. The thing is, he is Chris's best friend. Best not to say too much at the moment.'

'Well,' she said, putting a hand on my shoulder. 'For what it's worth, I think you're a brave lady, staying on by yourself. You can't let 'em stall your whole damn life. There just ain't enough time for that.'

She gave me a sympathetic hug. Hughie, who was working a few yards in front, chose this touching moment to announce out loud that he'd 'like to get that Binnie down on some canvas' and proceeded to paint me – boobs first, judging by the huge, almost symmetrical circles already staring out from the centre of the page. 'Och, yer an awfy flirt,' Greta told him. I think. Despite my private misery, I couldn't help but laugh.

By the time Chris announced a break for lunch, I was beginning to feel sick under the midday sun and my stomach was badly in need of the kind of sustenance only half a loaf of bread and a humungous plate of chips could bring. I was so hungry! However, when Mita appeared with two huge Greek salads, floating in olive oil, my gut lurched again. If vomiting was an Olympic event, I was about to go for gold.

'Chris? Do you have a toilet I can use?'

He pointed to the empty apartment below his villa. 'Use the one in there,' he said. 'It's closer.' I was already off like a rocket – running straight out of the clogs which stayed behind at my easel.

'And for the rest of today, Binnie will be working while invisible,' Chris said.

Emerging exhausted and dazed from the bathroom following an unproductive bout of heaving, I looked around the tiny, unlived-in apartment. Dusty and strewn with discarded canvases, it was a quaint single room with a kitchenette partitioned off. The open door revealed a sunny haven I had missed in my rush to get to the toilet. White curtains around a small patio provided welcome shade from the searing heat, as well as a screen between the apartment and Chris's villa. A garden table and chairs faced over a glorious array of flowers to the horizon beyond. I batted a sudden sting on my arm and realised the air was alive with biting insects, yet I imagined anyone would feel quite happy sitting here on a balmy evening with a bottle of wine and a mosquito swatter.

Toying with the trinkets and vases scattered on shelves, I saw a woman's face in the mirror on the wall. A woman I barely recognised: tired, sad and resigned, with heavily lined eyes. Good God, where had my spark gone? Once again I mourned the carefree, happier me who had flopped in a disorganised heap beside some guy who'd also arrived alone at the christening of a mutual friend's daughter.

'Do you come here often?'

It was a cheesy line to match his cheesy grin but, for a second at least, I was sceptical. *He's a bit full on. Do I come often to a chapel? What if he does? What if he just wants me to as well? What if . . . oh, wait.* Glancing up at astonishingly deep brown, teasing eyes, I met the face of my future. Towering over me by at least a foot, David looked slightly older than me, with a lick of wavy, dark hair and an assured, over-confident air. I was enthralled, captured and pretty much thrown over his strong, slender shoulders in that instant that I looked at him. For the rest of the day, as we weaved around each other chatting to the rest of the guests, it seemed his magnetism was in the air around me everywhere I went. I knew where he was at any given time without turning my head to look. The attraction was almost superhuman. In the blink of an eye all my cynicism fell away and, deciding he probably wasn't working in enrolment services for the Almighty, I answered his prayers. 'A date? Sure. Next Saturday, 7pm? See you then!'

And that was it. He'd been the first person to ask me out since my split from Michael.

It was just four weeks and six further dates before I told him.

'I love you, David.'

'You do?' he'd said, looking astonished. 'Well, that *is* nice.'

I had waited for him to tell me he loved me too, but he just smiled, squeezed my shoulders and turned back to the television. Then, he jumped off the sofa and shouted:

'Yahhh beauty!!!'

It was three nil to Chelsea.

Turning from the mirror, my face clashed with something jangly.

'What the . . . ?'

A mobile made from miniature Ouzo bottles was swinging from the ceiling. Great. There was nothing to beat crashing face first into some dingly-dangly reminders of why I looked like death. Rubbing my forehead, I blinked again at the Binnie in the mirror who gazed back with bitterness, anxiety and regret etched on her face. *When did I get so old?* The Binnie in front of the mirror oozed boozy fumes. Still feeling awful, I stretched out my chin, trying to smooth away the extra one underneath and finding . . . Oh dear God . . . more fluff. *Tut!* I leant in closer for the beard check. *THOU SHALT NOT CHECK FOR EVIDENCE OF BEARD!*

'That isn't me,' I told myself aloud.

'Are you sure?'

Chris's voice made me jump. I laughed a small, nervous laugh. Being caught talking to yourself was always embarrassing. Being caught stroking your sideburns at the same time was just too awful for words.

'So sorry, I was just admiring . . . things. What a great apartment,' I said, hiding acute mortification – I thought – pretty well.

'Yes it is. Just needs some work before I can advertise for holiday lets and start making some cash from it.' He smiled at me and I felt myself blushing again. For a few seconds there was that awkward silence thing – the kind I always had to fill with just about the first thing that popped into my head. I stroked the mattress. 'Lovely, inviting bed, though.'

Nooo! Way, way too sleazy.

'Er . . . not that I've tried it or anything . . .' I continued. 'Or that I'm inviting you . . . er . . . to.' *Oh, stop talking, Binnie!*

I felt in my handbag for my SPF 15 sun cream before holding it out to him. 'Here. You're going to need this to protect yourself from my face.'

He laughed. 'Invitation? Perish the thought.'

'Gee, thanks,' I said.

'The one I have upstairs is much more comfortable,' he continued, winking at me and just about sending my facial temperature to the moon. At least we were falling back into our old, familiar, mickey-taking ways. At least a part of me was beginning to feel normal.

'Aha, I see,' I said, guffawing like a moron.

Looking around the quaint, white-washed room again, I had an idea – one that meant never having to face hoards of loving couples or any of the similarly dressed honeymoon hotel staff again. One that meant not having to be with strangers for the whole of my holiday. One that meant I didn't have to be alone. However, it was also one that meant I might need to tell Chris my marriage to David really was over and at least some version of why.

I guessed I was going to have to face this situation with everyone sometime soon, especially myself.

'Look, in all seriousness, this place looks just ideal for me. Are you sure it's not ready to let?'

'For you?' he said, looking surprised. 'Aren't you booked into a hotel?'

I nodded unenthusiastically. 'Yes, but it's a little . . . shall we say awkward? Some space just to be alone would be wonderful,' I said. 'I just need to breathe again.' The last part was more to myself than Chris.

He scratched his chin. 'Well Bernice, I don't know, I . . . er . . .'

Knowing he wasn't keen to have me hurt a little. So, he was unhappy with me. I really needed a friend right now, but Chris's friendship clearly belonged to David.

'I won't be in the way, I promise. It's this or another hotel. Probably on another island as there are so few here,' I reasoned. 'Please?'

'Well, okay, why not?' he said, still not looking convinced. 'I guess I can have Mita clean and clear it out for you this afternoon. If you're sure this is what you want?'

The question, I knew, was about more than just about taking the apartment. Turning back to Boozy Binnie in the mirror, I sighed. 'Yes Chris, I'm sure. This is just the away-from-it-all haven of peace I need right now.'

He rested a hand on my shoulder and sighed. He didn't want me here, I knew it. Maybe he thought if I stayed at the hotel David could find me and we could patch things up.

'Right then, I'll consider it let.' he said at last. Then, a wry, mischievous grin, the Chris I remembered. *Cha-ching!* 'Two weeks rent up front okay?'

Chapter Six

Had a whole day of expert painting tutelage
and got full marks for artist impression . .
. after accidentally sitting on the palette
and ruining three good chairs.

Posting today's status told my Facebook world –
including Smother – all was well and going to plan
on the Dando honeymoon. Taking one last look round
the hotel suite, I patted the honeymoon bed – thinking
it must be the easiest five days it had ever had – tipped
my sunglasses from the top of my head onto my nose,
and headed out, with a nod to Suck-Face couple's door,
dragging my case behind me.

'See ya later . . . not!'

No sooner had I passed it, than the door opened and a
guy came flying out, landing on his backside – followed by
what looked like a pair of red knickers – which smacked
him clean in the puss. He lay stunned, giving me time to
race into the waiting lift without having to face him – to
join an old couple who'd just got in. As the door began

to roll shut, a woman's voice bellowed out, '*Accidentally* kept your trollop's knickers in your case? Huh!'

Finally ensconced in the lift, I breathed a sigh of relief.

'First floor?' the gentleman asked.

'Could be,' I said. 'Or maybe she's thrown him down before.'

The hotel concierge helped me strap my suitcase to the back of the moped, but not before expressing concern that the whole thing might tip up, and offering to get me a taxi instead. But nope, the newly independent me was going to do it by myself. Happily, my little scooter proved it could cope with the extra weight of my case and was soon carrying us uphill towards Chris's villa, a carrier bag containing a bottle of sparkling wine swinging from the handlebars.

Woman and cargo made it almost three quarters of the way before finally remembering to drive on the right side of the road. How lucky for me that they were quiet and that my phrasebook-assisted grasp of the Greek language didn't include profanities.

'You drive on the right hand side of the road, I get it. How hard can it be?'

Pulling up for the second time that day at Chris's gate and seeing the door to Villa Miranda closed, I rummaged in my pockets to find the combination number for the lock and the apartment key he had given me earlier. He'd be out for his daily kayak session no doubt, whatever one of those was. Although it was early evening, the sun still burned hot on my back, making the effort of pulling my luggage and carrier bag from the moped up the path of jaggy, loose gravel – which kept jamming the wheels of the case – all the more difficult. Hot, bothered and tired, no sooner was my key in the lock of the door than I'd thrown aside my bag, parked my case, pulled back the bed covers and flung myself onto the bed.

Something coarse and wet was rhythmically sweeping my foot.

'Don't!' My voice echoed in the lonely room.

Wait a minute, I'm in a *lonely* room! Sitting bolt upright and flinging the surprisingly heavy duvet off me, there was a loud, 'MIAOW' as the cat whose sleep I'd just rudely interrupted with an unscheduled flight on said duvet, landed safely on its feet and bolted out of the half-open door. But it wasn't the sight of the low-flying kitty that made me scream like a banshee. It was the goat at the foot of my bed munching the sheets – something it forgot to stop doing as it first looked startled, then ran out of the door to get away from the mad, wailing woman, trailing the sheet behind it. Before I could run after it, I heard the squeaking of a gate outside and footsteps crunching up the gravel.

'Oh shit!'

Jumping to my feet, I peeped out of the door in time to see Chris, face aghast, staring at a different goat which was standing on the roof of his car, bleating loudly as if in protest at his audacity. What's more, at least ten or eleven other goats, besides the one I'd just encountered – which now stood by the patio table still chewing my bed sheet – were scattered across the gardens, munching away at trees, flowers, bushes and even a curtain from my patio. Grabbing my carrier bag, I made my way over towards Chris, scattering goats in my wake.

'I'm so, so sorry! I was really tired and . . .'

I held out the bottle of wine, bought to say thanks for his letting me use the apartment, and finished with a feeble (and obvious) 'I forgot to lock the gate.'

'I was only gone . . . an hour . . .?'

Before Chris could say any more, the sound of hurried footsteps made us turn around, to see Mita and a younger woman appear, one carrying brooms, the other, a crockpot.

'Oh dear, my Cristos, what has happened!' The younger woman cried, handing him the crockpot which was wrapped in a towel. 'Stifado for you,' she said, pausing to swoon at him, until, tugging at her skirts, Mita brought her back to her senses. The pair were soon rushing around shooing the goats from the property, with help from me and my carrier bag. Within minutes, all the goats were bleating and scuttling down the lane followed by the two women waving brooms at their behinds.

We perused the damage. Broken plants and flowers lay all over the garden, Chris's car had scratches all over the roof and the privacy curtain that had been around my patio was now a marquee between two oleander bushes. Looking at his stunned face, I said, 'The hotel might give me back my room.'

Oh God, whatever I've done in the past, he must really hate me now. But to my relief, I saw him break out into a huge smile. Seconds later, he erupted into fits of raucous laughter.

'Then I'd never find out what you do for an encore!'

'Oh Chris, your beautiful garden,' I said, wondering if he was delirious or something. Still chuckling, he bent down to pick up some of the wreckage, still carrying the Stifado. I put aside the bag containing the bottle of wine, and pulling the crockpot from him in a feeble attempt to help, knocked off the towel, wrapped around it to stop anyone burning themselves with it . . . and burned myself with it. With a howl of pain, I threw the dish and its contents to the floor . . . right at his feet. My face burned almost as much as my hands. Chris, whose sailing shoes were now covered in hot, thick gravy, looked down at the mess before him and burst out laughing again. Okay, now I *knew* he was delirious.

'I . . . well . . . your dinner . . . your car,' was all I could say.

He stopped laughing and his face softened, probably because I looked like I was about to burst into tears. I felt awful.

'Oh, don't worry,' he said. 'It's a very old car and I'm the poor English bachelor everyone wants to mother. They're Mita's goats. She'll be back with a gaggle of local women in about half an hour and they'll no doubt clear everything up. There isn't much damage done really. Relax!'

I thought of the adoring looks Mita and her friend had given to Chris earlier. 'They'd like to do more than mother you.'

Chris grinned. 'Who wouldn't?' he said. 'I'm surrounded by unmarried Greek ladies who'd all like to be the lady of my manor.' Putting a friendly arm around me, he led me back up to the villa. Despite my mortification at the chaos I'd caused, I fought a peculiar urge to sink into his friendly embrace. It was wonderful to be with someone who knew how bad things were for me right now, but crying on Chris's shoulder might not be the right thing for me to do. He was David's best friend – not mine.

'I'm quite the catch you know – check my swanky new gravy shoes,' he continued, squeezing my shoulders some more. 'Come on, let's open this bottle and eat together. I've already got a dinner big enough for two stewing in the slow cooker anyway.'

As the sun began to set that evening, we enjoyed a

fantastic meal (which I ate hungrily while he shared some wonderful stories of life on the island with me) without drinking any of my sparkling wine – which had rounded the afternoon off perfectly by exploding like a cannon all over the table. Sparkling wine, it transpired, tended to be eager to get out after a bumpy moped ride and some vigorous goat-shooing work. I wondered at Chris's calm nature; taking mishap after mishap in his stride. Greece had certainly relaxed him. I wanted so much to ask him why we'd stopped talking to each other, but it was such an awkward thing to bring up at a time like this. In any event, it was lovely to have an evening unspoiled by thoughts of a bitter past life.

'Laughter,' he said, pouring us our umpteenth glass of wine, 'is not only the best medicine but the best way to keep a healthy perspective in life. Everyone should have the ability to laugh at themselves.'

'Everyone seems to have the ability to laugh at me,' I said. 'Do you know, my father used to call me Calamity Jane.'

'Ah well,' he joked. 'He had a point there.'

We clinked glasses in a toast to my incessant clumsiness and watched the sun sink down to the cricking of an island-wide cricket's chorus. I was so chilled out I even sank back in the chair instead of perching on the edge, sucking my stomach in. Then, just as I found myself *really* beginning to relax in Chris's company, the spell was broken.

'Look, Bernice, I really don't want to pry,' he said. 'But are you going to tell me anything about what happened with you and David? Because, I have to admit – and I apologise, but he is my friend after all – I tried to call him this afternoon.'

'You did?'

He looked at me seriously. 'Not to tell him you're here. I don't want to interfere of course, so I wasn't going to say anything. You are, and will always be my friend too, providing you didn't do anything . . . and, well, I don't believe you would . . .'

'No, I didn't. It wasn't that.' I cut in.

'That's fine; you don't need to tell me everything. I just wanted to check he was alright.'

I had to ask.

'And was he?'

'I should imagine that he isn't right now, but he didn't answer. Is there at least a *part* of this you can tell me to help me understand?'

As I struggled for the right words, the goat bell sounded out, saving me. Chris put down his wine glass and leaned over the balcony to see who was there.

'Oh, it looks like Ginger. I'd . . . er . . . forgotten she was coming,' he said.

'You have visitors? At this hour?' The clock on the wall showed it was coming up for ten o'clock. 'Maybe I'll just get off and . . .'

'No, no. It's Mrs Persson. You remember, from the painting class? Edvard and Ginger? I better go see what she wants. Wait there.'

Recalling the Nordic-looking couple from the class, I said, 'Her name is Ginger *Persson*?' But Chris had already taken off down the steps without hearing me. Five minutes later they were climbing the steps together.

'You remember my friend Bernice?' Chris said, leading her onto the balcony.

'Yes, sure. Hi.' She was smiling, but there was something behind the smile that made me sense she wasn't

65

altogether pleased to find me there. Chris disappeared into his kitchen, inviting her to sit beside me, which she almost did, choosing to balance on the arm of the chair instead. There were a few moments of awkward silence, so I took the conversational plunge.

'So, where are you from if you don't mind my asking?'

Her annoyed look revealed that she did. 'I'm Swedish.'

My reply revealed I'd drunk rather a lot of wine.

'Ah, I'm partial to a bit of that myself. Great in vegetable soup.'

I was joking of course, but the ensuing silence helped me wake up to one, tiny, minor detail. I was talking absolute bollocks. *That's it, funny farm time.* I half-laughed and leant forward to top up my wine glass, deciding awkward moments like this required nothing more than immediate, additional drunkenness. Ginger stared over towards the kitchen without saying another word, looking keen for Chris to come back and save her from the stupid woman. Which he did.

'Here it is,' he said, walking towards us with a piece of card in his outstretched hand. 'This is my painting of the harbour where you came in. I knew there was a spare print somewhere.'

Ginger faltered for a second, seeming confused.

'Ah, erm . . .yes, that's the one,' she said, taking it from him and tucking it into her bag. 'Well, I er, won't keep you any longer.' She threw me a stiff, sideways glance and I thought perhaps her vegetables weren't so nice after all.

Chris, on the other hand, was his usual, good-natured self. 'Good, well please take it with my compliments.'

It seemed he was almost *dismissing* her. Feeling awkward, I asked 'So, where is *Mr* Persson this evening?'

Visibly flustered, she got up from her seat, saying, 'Oh, he wanted to have an early night. I shall see you again soon, Binnie.' Chris took her arm and they walked down the stairway towards the path. I couldn't resist a little peek over the balcony, and saw they were deep in conversation at the gate. Ginger touched Chris's arm before turning to look back up towards the balcony – sending me diving down to my knees out of sight – then I heard the gate close behind her, the sound of a car pulling away and the crunch of Chris's footsteps on gravel, as he made his way back up to me.

Chapter Seven

Cooking chilli today. Not the country.

At exactly ten to ten on day two of The New Bernice Plan the following morning, tongue in cheek, Facebook update posted, I arrived twenty minutes late to the glorious outdoor kitchen of Taverna Antipodes in the village square for the next item on the tour group itinerary: a Greek cookery lesson.

Our instructor for the day was Michaela, a tall, slender, flame-haired young woman who continued with her talk as I hustled in. The rest of the group had already arrived and I spied Linda, who beckoned me to stand beside her. Edging past Ginger and Edvard, I nodded a 'Hi' to which I received a curt 'Hello' from Ginger – who had a definite flush to her cheeks on seeing me; similar to the one Chris had had when I'd made my excuses to go back down to my apartment the previous evening, following her departure. If she'd really gone to the villa alone just to collect a print from him, I'd eat my oversized, floppy, pink sun hat. I'd always thought of Chris as a complete gentleman. If my suspicions were right, this new life in Greece not only suited him, it had changed him.

As I made my way to the space beside Linda, a familiar 'How're ye doing lassie?' at my ear and a pinch of my waist told me Hughie had followed behind me.

'Greek food is a fusion of cultural influences,' Michaela was explaining. 'Tzatziki, for instance, is from the Turkish cacik.'

'And isn't hummus an Arabic word?' Linda asked.

'It is indeed. I'm sorry, what is your name?' Michaela said.

'Linda.'

'Well, Linda – nice to meet you – it is widely assumed that hummus is of Greek origin. However, it is a Middle Eastern dish. It is only because of its regular inclusion in the menus of many restaurants throughout Greece that hummus is considered to be Greek.'

'So ye willnae be teaching us tae make that the day then?' Greta piped up.

'No,' she replied with a smile. 'Our first course of the day will be *saganaki*.'

'Great,' Hughie whispered, so that only Linda, Greta and I could hear. 'Cos me an' Greta are saggy *and* knackered.'

'You speak for yersel',' Greta chided.

When it was time to go to our places and make the *saganaki*, which I discovered to my disgust was an oily, deep fried cheese, I found a place beside Linda. Being a bit of a short-arse, I found the table-top hob out of my reach on the far edge of the bench and my chuntering complaint to Linda brought Michaela across to slide the hob - which wasn't actually *attached* to anything - nearer to me. Linda chuckled and shook her head.

'You make me look so great at everything, Binnie. Can you stand by me for every class?'

'Oh, you sound just like my mother. Now, let me see. Will this particular piece of deep fried cheese be going to my muffin top or up here?' I held up my spoon-wielding arm and flicked my wrist a couple of times to wave a bingo wing.

Linda laughed. 'You are one crazy lady,' she said.

Half an hour later we were all sitting at our tables eating fried cheese and salad for breakfast; not the most obvious choice for the first meal of the day but, after a sniff, I had a little taste and then wolfed it down. I liked it, in fact – it was wonderful – an oily, moist, splendiferous pleasure. We even broke some bread to scoop up the excess olive oil as Michaela brought out two enormous bottles of wine and began pouring glasses for everyone. Wine, here, was also for breakfast. I liked Michaela too.

'*Yammas*!' she said, handing me a glass.

Recalling the state I had been in the morning before, I wondered if I should give my poor, bursting-at-the-seams body a break. It was then that I spied Hughie licking olive oil from his lips and grinning at me.

'Thanks,' I said, clasping the huge glass of wine to my bosom, as if the opaque wine could hide it from him.

'One for you too, Linda?'

'For breakfast? Yes missy!' she replied, throwing one end of her gorgeous pink silk scarf over her shoulder and grabbing a glass.

As we ate, Linda explained she'd come to the island, not only for a holiday, but to meet her girlfriend.

'Eydis travels the world with a troupe of gay dancers,' she explained. 'She's bringing them here for a show at the Mehrocca Lounge.'

'Well, that's lovely,' I said. 'So, when you say you came to meet her . . . ?'

'We've never met before. I got to know her online, in a lesbian chat room. Modern, eh?'

'Seriously?' I said. 'That must be difficult.'

She laughed. 'Yep, real, real hard. I decided it was time to make a move, find out what a proper relationship would be like. Darlin', I've lived on ma own for forty seven years.'

I couldn't comprehend being alone for forty seven days, never mind forty seven years.

As we sat watching the sea, she pointed to a young Greek lad, leaning against a tree and staring in our direction. Shining wet from a recent swim, wearing nothing but a pair of shorts, he had the most beautiful body, wavy black shoulder-length hair and was a magnificent shade of sun-kissed bronze. Seeing me gawping – 'Close your mouth, darlin',' Linda told me – he nodded in my direction.

'Who's he nodding at?' I asked, spinning round and finding no-one else there. My face burned red.

'You,' said Linda.

'No, he couldn't be looking at me,' I laughed, tugging the hem of my vest top down over my belly,. 'I'm at least twice his age.'

Linda shook her head at me. 'Hell, woman, enjoy it. Why would you think he wasn't looking at you?'

Before I could reply, Ginger appeared beside us. She waved to the young man, who waved back at her, and said, 'That's Argos, our tour guide for the volcano walk this week. Lovely, isn't he?'

I looked back to find him still staring and smiling my way. Perhaps I looked younger from a distance?

'Some people seem to think so,' said Linda, nudging me.

'How do you know he's our guide?' I asked, tearing my eyes away from him at last.

'He also does the parascending sessions. Edvard and I met him last week. So, you're staying with the painter now?' Ginger had added the question almost too sharply.

'You are?' Linda said, looking surprised.

'Yes,' I said matter-of-factly. 'In the apartment below his villa. Though, not *with* him. He's an old and very dear friend.'

I turned again to look for Argos but he had disappeared. I felt oddly disappointed.

Ginger continued her line of questioning. 'Just a friend?'

'Yes.'

'I see,' she said, smiling as if satisfied. 'How nice for you.'

'Yes it is,' I agreed. 'He's a very good man.'

'Very good of him to let you stay,' Linda added.

'Indeed,' Ginger replied.

There was a brief, uncomfortable silence until Michaela cleared her throat loudly and I spied Edvard beckoning Ginger back to their table. I pointed to him so that she could see.

'Oh well, it looks like the teacher is preparing for our second lesson,' she said. 'See you later.'

As she hurried back to her seat, Michaela stood up.

'The main dish we are going to make this afternoon is baked fish in a salt crust,' she said. 'It is a tender and very beautiful meal. You will feel you are eating at the table of the Gods of Olympus.'

'Not if you don't like fish,' I said.

'You have tasted every fish in the ocean?' she asked, with a kind smile.

'No, I guess not, unless they're all fish fingers,' I replied.

Seeing Ginger whispering to Edvard, I pulled myself upright. If they were talking in Swedish about how dippy she thought I was, sitting up straight would let her know I was on to her. Look at me; I'm a normal, non-slouchy, intelligent person. *I know fish fingers can't swim.*

'I hope, in this short afternoon, I can help you find the joy not just in cooking but in *really* tasting,' Michaela continued. 'This island has a sumptuous variety of foods to offer. One of the best is the fish, fresh from the ocean.'

Some staff from the kitchen began clearing away our plates before bringing out trays of fish. I tried not to meet the glassy, unseeing eye of my own unfortunate dinner-to-be as it was placed in front of me. It was the biggest fish I'd ever seen on a plate.

'Am I just feeding myself or the whole island?'

Michaela laughed. 'The kitchen staff enjoy helping with the leftovers. Nothing will be wasted. Now,' she continued. 'The purpose of today is for you to explore the flavours of Greece and learn some traditional cooking skills. All the better if you can experiment a little, doing as the Greeks do – cooking with *meraki*.'

'Mer whattie?' asked Linda.

'That word again!' I said. 'Mita used it at the painting class.'

'*Meraki*,' Michaela explained, 'is a word Greeks use for, say, creating a piece of art or cooking a dish, and really loving what you do. If you are putting all your effort, creativity and love into it – a bit of yourself – you are doing it with *meraki*.'

'What a wonderful word,' Linda sighed.

'I like it, so romantic,' I said.

'Which bit of yersels do we hae to put in the fish?' Hughie piped up.

My mind boggled. I really didn't want it to . . . the pictures I was getting were terrible.

Michaela shook her head and laughed. She seemed so patient and lovely, with a wonderful warm sense of humour. I imagined she did everything with meraki. As she showed us how to prepare the fish, whilst explaining the many kinds that were available and even sharing tales about the toils of Greek fishermen, I marvelled at the obvious love she had for her work and wished that I had that too. It was quite beautiful to watch.

'So, the salt insulates the food, cooking it gently and evenly,' she said, putting the final touches to her fish. 'When it comes out of the oven, we will simply crack open the hardened salt shell to unearth a moist, evenly-cooked and fragrant dish. And there you have it. A very easy and delicious meal.'

Clapping her hands, she invited us to start. I began by prodding the belly of my fish and was rewarded with a sickly squelch.

'Yeuck!'

Something told me I *wasn't* so beautiful to watch at work.

'What are you doing, Binnie?' Linda asked.

'I'm checking to see if Ishmael's leg is in there.'

'Eh?'

'This has got to be *the* Moby Dick,' I answered.

Hearing his favourite four-letter word, Hughie began, 'Do you want to . . .'

'NO!' Greta, Linda and I all shouted together.

'The salt is over there,' Michaela called over, pointing to a shelf of labelled white tubs behind us. 'Please help yourselves.'

Leaning over to Linda at the next bench to mine, I whispered, 'It's looking at me!'

'Who is?' she asked without looking up.

'The fish! I can't cut it open and stick things in its belly while it's watching me.'

Linda, who had already begun wiping down her fish, looked up at me with smiling eyes. *'Moby Dick seeks thee not. It is thou, thou, that madly seekest him!'* she said. 'But if it makes you feel better, just put a sprig of parsley over its eyes.'

I went across to the basket of herbs, picking up and sniffing everything I could find. Although experimental cooking had never been my thing, experimental eating was. I chewed on a couple of leaves and pulled a face. They smelled *far* better than they tasted. By the time I'd tested several green things the rest of the group were back at their stations and I found there were no salt pots left.

'Erm, excuse me Michaela?' I called. 'There's no salt left.'

Michaela looked up from helping Greta cut her fish's belly open. 'Oh, they must have miscounted,' She said. 'Georgio!'

When no-one came out of the kitchen, she turned back to me. 'Oh dear,' she sighed. 'No-one can hear me.'

'It's okay,' I told her. 'I'll go get some myself. What shall I ask for?'

'*Alati*,' she replied, looking relieved.

As I walked across to the kitchen, my phone buzzed. It was a text from Sal.

Hey, Mum. Hope you're having a great time. Just want to let you know I passed my audition for the band! Woohoo!

I grinned from ear to ear. At Sal's age, my instrument was my voice. For her, it was her beloved guitar. Feeling as pleased as I knew she would be, I texted her back:

```
That is fantastic news! Well done you! Love
you too, too much. Will call you later XXX
```

Her reply was almost immediate.

```
Don't be silly, it's your honeymoon! Enjoy!
I just had to tell you right away. Plenty of
time to speak when you get home. Love you
too XXX
```

Feeling a strange longing to call, mixed with despair at not wanting to lie to her, I sighed. She was so happy. There was no way I wanted to spoil that right now by making her worry about me. Beth and Sal would be fine; both of them staunchly independent. They were so much stronger than me.

I pushed my phone back into the pocket of my shorts and trundled on into the kitchen, trying to remember what to ask for. What was salt in Greek again? Turning back to ask, I saw that Michaela was still busy helping Greta and so, deciding not to trouble her any further, I carried on further in for a look around. No-one appeared to be about, but there was an enormous pot of what looked like squid rings on the surface beside a gigantic bag of flour. Someone had been making calamari. Next to the flour was a white bowl like the ones outside, only it was empty. Next to it was a pot, which I picked up to examine. On the label there was Greek writing and a picture of a teaspoon in white powder. Bingo!

Feeling pleased with myself, I picked up the pot

and returned to my herb-shrouded fish – all the while humming the theme tune to *MasterChef.* Let my cookery masterpiece begin. Glancing over at Linda slicing away her fish belly, I almost heaved. Okay, masterpiece it may be but I was *not* cutting open a fish's stomach. If I had to go in, I was going in through the mouth . . . if it would just stop looking at me!

'Would anybody like some more wine?' Michaela called, beckoning to a young lady who was weaving her way through the tables with a bottle on a tray.

'I could really begin to love this woman,' Linda laughed, holding up her hand and winning a refill for both of us.

Pushing spoonfuls of freshly squeezed lemon juice, bunches of herbs and – oh why not, I wasn't planning on eating it – a few big handfuls of the salt down through the gullet of the fish, I removed its herby eye mask. Standing it on its tail to shake everything down, I noticed the salt dissolving in places. Oh, for some good, sturdy, British salt. Maybe not cutting it open had left the innards a little moist?

When the insides looked as though they could hold no more, I lay my now bloated prize on the baking sheet and took a large gulp of wine before patting more salt all over it, which was fast dissolving on contact. Looking about me, I could see everyone pouring lashings of salt on top of their fishes. Not wanting to bother scraping some of the salt off to dry my fish properly, I poured the entire remaining contents of the pot over it.

'Linda?'

'Yes darlin?' Linda answered without looking up, focussed on the task in hand.

'Why is this Greek salt so bloody powdery?'

'What?' she said, still distracted.

I shrugged, knocked back the final dregs of my wine and stuffed my fish's mouth with a huge wedge of lemon. It didn't look at all appetising; but I'd made it with *meraki*. It was bloated and holding far too much inside. *Just like me.*

'Mum, I made rice pudding at school! Can we have it for dessert tonight?'

'Oh, that looks quite nice, Bernice. Do you know who I think might like that?'

I shook my head, all the while thinking she, Dad, Suzy and I might like it. 'No?'

'Old Tom next door, he'd love it. Poor old soul, I'm sure he doesn't eat right. I'll take it round to him, shall I?'

In a moment she was gone with the pudding. My pudding. I hadn't even had time to reply.

As our fish were being put in the oven there was a buzz in my pocket alerting me to a phone call. It was my sister, Suzy. Signalling to Linda that I had to take a call, I walked over to a private spot by the sea wall and answered it.

'Suzy, you know I'm in Greece, right?'

'Yes, sorry sis, I hate to disturb you on your honeymoon but I thought I'd better let you know, Mum's in hospital.'

'Again?'

I heard her sigh. When two women talk about their mother being in hospital you would expect one to sound upset and the other to ask a concerned – maybe even panicked – 'What happened?' But, this was Smother.

'The usual,' Suzy said. 'Vague, non-specific dizzy spells. You had to go and get married and hog all the limelight, didn't you?'

We both laughed, albeit half-heartedly.

'Sorry,' I said. 'Has the hospital diagnosed Attention Deficit Response yet?'

'If only,' she sighed. 'As per usual, they're all looking at me like I'm the daughter from hell because I don't look distraught. They just don't get it.'

I felt her pain, having been in the presence of medical professionals and staff at the sheltered housing complex where Smother now lived, looking at me like I was the Devil incarnate for seeming not to care about her many and varied ailments. Nobody but Suzy and I knew they were almost always invented or brought on by her 'forgetting' to take some important medication – attention seeking by any means necessary.

'I know, it's hellish. I'm sorry I'm not there to help.'

'Don't be silly, we both know she wouldn't be in hospital if there hadn't just been a major family celebration that wasn't about her. I just thought, you know, I should let you know. I don't want to spoil your honeymoon, but it felt wrong not to say.'

'I understand,' I replied, taking a deep breath as the guilt of pretence washed over me at the mention of my honeymoon. 'Look, Suzy, I'm going to give you a call later. No doubt sm . . . *Mother* will be home with a clean bill of health in a day or two, but there's something else I want to discuss with you. Something . . .' I paused. How I hated lies. 'Something I need your advice about. Is that okay?'

'Really?' she said, sounding concerned for the first time. 'Well, okay, that's fine if you need me. Is everything alright there?'

'Yes,' I lied.

'Okay, fine. We'll talk later after I've done the perfunctory evening visit.'

'I'm so sorry you have to do this on your own, Suzy.

Just buy Mum some magazines, stroke her hand and tell her to cheer up.'

'Cheer up? She was taken in at midnight in an emergency response ambulance and by two o'clock this afternoon she was laughing and chatting up a student doctor from Pakistan! If she's sick, I'm the Queen of bloody Sheba.'

There was some commotion behind me and I turned to see a band setting up beside the taverna, getting ready to serenade us during lunch.

'Right, I've got to go now. Let me know if there's any change or it turns out she actually is ill this time and we really are terrible women. How are the girls?'

'Oh, they're fine, of course. They won't call you, as it *is* your honeymoon after all. But they send their love.'

'Well, send mine right back and tell them I'll see them soon.'

We said our goodbyes and with a heavy heart I hung up, pushed the phone back into my pocket and headed back towards the group. I needed to speak to someone and even though she had her own worries right now, all at once I knew that someone was Suzy. She knew me better than anyone did. But as for my daughters, I couldn't tell them and equally, I couldn't face them and lie. I was happy to have them think all was well for the time being.

'You break the salt crust with a fork, like this,' Michaela explained later, as the cooked fish were delivered back to our tables. She gave Greta's fish a tap to demonstrate, as we all gathered round to watch, the crispy, salt crust fell away to release a cloud of steam and a juicy, fragrant, baked fish. I had to admit, it smelled wonderful.

'Okay, your turn now.'

I looked down at my fish which fizzed and bubbled, seeming to have expanded to twice its original size.

Picking up my fork, I continued on to the pièce de résistance.

'So, how does it go?' I said to Linda, who was busy with her own meal and didn't reply. 'You tap the crust with a fork . . .' Even though there was no actual 'crust', I gave my heavily bloated fish a good, strong thwack . . .

BOOOOOOOOOM!

The first thing I was aware of was that the band had stopped playing, swiftly followed by the flapping of what seemed like hundreds of wings as a flock of birds took to the air. Through the smoke, that hung like a cloud before my eyes, I saw Michaela wiping bits of fish from her face. Before I could say anything, I felt a mild stinging sensation on my chest and looked down to see hot, white, foamy flecks splattered up the front of my top.

Then somebody screamed.

As I dared to look down at the dish, fork still in hand, I saw that my dinner had all but gone – to outer space. All that remained was a frazzled piece of parsley. I almost wept at the irony of this herby eye mask being the only thing left; the very thing I'd used to protect my now-in-a-thousand-pieces dinner from watching me couldn't save it from Boomtown. Wiping foamy, lemony mess away from my hair and eyes, I heard the sound of people running and, before I knew it, a crowd of startled onlookers, including the hunky Greek god from earlier, had surrounded me.

Hughie broke the brief, shocked silence that followed.

'So this is whit happens when you put a wee bit o' yerself intae yer cooking.' He picked at some lumps of fish that had landed on his head and ate them. 'Well, it tastes grand oanyways, lass. All we need now is some breid to go wae it.'

Argos looked from Hughie to me in a state of confusion.

'Bread!' I repeated, before turning to the crowd and mimicking putting a piece of bread in my mouth. A sea of blank faces stared back at me. *Awkward*. I had to explain; break up that terrible, what-the-hell-are-you-doing-crazy-English-lady silence. I turned back to Michaela and the rest of the group. 'Oh,' I said, scratching my head. 'What's Greek for bread?'

'*Psoli*,' Hughie piped up.

'Ah, yes, that's it!' I exclaimed, pointing to my mouth again. 'I need *psoli*!'

'You need . . . *psoli*?' Argos asked. His face was aghast.

I mimed putting something in my mouth again, saying, 'Yes, *psoli*. *Psoli*!' Turning back to the crowd who all looked as confused as Argos, I pointed again to my mouth. 'I need some *psoli*!' Some of the onlookers began shaking their heads and turned away.

'Oh, Binnie, no!' Michaela cried out.

From the remaining crowd there came some low, supressed titters, until everyone was roaring with laughter. I turned back to Michaela and saw that her cheeks were bright pink and she was covering her ears.

'All I'm saying is I want some *psoli*. What's wrong with that?'

Behind her, Linda and Hughie were doubled up in hysterics and had been joined by some of the people from the kitchen. Everyone was laughing. Even Michaela had tears in her eyes that revealed she too was trying to stifle a snorting fit. It was only Greta who seemed as confused and oblivious as me.

'Oh dear God, stop!' Linda cried, grabbing my hands, tears of laughter streaming down her face.

Feeling that all too familiar, embarrassed glow in my

cheeks, I waited to be let in on the joke. Her explanation sent me chasing Hughie out of the taverna, across the beach and into the sea.

'Binnie,' she said, '*Psoli* means cock!'

Chapter Eight

So, apparently 'blow fish' is not an instruction.

B ack at the apartment, I posted a snap of my cookery class disaster on Facebook before refreshing the page a minute later, by which time there were three likes, including one from Caroline. I was not, however, going to let her, or the fact that I'd managed to concoct a science experiment instead of a cooked meal, spoil my day. That afternoon, having never wanted to eat fresh fish in my life, I had discovered two things:

1) Fish baked in lashings of salt actually tasted rather delicious and

2) Fish with cupfuls of baking soda and a lot of lemon juice all pushed into a cavity made airtight by various herbs and a chunk of lemon could send your lunch into orbit.

It didn't matter that by the end of the class I was still a terrible cook. After my embarrassment from the 'telling the whole of the island I need cock' thing had abated, we had all laughed so hard the rest of the class had been abandoned. I couldn't remember having so much giggly, juvenile fun in a long, long time. The only thing muddying my try-to-be-happy waters was the feeling that Chris was perhaps not the true gent I'd always thought he was. Not that it was any of my business – but Ginger had treated me all day like the 'other woman'. Knowing she and Edvard had been on the island at least a week longer than me, I couldn't shake the thought that something untoward was going on and that now I was staying at Villa Miranda, I was in the way.

I took a sip of from an ice-cold glass of water and sat down at the porch table before taking out my mobile phone, remembering my promise to call Suzy. As I played through the conversation to come in my head, that all-too-familiar angst grabbed me. What would I say?

'You know my fabulous husband and my fabulous honeymoon?'

'Yes?'

'Well, he isn't and it kind of isn't – or might not be – a honeymoon anymore.'

Gah! I needed a drink. I sent her a text:

`Something's come up. Will call tomorrow`

Before heading out for dinner, I began the day's essential ten minute pelvic muscle training session as per my 'Five Daily Steps' and pondered serious issues of life back at home – as you do whilst electronically stimulating your pelvic floor muscles. With sudden, incredible clarity, I realised that nothing I did back at home held any real challenge for me any longer. My job as a clerical assistant for a legal firm bored me to tears and there were zero promotional prospects. I stayed in most weekends, losing touch with all of my own friends, occasionally going out with David's – all lovely, responsible, professional people; people I couldn't imagine saying the word 'cock' in front of, never mind laughing about it. It was only Chris I'd ever really hit it off with as we had the same sense of humour. Only now, as I pondered my relationship with David from this distance – almost as an outsider – it was becoming clear. I'd been dumping my own identity whilst moving into someone else's. Today, spending a few hours with new people, laughing 'til I cried and just being *myself* had made me think about what I'd been missing.

Laughing 'til I cried. It could have been much, much worse were it not for my ten minutes a day of pelvic toning. Checking the timer, I realised that in all my day dreaming I'd done eleven minutes of squeezing instead of ten. Why didn't these things ping to let you know you're done, like a microwave or something? It had arrived with only German instructions, so I'd had to guess the correct timing and settings. Ten minutes a day for leaky-pee-free laughter following fish explosions, fifteen for the ultra-pleasing, sexual grip of a nineteen-year-old, twenty to make his face turn blue and have him screaming to be let out. *If only . . .*

After several wardrobe changes, rejecting the blouse that had to have a safety pin between buttons to prevent gaping, the strapless dress that could only be worn without a bra, making me look like I had two bellies, and the top with the spaghetti straps I'd been forced to cut and tie to hold my boobs up, I dressed in super-safety black again.

I decided against my initial plan – to go upstairs and invite Chris to come out with me – and called a taxi back out to Taverna Antipodes, where the tour group had gone for a Greek night. Ginger and Edvard would be there and I didn't know just how comfortable it would all be if I brought Chris along. Maybe I was wrong, but if something was going on I didn't want to be a part of it by inviting him further into the circle.

'Hello darlin',' Linda shouted as my eyes sought out the gang in the now bustling taverna that evening. 'A drink for the lady who started a Greek fishing boom?'

'Yes, hello!' I shouted to be heard over the band, which was filling the taverna and, it seemed, the entire locality with beautiful music. The party was already in full swing and everyone, including a very rosy-cheeked Linda, appeared to have spent the first hour throwing down a lot of liquid while I'd been back at the apartment, training my pelvic floor not to.

'It's a help yersel' buffet,' said Greta, pointing to the food table as she hiccupped and swayed with a big grin on her face. From the far end of the table, Ginger afforded me a frosty glance – while Edvard looked pleased to see me.

'Ha ha!' he cried. 'It's Boom Binnie Boom!' So, even he was drunk.

Hughie nodded whilst waving a leg of chicken about, casting me one of his classic suggestive looks – one which seemed to say, 'I've detached my willy for you and dipped it in honey, yoghurt and spices, would you like some?'

I shuddered and turned back to Linda, who pointed me towards the busy buffet table.

'Shall we go eat? I could go for a second helping,' she said, downing a full glass of wine and taking my arm. Brushing aside my inborn wariness of new taste experiences – after all, the New Bernice Plan included doing one thing a day that scared me – and with only a transitory fear of looking for lamb and finding goat, I allowed Linda to drag me towards the buffet table. I kept my eyes glued to the floor to avoid Hughie's suggestive chicken waving and my head collided with what *felt* like a muscular chest – but all I could see from my view of the floor was a pair of white slippers, each adorned with an enormous red and gold bobble. I muttered, 'So sorry, madam,' before looking up to see Argos. The same gorgeous guy who had earlier been wearing nothing but a pair of shorts, now wore slippers, a bright red and gold waistcoat, a skirt and tights.

'Hello, lady,' he smiled.

Caught off guard, my oft-practised blurting technique came into play.

'Hey, nice skirt!'

He held his 'skirt' aloft – reminding me of a five-year-old girl showing off her favourite party dress. 'You don't like my *vraka*?'

'I'm sure your *vraka* is very niceshh, thank you for drawing our attention to it,' Linda cut in.

'It is a uniform just for tonight,' he explained, 'to serve you lovely ladies.'

Tearing my eyes away from his – with some effort as there was no getting away from the fact he was just beautiful – I pulled in my tummy, which thankfully didn't make that vehicle reversing sound, and turned back to the gang.

'Would anyone like another drink?' I asked.

'ME!' The group shouted in unison.

Hughie stopped playing with his food to lean over and tug at Argos's *vraka*. Greta slapped his hands and uttered . . . well . . . something.

'Where's your sporran, laddie?' Hughie said, confirming my theory that he really *would* pester anything in a skirt.

As the band finished a song and began calling people up to join the professional dancers, Argos said, 'I have to work now. Of course, we can bring you wine. No charges. My uncle owns here.'

'Well, that is so kind of you,' I replied. 'Can we have . . . erm . . .' I looked over at the table and noted several almost empty bottles of wine, 'a couple of bottles of white?'

Argos opened his mouth to speak just as Ginger dived in and dragged him to the dance floor to join the waiting crowds of dancers and assorted merry tourists, the latter faltering through the steps of the traditional *Sirtaki* dance.

'Anyway, the *metzes* are jusht delicious,' Linda gushed, taking my arm again. 'Letsh go get 'em.'

'Linda,' I said. 'You do a great Shhhean Connery when you're drunk.'

The taverna was heaving with people, making it a slow process to pick our way through the crowds to reach the buffet area where we began piling our plates. My food stayed on my plate, whereas Linda was unwittingly feeding the scrawny-looking wild cats that were all around the tables with more dropped food than I imagined they usually consumed in a fortnight.

'I've been meaning to tell you,' Linda shouted to be heard above the noise, whilst searching her plate for the chicken she'd put there a second ago, deciding she hadn't taken any after all and adding more. 'Tomorrow ishh the big day.'

'Ah yes, the volcano climb.' I said, watching four cats behind Linda fight over her dropped chicken leg. 'It will be a toughie. But hey, extra olives and feta cheese for all the calories we will burn,' I said, picking at a pile of green stuff on the table. 'If that's what this is?'

'No, honey, I mean I'm meeting Eydis. She and the danshers have arrived tonight. They'll be with ussh for the climb tomorrow. Some pre-dansh training.'

'Wow, Linda, you are so drunk,' I said, almost unable to contain my laughter. She looked hurt, so I changed tack. 'But that's lovely!' I said, more seriously. 'Aren't you excited?'

'Like a silly school girl,' she replied. 'All nervoush and thinking, what if she doeshn't like the real me?'

'Of course she will. Why wouldn't she?'

'It's jusht that, oh the wine here really is shtrong. Forgive me for the oversharing, but, when we make love . . .'

'Make love? I thought you said you'd never met?'

'We haven't, but we have – you know – shhybered a few timesh. God, I can't shpeak, this wine ishh great! Horrible, but great. Where wassh I? Oh,' she continued. 'She said she had multiples.'

I didn't want to know, really I didn't. All at once we were embroiled in one of those inappropriate, somewhat disturbing conversations worthy of Smother. So why did I have to ask . . .?

'Multiple whats?'

Slapping a spoonful of what looked like mayonnaise onto my plate, she answered loudly, 'ORGASHHMS!'

It was an announcement almost like a call to the buffet, like *'Grubs up!'* or *'Metzes anyone?'* A grey-haired woman standing nearby held out her plate and said, 'Ooh, I'll have some of those!'

I pulled a chuckling Linda to one side and whispered, 'Do you mean cyber-sex?'

'Yeshh.'

'You get those from that?' I asked, unable to stop myself

thinking back to David's internet exploits. If Linda could have a whole, loving, sexual relationship online, how could he claim he wasn't cheating?

'That *is* interesting.' I mused.

'Is it?' she asked. 'Are you conshidering a shexual turnabout?'

'And you're faithful to her?'

'Binnie,' Linda said, 'I *am* taken you know. If thissh ish a come on . . .'

'No, no! I'm just interested in the sex . . .'

A tap on the shoulder made me start and I turned around to find Ginger standing behind me – looking appalled. It was clear she had just caught the latter part of our conversation.

'Argos . . . erm . . . asked me to come and get you,' she said, with a distinct look of distaste on her face.

'Ah, okay,' I said. 'He must be bringing the wine. Come on, we'll follow you back.'

'Er, no. I'm going to be going home just now, I've a terrible headache,' she said.

'You do?' Linda and I had spoken together.

'Yes, it's been coming on all day really. I'm just going to have an early night.'

'Well,' I said, sighing – although not through pity. I didn't believe her. 'That's a shame. Will Edvard be leaving with you too?'

Even though the light was dim, I could swear I saw her cheeks flush. 'No,' she replied. 'I'm just going to head off in a taxi. No need to spoil his night too.'

When Linda and I got back to our table, I could see people had gathered around the dance floor to watch some kind of display. Edvard remained seated with Michaela, Greta and Hughie, chatting away. My thoughts turned to Chris, who I felt sure was about to get a visitor. He had always seemed so honest and respectable. *Was he having an affair with Ginger?* I wanted to race home and confront him, but it wasn't my business really, was it? Could I just I ask him out of concern, say I was worried about him and sorry for poor, unsuspecting, Edvard?

Before I could consider the matter any further, Linda was ushering me over to the dance floor.

'What's happening over here, then?' She said.

There in the centre of the crowd was Argos, making his way across to me with a bottle – spilling some in all the kerfuffle. For a moment, our eyes met and his face was so soft and sexy in the evening glow, I felt my stomach sink to my shins.

'Oh, that's so lovely of you, thank you, Argos,' I shouted over the music as he stood looking at me as though he was mesmerized. I turned round to beckon to the rest of the gang and shouted, 'Look, Argos has brought us some free wine!'

I stepped forward, took the bottle from him and began to amble back towards our table, now a sea of excited faces with everyone on their feet waving at me. Greta had even grabbed the edge of the large paper tablecloth and was holding it up, catching her skirt at the same time to reveal a huge pair of floral grannie knickers. *Well, they are certainly excited.* Shielding my eyes from the sight of Greta's frillies, I tried to be as upbeat sober as they were drunk.

'I know! Free wine!' I exclaimed.

My face beamed . . . and then fell, as Michaela came charging towards me, arms outstretched and grappled with the bottle in my hands, almost taking me down to the floor in the process.

Someone shouted, 'FIRE!'

Whipping the bottle free, she pointed behind me, to reveal a long line of burning booze leading from my heels to a stunned-looking Greek man in the centre of the dance floor, lighter in hand. There was screaming, clapping and drunken cheering. The screaming was me.

'WHAT ON EARTH . . . ?'

Argos raced towards me, stamping out the line of fire between the man and me as he ran. The crowd roared over my screams and at once, the man with the lighter snatched the bottle from Michaela and proceeded to spill more of the liquid over the floor before lighting it again, forming a perfect circle of flames before the cheering crowd.

Seeing my nonplussed face, Argos shouted into my ear, 'It's brandy.'

'But I didn't ask for brandy,' I said.

'It's the 'ring of fire' dance, see? I wanted for you to see it. I didn't want for you to be in it though. I'm sorry, lovely lady,' he said, as another of the dancers tugged his shoulder. 'I must go back and finish.'

Nobody had moved yet – not even Greta who was still holding the tablecloth in terror, still flashing her knickers. The only one too inebriated to notice my near ritual burning was Linda, who cackled with delight as a waiter delivered three more bottles of wine to the table, trying hard not to look in Greta's direction.

'Woohoo!' She sang out. 'Now it's a party!'

Chapter Nine

The Greek dancing was fun. I was on fire!

On day three of The New Bernice Plan, I posted a photo of myself and Linda to Facebook, arm in arm, performing the 'ring of fire' Zorba dance. Within minutes of my posting, the well-wishing messages began to ping through in a series of mobile notifications.

Hope you are having a wonderful time, Mum! Miss you!

Many congratulations to you both! Love Caroline & Michael XXX (Yawn)

Greece looks fabulous!

The last message was from David's secretary, Iris. So, he wasn't back at work. Having now set my phone not to accept his calls, my voicemail box was full of pleading messages that I couldn't bear to hear, at least, for the time being. However, the text messages just kept on coming:

```
Missing you! Please answer or call me back.
It's not supposed to be like this, we should
be together. I love you so much Mrs Dando.
```

Reading the last line again, tears welled up in my eyes as his words poured into my conscience uninvited. *I love you so much Mrs Dando.*

'I love you Mum.'

My mother looked up from her newspaper and grinned. 'And so you should,' she said. 'Now shut up, I'm reading.'

Looking back down at my drawing of Adam Ant, I bit my lip and sighed. I loved Adam Ant too. I bet he wouldn't tell me to shut up about it though. He would kiss me on the top of my head and tell me how lovely it was to have the loyal, unconditional love of a nine year old.

With a thumb rested over the reply button, I faltered in my resolve not to think about any of the disappointments of my life. David loved me, but he didn't want me; all those nights when he'd left me in bed for a television rendezvous with some bum-waggling porn star had taught me that. My mother too had always seemed to do that showy love thing that is required of a parent, but it felt hollow somehow. The words 'I love you too,' would wrap around me like a very thin cloak; placating me, yet offering no real warmth. Even my father, right up until the day he died, had just seemed let down by everything I did. He must have told me he loved me at some point, but I couldn't remember when.

Recalling the familiar yearning for sex that Argos had stirred in me as I'd watched him dance last night had brought it all home. My relationship with David marked the beginning of a sexuality death: mine. It was a wonder it wasn't me switching over from squeezing my way to more painful thighs on the shopping channel to watching a *guy* writhing about in nothing but a tool belt. Then again, I could just see myself calling him:

'Hello caller, what's your name, honey?'

'No, it's Bernice.'

'Hi sexy! What can I do for you?'

'Erm . . . I don't know . . . Are you any good with flat-pack furniture?'

I deleted the long line of texts on my phone. I mustn't dwell on things. This could all wait until I go home.

A fishing boat was to take us out to a tiny, neighbouring island for the volcano climb today and Chris had agreed to drop me off at the harbour. As I walked towards his car, I saw that he was chatting to someone on his mobile.

'Yes, er . . . okay, that will be good. Make it five if you like?'

With his free hand, he gestured at me to get in the car, before ending the conversation abruptly.

'Cool. Anyway, I have to go now. Bye!'

I opened the door and climbed into the passenger seat which burned my backside for my trouble.

'Ooh, hot!' I yelped, drawing up my knees only to feel the thick skin of my thighs peel off the seat with a loud and very attractive schlupppp.

Chris grinned, pointing out the wicker seat pad under him, which had no doubt saved his legs from a scalding.

'Yeah, two of those would be useful,' I said, reaching under myself to pull the legs of my shorts over the backs of my legs. As Chris watched me in amusement, I realised that the process had lifted the hem of my blouse to reveal the 'sit-down spillage' – a plumptious roll of belly fat spilling over my waistband. I pulled my hands quickly out from under me to tug it down, and felt my thighs singe on the seat again. 'Oooh ya!'

'You okay there?' Chris grinned.

'Never been better,' I lied.

'Sorry, I very rarely have passengers in this old thing so I only have one seat pad,' he said, before starting the engine. 'So, how's it all going so far, Bernice? Are you doing okay?'

I thought of the long version:

'Well, I've been chased by Greek hit men for stealing their pencil; treated a little old lady and her lemons to a flying lesson, almost set my new group of friends on fire, oh . . . and I made a fish explode.'

But instead I gave him the short one,   'Oh fine, Chris. I'm having a blast.'

'Well that's just great,' he replied. 'Because, I don't mean to pry, but, did I hear you crying last night?'

Crying had occurred from time to time in my room, late at night after a wine or two, but I was pretty sure it wasn't ever so loud that he would hear me upstairs. *Wait a minute . . .*

'There may have been singing as I rolled up to my front door after last night.'

'Ah,' he replied. 'It's a good job I didn't come down to check on you then. Because I thought about it, but I, er . . . well . . .'

'Wasn't alone?' I said, matter-of-factly whilst trying to recall what it was I'd been screeching in the early hours of the morning.

'No, I wasn't, to be honest.' Taking off the handbrake, he pulled out of the drive.

'A girlfriend?' I cringed at my own nosiness. *Why did I ask that?*

'Do you think you could jump out and lock the gate behind us before we go on?' he said, ignoring my question and not taking his eyes off the road.

Even though I knew I had no right to have feelings about any 'girlfriend' Chris might have, my heart sank. It was Ginger. I knew it! For the briefest of moments, I hesitated, wondering whether to just dive in and ask him about it. But it was such a nosey, mother hen thing to do. No, I couldn't do it now. Maybe later, with some assistance from my old friend, Dutcheous Courageous. I opened my door and jumped out of the passenger seat to lock the gate.

My mobile phoned beeped as I climbed back in. The text was from Suzy.

All fine. Mother home X

'Oh, I really should call my sister,' I said, to myself really.

As we rounded the bend towards the harbour, I spied Argos in nothing but a pair of shorts and hiking boots, standing beside a beautiful, blue fishing boat. As Chris pulled the car up in front of the boat, my tour guide for the day flashed me his most gorgeous smile. I belly flipped.

'Catch you later then?' Chris said.

'Huh?' I answered, fixing my huge, floppy, straw sun hat in place, sucking in the sit-down spillage and smiling back at the young stallion before me. *Sigh.*

Chris looked from me to Argos, before asking, 'I meant to ask you, have you had any word from David yet?'

I turned to face him and touched his arm in earnest. It

was time to tell him *some* version of the truth. If I practised saying the words to him, I could say them to Suzy tonight, hopefully getting some insightful answers from her.

'Chris, I think I should just tell you before we go any further, what has happened between David and me goes back a long way in our relationship. We have a lot to work out, even though the wedding was only last week and it sounds . . . well . . . ridiculous. I'm sorry; I know you're worried about him, but I need to focus on myself for a little while. It sounds selfish but that's just how it is.' I wondered if Chris had called David. It seemed highly likely, but I went on with my speech anyway. 'I just hope that you and I can still be friends.'

I breathed a sigh of relief. One awkward conversation down, now I could call Suzy and have the full, proper one. I resigned myself to having to call her tonight when I got back to the apartment.

Chris lifted his cap and scratched his head. 'I don't understand,' he said. 'You seemed so happy. What was he doing? Cheating?'

'I honestly can't answer. If you want to know if he's hurt me, then yes, he has. But I'm not sure how much of it is my fault as well as his. Just don't hate me. I promise you, there's no need.'

He shook his head and guffawed. 'I don't hate you. And you know you're welcome to stay at the villa,' he said. 'But please, I know it isn't my business, but don't bring anyone back. It wouldn't be right.' He looked again at Argos, who was still watching us as he greeted other guests boarding the boat.

I swallowed hard. 'Oh God, no way!' *What must he think of me?*

Before I could consider this a moment more, I heard

Linda call out my name and turned to see her standing with a blonde, frizzy-haired, slender woman with huge, white-rimmed sunglasses that were much larger than her face. This, I supposed, was Eydis. They were waiting to board the boat. I waved them on, mouthing 'Just a minute!'

Chris started up the car before turning to look at me again. I don't know why, but it was a look that hurt my heart.

'Of course,' he said. 'It just feels sad and, well . . . weird, you know? David and I have been friends a long time.'

'And you don't like to see him hurt. I know. I remember.'

Still looking at me, he pursed his lips as if he was about to say something but had changed his mind.

'Look, I have a lot of thinking to do,' I continued. 'I'm not even *about* to think of moving on or doing anything silly and this honeymoon alone thing is no picnic in the sun . . .'

'Binnie!'

We both looked up to see Linda calling, raising a huge glass of wine to me from the boat, and before us the most fantastic sight which instantly changed the mood. Six shirtless, hunky guys with ripped torsos – all wearing luminous green shorts, green fluorescent sunglasses and flip flops – were lining up to board the gang plank, carrying picnic baskets and holdalls, chattering away like old hens. One of them was – rather bizarrely – carrying a snowboard. Chris's mouth fell open, just as all the men, spotting Linda gesturing, turned in unison and waved at me.

'Woo hoo! Hurry up, Binnie!'

'That'llbethedancetroupeLinda'sgirlfriendwasbringing along today,' I told him, squirming but not able to stop myself from grinning. 'Today is supposed to be fun. Just the tonic for . . . erm . . .' there was a pause as I turned back to see his still-astonished face. 'Taking my mind off things,' I finished.

'Well,' he replied. 'I have a feeling it's going to work. Enjoy! But, can you at least try to stay a bit more sober?'

Maybe I looked doubtful at that point, but I didn't mean to. Chris took a deep breath. 'Okay,' he went on. 'No more singing at two in the morning, okay? And no getting into any of that Binnie-esque mischief you're famous for.'

'I'll be on a tiny island with nothing on it but a volcano that's been asleep for thousands of years,' I laughed, giving him a hug. 'What mischief could I *possibly* get into?'

Chapter Ten

Climbing up a volcano to throw something in as
a sacrifice to the Gods. All I have is my picnic
and David. I can't tell you how much I'm going
to miss him.

Eydis turned out to be from the East End of London
with 'a Cambridge education,' to use Linda's gushing
words as she introduced us.

'Looking forward to the volcano climb then, Binnie?'
Eydis asked me as we sipped way-too-early glasses of
boozy Tsipouro. She looked for all the word like she could
be up and down several mountains in a day and still have
time and energy for an evening jog on the beach.

'Absolutely,' I lied. 'It should be a piece of cake in this
heat.'

Behind us Roman – as I learned his name was – the
snowboard-carrying dancer, was chatting to Argos in the
most wonderful Italian accent, and looking completely
smitten. 'This Titsy-pouro is magnifico!' he said, 'Dove
posso comprare?'

'You are aware there was a mini eruption on a nearby island a few days ago, aren't you?' Eydis continued.

'Oh, that's exciting!' said Linda.

'Yes,' I said, grimacing. 'Near death experiences are what I live for. Shall we go there next?'

'Good,' Eydis laughed. 'You will get on well with my boy, Roman.'

'I will?' I glanced back at him, arms now draped over Argos's shoulder, laughing like a hyena.

'Sure! You wouldn't think it to look at him, but he's an ex-member of the Dangerous Sports Club at Oxford Uni. Crazy bunch! The board is for a bit of additional thrill seeking,' she explained.

'Sounds like fun,' I said. 'But I don't think they'll get to do much snowboarding in Greece.'

'Haven't you heard of people snowboarding down volcanoes?' Eydis asked. 'That's what he plans to try.' She pointed to another of the troupe who was carrying a large, black holdall. I cloaked my chest and shoulders safely under the sarong and turned to look. 'They have a camera to make a video for YouTube,' she finished.

'Snowboarding on volcanoes? How is that possible?' Linda asked the question that had been in my head too. But just as Eydis was about to reply, Ginger, Edvard, Hughie and Greta came over to us. Much to my amusement, Greta was almost tripping over herself to ogle the dancers.

'Hullo, lassies,' Hughie said, to my boobs.

'Hello, Hughie,' I said, pulling my sarong protectively over my chest.

'Ye know,' he said with a smile. 'Ye shouldnae hide those things. Now whit were ye saying aboot snowboarding?'

'Nothing,' laughed Eydis, tapping her nose to indicate secrecy.

Greta looked nonplussed. 'Weel, they forecast a wee bit o' rain,' she said, 'but ah didnae hear aboot any snaw.'

Unable to contain her disinterest, Ginger strode away.

'Argos!' she said, grabbing his arm. 'How lovely to see you again.'

Turning to look at the young tour guide myself, he winked at me whilst accepting Ginger's hand and kissing it, I giggled and went all a-quiver like a silly schoolgirl. Oh, grow up woman! What was I? Twelve?

'You don't have a spare twenty in there do you?'

I tugged David's wallet out of his back pocket and made off with it, laughing as he grabbed at my hand to get it back, and missed.

'Hey, give that back to me!' he said, sounding angry.

'What's the matter, David?' I teased. 'Afraid I'm only after you for your money?' As I snapped the wallet open, he lunged for it again and I pulled away. 'Hah! You can't have it!' I squealed, utterly delighted to be winning the game.

'Just give it to me!'

The fury in his voice began to scare me and I stopped laughing. 'What's your problem?' I asked, feeling hurt. I looked down at the now open wallet, intent on closing it and passing it back, when a flash of familiar colour met my eyes. Tucked into one of the pockets there was a photo, with the edge just poking out. 'What's this?' I said.

'BINNIE, GIVE THAT BACK!'

I pulled the photo out and gasped, staring at it in disbelief. 'Why would you have this?' I cried. 'Why is it in your wallet?'

David made a final swipe at the wallet and won it back from my fingers, which were now limp and unresisting.

'Why, David?' I pleaded for an answer, needing one badly, but guessing that I knew it already.

'I didn't know that was there,' he said, sounding sheepish. But in another moment, he seemed to rethink things and his anger returned. 'Why are you going through my stuff anyway? This is mine!'

'I wasn't going through your stuff,' I retorted. 'I just wanted to borrow some cash for petrol.'

'Well, next time I'll get it for you. For God's sake, woman, can't a guy have any privacy?'

Tears pricked my eyes, pain searing my heart like a hot knife through butter.

'I . . . I didn't mean to pry,' I began, all the while not being able to believe I was the one apologising. He was the one with the photo in his wallet! And of all pictures, it had to be that one.

'Please, David,' I begged, waving the photo at him. 'You have to tell me. Why are you carrying around this photo?'

He shrugged. 'Oh, I don't know. I think I picked it up off the floor one day and shoved it in my wallet intending to hand it back to you. What's the matter? Are you crying?'

I shook my head.

'What, do you think, that I kept it in there on purpose?' he went on. 'Don't be silly.'

'I'm not being silly,' I cried. 'You had that in your wallet, David. And, for that matter, not one photo of me! How am I supposed to feel?'

I hugged the picture to my heart, like it could somehow stop it from breaking. It was one of my favourite photographs; I'd taken it myself. In the shot were four of my girlfriends at a hen party weekend we'd gone to in Spain, several years before I'd met David, back when I still had my own friends. All four of them were waving glasses of champagne and all were sporting tiny, string bikinis.

'What do you think, that I have it there to ogle your mates or something?' he boomed, still intent on making me feel silly. 'You are bloody paranoid! Why don't you stop being so pathetic and grow up! I love you, goddammit. This stuff,' he said, taking the photo off of me and tearing it in half. 'It's all in your own head!'

Within the hour we'd reached our destination, a little early-morning merry thanks to our additional shared liquid breakfast from Hercules' rucksack – the videographer for the dance troupe. I held on to my oversized sunhat, which was flapping away in the breeze and followed Eydis down the line to introduce us to them all – Roman (Italian), Hercules (Greek), Dominik (a Scot), Feargus (an Irishman), Bertrando (French-Italian) and Jasper (Philippine) – she explained a bit about their act. 'My boys are all incredible athletes and dancers who tour with the troupe only in the summer at the moment. I hope to make it a full time career for them.'

Greta was especially enamoured with Dominik – a smouldering, dark-haired 'hunk of Scottish beef' as she called him.

'Oooh, if I wis forty years younger, ye'd be in stokin' up ma fire,' she said, pinching his cheek.

By the way she was pawing and drooling over them all, I wondered if she knew, as I did, that every one of them was gay. Even forty years ago she couldn't have had any of them 'stoking up her fire'. Unattainability aside, they were gorgeous, fun guys; all international graduates from British universities, brought together by Eydis. The group was called Gelle.

'What is that terrible smell?' asked Hercules, covering his mouth and nose with a handkerchief as we all stepped off the gang plank at the end of the journey.

'Aww, Hughie, ye huvnae, huv ye?' Greta asked, punching him on the arm. He smiled, seeming proud to take credit for the overwhelming smell of fart that was in the air.

'It is the sulphur,' Argos explained. 'There was an eruption here a day ago. It is the gases from the volcano.'

'Hold the phone. There was an eruption here a few days ago?' Linda gasped.

'I thought it was on Santorini?' said Eydis.

'Yes, there was one there too. But the one here was very, very small. Nothing to worry about. They happen all the time,' Argos assured us.

'Should we really be here then?' My stomach did a little somersault as I asked this, and not just because of the stench. What exact thrill had David planned for us, bringing me to Death Valley?

'Here we are, Binnie, the old volcano tour I've been dying to do for years!'

'David, what is that glittery red line down the side of the mountain? It's heading straight for us!'

'Oh, it's nothing. Did I mention we were going for a swim? JUMP!'

'Really, it is fine,' Argos said, offering me a kind smile. 'There has been no major activity on this island for many, many years.'

'There was enough to bring the army out here,' I said, pointing to some camouflaged jeeps parked on the road near the shore.

'Oh, they are . . . what do you call them in the English? Scientists?' he replied.

'Volcanologists,' Eydis corrected him.

He blinked at me through dark, long eyelashes and our eyes locked, until mine became unable to resist the hike south to eye up his muscular torso for the hundredth time. If this guy fancied me as much as his eyes were telling me, there was a God after all.

Trudging our way up to the volcano caldera, my group found ourselves lagging behind the rest, overtaken by eager and much fitter tourists from the three other boats anchored at the island. As our group, with its six sexy, flamboyant men in scant, fluorescent clothing passed three male volcanology-types standing beside a military Jeep checking a map, they looked up. As they stared, Hughie offered them a staunch salute.

It was forty minutes later when we reached the caldera, shattered and full of Tsipouro. My heart was thumping so hard, I had started to accept death.

'Hey, look at that!' Argos was pointing up into the sky. Everyone followed his gaze to see a large bird of prey circling overhead.

'Now I know I'm unfit,' I said. 'I'm a drive thru menu for vultures.'

As we continued to watch it circle overhead, Hughie said,

'Looks like that rain's coming in after a' Greta.'

The skies had indeed begun to look darker and there was an ominous rumble of thunder in the distance.

'Okay!' Argos announced, clapping his hands. 'I think it is time we started back down.'

'Already?' I complained.

Linda grabbed at my hat and pushed it back on my head. 'Come on, sugar,' she said. 'Time to go.'

'Mr Argos?' Roman was on his feet, tapping him on

the shoulder. 'Is there anywhere here we could-a board down?'

'Board down?'

'Yes, board down. Like with the snowboarding?' He waved the board at Argos and grinned hopefully.

'Sorry, it is not possible here, the land is too dry.' As he answered, a further rumble of thunder and some first spots of rain disagreed with him. Turning to the rest of the group, he shouted, 'Time to make ways back to the boat!' Again he clapped his hands, just as a loud clap of thunder simultaneously crashed. Perhaps believing he had ecclesiastical backing, everyone began to pick up their things more quickly and make their way back towards the path.

'It's very busy up here,' Hercules said quietly. 'We could just hang back. How dangerous could it be?'

'Getting hit by lightning on top of a volcano?' Linda said sardonically, 'Oh, I don't know . . . quite?'

'Excellent!' Roman cut in excitedly. 'Let's do it!'

'Yes, wonderful idea,' Eydis replied, grabbing a concerned-looking Linda by the arm. I could see my friend wrestling both with a desire not to lose her cool in this first meeting with her much younger girlfriend and her instinct for self-preservation.

'Aye,' Hughie agreed. 'We just need tae look oot for any o' they sploótering gases!'

'Ah willnae walk ahint you then!' Greta chuckled.

'We can catch up with the group shortly What do you think, Binnie? Fancy a little adventure in the rain?' Linda winked at Eydis. So, looking cool and agreeable won. I'd rather have been following Argos down the hillside with my tongue hanging out, but found myself nodding in agreement too, even though I had no-one to impress. Not anymore.

*

109

'Bride or groom?'

The elderly usher tapped a carnation on my shoulder as I stared in wonder at the incredibly high ceiling inside the chapel at Oxford University. Behind me, Michael, his mother, father and sister were greeting lots of well-to-do relatives they hadn't seen in an age, in a series of stiff handshakes and air kisses.

'Thanks,' I said with a smile, taking the carnation from the man. 'I'll eat it later.'

Michael's mother watched me with raised eyebrows before giving her husband one of her familiar, 'Where DID our son find that girl?' looks. Michael lurched forward, grabbed my hand and dragged me away to our seat.

'Can't you at least try to behave in a civilised manner?' Michael hissed into my ear. 'They are my family!'

'I was only being jolly,' I said. The truth was, I was just being myself.

His father directed us to a pew as far away as he could from any relatives who might notice they'd brought a commoner with them. At least, that was how I had interpreted it at the time. At just nineteen, I'd begun to tell myself the whole world disapproved of me.

'Michael,' his mother said to him just a few weeks later. 'What do you see in that girl? She just isn't, well, like us.'

*

Nobody in the group ahead, hot on the heels of Argos and the other tour guides, was in any hurry to look back, which was perfect for our plans. The rain was heavy, but it was a lovely warm rain, the kind you could dance in naked. If you were Gelle. Or Hughie, I thought . . . and then shuddered.

'There's some bubbling activity here in the ground,' Linda said, leaning over what looked like a small, hot puddle. We had reached the cordoned off area of the caldera – thrill seekers in forbidden territory – armed with a snowboard, binoculars and flip-flops. Wrenching her backwards to safety I jeered, 'Do you want a melted face?'

'Ooh, yes please,' she said. 'I laugh in the face of a melted face.'

'Not before we have seen the volcano-boarding Roman!' Roman shouted, putting his snowboard at the edge of a very steep embankment.

'Wait for the camera!' Jasper shouted. 'Hercules, get ready!'

Hercules did as he was told, taking the video camera out of his holdall and pointing it at Roman.

'Ready!'.

Maybe it was one *Tsipouro* too many, or maybe I was just willing to exchange death for a great Facebook status photo. But, whatever it was that made me jostle Roman out of the way and get onto the board to let Linda take my photo, before pushing my feet into the bindings, it was a mean and impish arsehole.

'*Everybody's gone surfin'!*' I sang out, see-sawing on the board like a lunatic.

The gang howled with laughter. Then, Greta said, 'Ooh Binnie, there's a wee gecko thingy on yer bunnet.'

'*Surfin' US . . . AAAAAAAAAAAAARGH!*'

Before anyone could say, '*And there's a hungry long-legged buzzard swooping down to eat it,*' there was a hungry long-legged buzzard swooping down to eat it. The unfortunate gecko was a goner. I think. It was hard to look back while travelling at high speed down the side of a volcano on a snowboard, with my feet caught and tangled in the bindings.

'BINNIE!'

There was yelling and the pounding of feet behind me, but no time for a peek over my shoulder. A desire for self-preservation – which would have been handier ten seconds ago *before* I'd climbed on to the damn snowboard – took care of that.

CRASHHHHHHHH!

I couldn't imagine a more perfect time for the thunder and lightning to *really* get going. As the ground underneath me started falling away in all directions, unearthing a cluster of rocks, I let out a scream.

'AAAAAAHHHHH!'

There was no time to progress to the letter B. Rock, board and I all began tumbling down the volcano side, throwing up debris as I disturbed more ground in my wake.

'It's all over!' I cried in my own head, hurtling down and down like a rocket . . . on a snowboard.

Chapter Eleven

Dear God, if you can hear me now, I'm
guessing it's because I've just been killed
in a snowboarding accident. How unoriginal.
Trust me to die in a death hoax report kind
of way.

As suddenly as it had started, the earth stopped moving as I hit a clump of earth and the board came to a grinding halt, throwing me backwards so that my feet broke out of the loose bindings. I lay on top of the board, staring up at the sky, catching my breath and taking in the shock of what had just happened. Then I heard Roman's anxious voice not far behind me, yelling, 'STOP!'

Before I had a chance to try and sit up, the earth started moving again and the board carried me rolling on downhill, flat on my back, in what must have looked like some horrible, upside down body-boarding attempt. Thankfully, Roman had gained on me, and was now running alongside, still yelling. He dived across my path, throwing his whole body in front of the board. I was saved – but not before the snowboard had skidded over his leg, throwing me into a backwards body-roll. I heard an almighty clatter as it carried on un-womanned, before crashing into a huge, jaggy boulder that had been waiting to act as my brakes before Roman had dived in the way. There was dust everywhere.

'My foot! My foot!'

The other dancers came rushing across to help, picking me up off him.

'Oh, are you okay?'

'Where does it hurt?'

'Can you move your ankle?'

Even as I lay dazed, looking up at the heavens, I knew nobody was speaking to me. A noise somewhere above made me strain my neck to look up and there, out of the huge plume of debris in my wake, came Linda, Eydis and an out-of-breath Hughie, closely followed by a slowly lumbering Greta.

'Are you okay, Binnie?' Linda asked, reaching me first.

Somewhere in the distance there was a sound of people shouting and . . . it sounded like . . . screaming.

'Shhh! Do you hear that?' I said, still lying on my back.

No-one could see anything through the debris my volcano snowboarding antics had just stirred up around us.

'Oh, my goodness, it sounds like chaos down there,' I said. 'Maybe one of the volcanoes has erupted!' Forgetting my bruised and aching backside, I jumped to my feet, panic rising in my chest. It was time to run. *I knew I shouldn't have come to this cursed island!*

'Dear God,' said Eydis. 'Come on! We'd better hurry back down to the boat! It sounds like pandemonium down there.'

'I can't walk!' Roman cried out.

'Boys, carry him!' Eydis commanded. 'We need to get down fast.'

'I can't run!' said Greta, sounding panicked.

The rain was abating a little now, but thunder rumbled across the valley. We could see nothing but debris and dust behind us so no-one could work out where the eruption might be. All we knew was that we had to move fast or risk becoming part of the landscape.

Hercules and Jasper took Roman by the arms and legs to carry him, while the remaining three dancers lifted Greta, one grabbing her arms and the other two taking a leg each, and carried her spread-eagled – bloomers on show for the second time that week – down the mountainside. With elbows stinging and pride hurt, I followed.

It wasn't long before we came across the military Jeep, its officials nowhere to be seen. As the dust began to clear, I could make out streams of people, all tearing down the hillside in front of us.

It had to be another eruption. I saw that the driver's side door of the Jeep was ajar and the motor still running, I looked all around again to see if I could see the volcanologists, but couldn't see them anywhere. Thinking only of Roman's injured foot now, I shouted over to the guys.

'Quick, over here!'

Roman was soon piled onto the back seat, joined by Jasper and three other squealing guys who crammed in, backsides pressed to the windows as Hughie dived into the passenger seat with Greta jumping on his lap.

'I . . . I can't drive!' I squealed, realising I'd jumped into the driver's side, forgetting the right hand drive thing again.

'Just put yer foot doon on that wee pedal on the right and let's go!' Hughie yelled.

Of course I could do it, I'd had some lessons. With no time to think any further, I took to the wheel to make a getaway. *Brave, heroic Binnie to the rescue! I am Wonder Woman!*

I wound down the window and called to Eydis and Linda, 'Will you be okay?'

There were shouts from the team of scientists and at last, I could see them running towards us.

'Fine!' Eydis called. 'You go ahead, I'll explain to these guys. We'll see you at the boat. It's not far now!'

Releasing the hand brake, throwing the clutch into gear and hurtling off down the road to the waiting boats, accelerator pedal to the floor, I heard a running commentary in my head which sounded just like my father:

'I knew you could do it, Bernice. Go like the wind!'

'We interrupt this episode of Come Dine with Me *to bring you a newsflash. British tourist, Bernice Dando, has just saved a man's foot from certain amputation in the wake of a devastating volcanic eruption on a remote island in Greece, by selflessly forgetting she can't drive.'*

Within minutes – which may have seemed like hours to my wailing passengers, as the car swerved and bumped down the dusty hillside, taking every bend on two wheels – we were back at the beach, in complete chaos.

Tourists, locals, goats, locals pushing goats – everyone was thrashing through the sea to pile on to the four fishing boats that were berthed at the harbour. There was panicked shouting and screams of desperation all around us.

'Volcan!'

'Get us off this island!'

'HELP US!'

'My cigarettes! I left my damn cigarettes up there!'

I caught sight of Argos lifting people aboard our boat to safety and pulled over beside him, checked my reflection in the mirror (is my mascara running while Greece is burning?), threw open the door of the jeep and jumped out.

'Argos! Please! Help me get Roman on the boat. His foot is broken!'

All at once, the dancers fell out of the back door of the jeep with an almighty singular shriek and crashed onto the sand.

'Where did you go, lady?' Argos asked, panic etched on his normally calm, composed features.

Turning to point at the caldera we had just hurtled down from, my eyes met the sight of Linda, Eydis and Bertrando, who had stripped off his flip-flops and was tearing down the mountain barefoot, waving them frantically in his hands. Directly above them I could see the huge plume of debris I had stirred up around the caldera we'd raced away from. Thunder and lightning boomed and crashed all around it. It looked like a scene from a disaster movie.

'Wow, you'd think that one was erupting too.' I thought.

Turning my attention to the entire landscape, I searched for the real volcanic activity – a fiery, red, nose-bleedy line, smoke spewing out of a volcano top, anything – and saw *nothing*. All was calm, except for the area I had snowboarded down, crazy stunt-woman style. As panicked people continued to scream and run in all directions around us, realisation dawned . . .

A military helicopter swooped in and landed a few feet away. I watched as its occupants were pulled out hastily by screaming tourists, who then bundled into it. Behind me, Argos and the rest of the group had forgotten me, as everyone began clambering onto the boat, carrying a yelping Roman along with them. I looked back up at the 'erupting' volcano we had just raced from and spied four very angry scientists heading my way.

'Erm . . . everyone?' I said to myself, as no-one could hear above all the chaos and noise. 'I don't think there is going to be any need for us to rush.'

We are sorry to interrupt Sid going through Gemma's knickers drawer in this gripping episode of Come Bitch at Me again, but we have to bring you an update on our earlier newsflash. Bernice Dando is officially a numpty.

Chapter Twelve

I'm a changed man; I mean it! I'm not doing
anything with my phone.

The message had come from a new, unrecognised
number. So, David now knew I was blocking his old
one. As Chris turned the car into Villa Miranda's driveway,
a tear fell down my cheek and I brushed it away.

'Did you hear that on the radio?' Chris interrupted my
thoughts as he pulled the car up to the gate.

'What?'

He turned the radio up, but all I heard was the DJ
babbling away in Greek.

'Was there an eruption scare on that island you were
on today?'

'Er . . .' I gulped, finding time in my moment of internal
misery to feel embarrassed. 'Yes, there was.' As I turned
off my phone and tried unsuccessfully to push it into the
small, tight pocket of my shorts, I felt my cheeks flush
red. 'It was just loads of people panicking and rushing for
boats to get off the island.'

'I thought that's what it was saying,' Chris said, looking aghast – at my calm attitude no doubt. 'My understanding of Greek isn't perfect,' he went on. 'Why on earth didn't you mention it? Are you okay?'

'Fine,' I said, opening the door to go and open the gate. 'It turned out to be just a scare . . . a rock slide or something.'

'It was a big enough event to be on the local news.'

'Well, there were scientists in the area because of the recent mini eruption on the same island,' I admitted. 'So there was quite a turnout, what with the helicopters and people in army uniform. It looked like a scene from a disaster movie, but it was nothing in the end.'

I got out, unlocked the gate and watched the car crunch up onto the gravel driveway.

'And that's it?' Chris called back to me as he stepped out of the car.

'That's it,' I answered. I hadn't just escaped death by the skin of my bruised and battered butt cheeks. I had just escaped prison for stealing a jeep in a panic, though.

'Anyway, do you know what?' I said, more brightly. 'Today, for the first time in years, I drove a car. Isn't that marvellous? I don't suppose you fancy having dinner with me tonight to celebrate?'

I had changed the subject with the dexterous speed of a swooping falcon type thingy.

'You did?'

'I did. So, what do you think? Dinner? My treat?'

'Well, I'd love to but I'm actually meeting a friend tonight.' He checked his watch. 'In about half an hour, as it happens. Better get my skates on.'

'Ah, okay. Well, have fun with your friend,' I said, heart sinking. 'Maybe another time.'

'Sure,' he said with a smile. 'Another time.'

I watched him race up the steps and wondered what excuse Ginger was giving to Edvard to get away right now. My own reasons for asking Chris to go out with me tonight hadn't been entirely about sticking my nose in where it didn't belong, though. I hated eating alone.

I walked into the apartment and pulled out my phone once more, to leave the perfunctory 'Mr and Mrs Dando having a great time' Facebook status:

```
What a day on the Dando honeymoon! The
earth moved!
```

Knowing full well Beth and Sal would balk at the sexual innuendo in my post, I sent it anyway, with a link to a news story about the nearby Santorini mini eruption before switching on the shower. Before I could go anywhere, I had to wash away the volcano dust. And I had to – needed to – call my sister.

I slipped into a long, silky-blue maxi dress and eyed my reflection in the mirror. The material felt so fine against my skin and the pretty sea-blue flared skirt skimmed over my hips and thighs perfectly. It was almost as if I had no tummy. Thank you, Spanx.

'Hello, lovely lady,' I said aloud, doing my best Argos impression and throwing the tiny knickers I'd been intending to wear back into my open case. Despite the most horrendous day, a day in which he was probably aware I had played an, albeit unwitting, part in the furore, it was becoming evident that for some reason Argos found me – yes me – attractive. I felt a pang of guilt. I was, after all, married to David. But then, he didn't desire me. Why shouldn't I enjoy being admired by a younger guy?

My feminine mystique had returned because he hadn't seen me naked. Oh hell, here I am again, imagining that awful moment when a new dalliance is on the cards and you've been with the same, comfortable man who knows every curve of your body for so long. I looked down at my breasts and sighed. How would it feel getting these old puppies out to someone new? Oh, who cares! I drove a jeep today!

I couldn't help but laugh to myself. I clicked on the radio and reached into my open handbag on the floor for some lip salve. The news was playing:

'AAAAAARRRRGGGGHHHH!'

There was panic and pandemonium today on the Greek island of . . .

I flicked it off again and, as I did so, picked up my electronic pelvic toner lying next to it. *Dammit! I forgot to do my ten minutes today.*

'Never (cough), neglect your (cough) pelvic floor (splutter) darling.' After wiping her mouth with one hand and passing me a magazine article with the other, Smother tapped the accompanying diagram of a man and woman smiling at each other in bed, presumably after having had the most gripping sex ever, thanks to the woman in the photograph discovering this thing.

'It's amazing. You can watch TV, check your emails or read a book while it tightens your . . .' she pointed to the place on her own body I was never going to look, 'you know . . . intimate muscles. The ones that have gone now you've had your children. It's called a vaginal cone.'

'God, Mother,' I joked. 'Worst. Ice cream flavour. Ever.'

Of course, I knew all about pelvic toners and just wished – whilst putting a sofa cushion in the washing machine after she had left, still coughing – that Smother had, thirty years and four hundred and thirty thousand cigarettes ago. I posted my order form the same evening.

As I swung the bulb by its wire in front of my face, I wondered about the ingenious ways this electro-pulser of internal womanly things might improve my non-existent sex life. As my mind carried me, not altogether kicking and screaming, back to Argos's rippling chest, the 'time to zap your vagina now' alarm went off on my mobile phone, making me jump and drop the device. *How did it know?* I reached over to turn it off, reasoning with it at the same time.

'I swear, I'll do two lots tomorrow.'

I picked my handbag up off the floor, closed it and headed out for a meal alone. There would be time to call Suzy later after a few drinks, which should help me spill all the beans.

Finding a pretty tavern with a table facing out to sea, I sat down to watch the evening sunset, my mind drifting for a few moments, until a handsome young Greek waiter brought me a menu.

'Are we waiting for someone tonight?' he asked.

'No, it's just me.'

He smiled. 'Okay, well, can I get you something to drink? Perhaps a little wine?'

'That would be lovely. House white, please.'

He handed me the menu, brushing my hand in the process, and gave a little wink before heading off for the wine. My face flushed, but the prickle of pleasure I got from being flirted with by such a handsome young man was a nice addition to what could have been an awkward evening otherwise. I'd forgotten what it was like to receive so much male attention and couldn't really understand it. I recalled a line from the film *Cocktail*: 'Excuse me? Do I have "fuck me" written on my forehead?'

Maybe as a single, forty-something woman, it was time to consider a tattoo . . .

I watched his tight, sexy bottom disappear off behind the kitchen counter and my eyes wandered across to meet another, more familiar view.

'Edvard! Hi.'

He was standing over a cabinet display of fish at the counter with another waiter, watching me admiring the rear view of mine. *Awkward.*

'Hello,' he replied, pointing to something in the cabinet for the waiter before walking back towards his table, which happened to be opposite mine and occupied by a group of four others. There was no sign of Ginger. 'How are you this evening? That was a scary day, huh?'

'Not with Ginger this evening?'

'No, she has a yoga class every evening for an hour and tonight she is going to dinner with them while I watch the game.' He pointed to a large screen TV on the wall, so far silenced, which showed a couple of sports commentators having a pre-football match chat. Of course – tonight was the Euro cup semi-final. 'You are welcome to join our table?' he offered.

'No, that's okay. This is a lovely spot for drinking in the sunset and I'm not much of a football fan.'

Edvard nodded towards his table where two older couples I hadn't seen before were sitting. 'Are you sure?' he asked.

'Yes, quite sure, thank you.' As my waiter came back out of the kitchen carrying a tray with a half carafe of wine in one hand, he flicked a remote at the TV with the other so that everyone could hear the game. Placing my drink on the table, he winked again and proceeded to take my order.

I sipped my wine and stared out to sea and thought about Ginger. So, she has a regular yoga class? And tonight, she is at dinner with 'them' whoever 'they' may be. It was all looking too convenient. I really didn't know Chris at all.

'Why are you alone?'

The question came from a little girl sitting at the next table with her parents – who were both engrossed in the game. She had long dark hair, green eyes and peered at me over small, round glasses. I pretended not to notice she was speaking to me, and waved to get the waiter's attention.

'Could I have some water please?' I said, pointing to my glass and giving him a wink, in case it was international waiter/customer language or something. After dinner and a half carafe of wine, I was beginning to think I might need scissors to get the crushing Spanx pants off later. And wasn't I supposed to be cleansing myself of all this boozy living?

'Well, why are you?' the little girl continued to question me.

I looked at her and forced a smile. 'Because that's the way I like it,' I said.

'By yourself?'

She continued to stare without blinking, making me shift in my seat like a Mastermind contestant on their fourth pass.

'What happens just before a man . . .'
BEEP BEEP BEEP!

'I've started so I'll finish . . . ejaculates?'

'Ooh . . . er . . . I used to know this one. Oh, it's been a long time . . . Erm . . . Oh, pass!'

'Evie!' The brusque voice of the little girl's mother brought me back to reality. 'Don't be so rude! I'm so sorry.' The woman smiled at me before turning Evie back round to face her. 'Leave the poor lady alone.'

The words, 'poor lady' stung a little. It was how I must have looked − a poor, lonely lady.

Sighing, I picked up my handbag and headed for the toilets. As I checked my reflection, I reached into my handbag for some lipstick, but instead found some kind of wire coiled inside. I tugged on it and out popped a bulbous object I recognised. *Oh, for heaven's sake!* I'd dropped the damn pelvic toner in my bag! I pulled the machine out and stared at the cone, wondering if this was a sign telling me I was to be condemned to Slack Vaginasville for forgetting today's session. Maybe I could just nip back to the apartment after my meal and have an early one? I could phone Suzy while I was squeezing. *Urgh, noooo.* Wrong, wrong, wrong! Anyway, could I hold a vaginal cone in for twelve minutes without a toilet break after a half carafe of wine? Deciding against it, I shoved it back into my bag, checked my hair in the mirror and hurried back outside.

As I strolled back to my table, there was a tug at my shoulder.

'What's that thing?' It was Evie, and the cheeky little minx was tugging on my handbag!

Turning to see what she was referring to, I froze on the spot. To my horror, I realised she was pulling on the wire from the pelvic toner, which was hanging out of my half-closed bag.

'Get off that!' I hissed. 'Don't you know it's rude to . . . ?'

'Wow! What *is* that?'

She had managed to wrestle the toner free and stood gazing at the cylindrical bulb in wonderment. It was time to think up some very clever explanation and fast. However, I was pants at that.

'It's a . . . it's a . . .'

Looking around the taverna it was clear everyone was – thankfully – focussed on the football, which had now kicked off.

'It's a mini karaoke machine,' I lied. 'But it's broken, so give it back to me please.'

'A karaoke? Oh, I love singing! Can I have a go?'

'Well, you could, but as I said, it's broken so . . .'

She rolled the vaginal cone around in her hands, fiddled with the buttons on the monitor and stared back up at me. 'How is it broken?'

'See, there's no music. Now if you'll just give it to m . . .'

'Mummy, look at me! This lady gave me a microphone! She wants to hear me sing! Can I?'

Her mother was still engrossed in the TV and without turning, waved a hand at her. 'Okay, that's lovely Evie, now shhh!'

'Water for you?'

My waiter had appeared which gave Evie the chance to break away. She skipped round the back of the tables holding the vaginal bulb to her mouth as a makeshift microphone.

'BAYBEE, BAYBEE, BAYBEE OHHHH!'

I looked at the waiter who was now watching her with a bemused look on his face.

'Please,' I said, grasping his arm. 'I'm actually feeling a little sick. Do you mind if I cancel the rest of this order and just pay my bill?'

'Oh no, it was not the food I hope?' His nonplussed expression turned to one of concern and he shouted towards the kitchen, 'Vasos!'

Two faces peered out at him. I grimaced, 'No, no, please. I don't want a fuss. It's not the food, it was beautiful. Just perfect! I think I just had a little too much wine.'

Out of the corner of my eye I spied Evie still skipping around. I flushed crimson.

'Please,' I pleaded now. 'Just the bill?'

Waving the watching staff away, he nodded and disappeared back to the kitchen, but there was no wink this time. Maybe women about to vomit in embarrassment weren't his thing.

It occurred to me that there were only two ways to get my machine back from Evie: tell her parents – drawing attention to the fact that their little girl was singing into a pelvic toner – or play along. I went for option number two.

'How about we sing one together, over here by the beach?' I called out to her. 'Then you can give it back to me.'

She nodded enthusiastically and I led her over to the wall to sit down, wondering why on earth her parents weren't watching her wandering away with a stranger.

'Now, what shall we sing? And don't say Justin Bieber because that's just not music.'

She grinned, a sweet, innocent-looking smile. This girl had a great face for undetected mischief.

'Do you know *LMFAO*?' she asked.

'Excuse me?'

Putting the bulb up to her mouth once more, she wailed, 'When I walk in the spot, YEAH this is what I see OK! Everybody stops and they starin' at me!'

Jesus.

'Your bill, madam?'

The waiter had been watching as we belted out our duet, sharing the vaginal cone 'microphone' with my joining in at, 'I'M SEXY AND I KNOW IT!' – the only bit that was familiar to me and something that singing into a pelvic toner didn't epitomise. I wasn't sure if he could tell what the machine really was, but I wasn't offering up the question for a round of *Jeopardy*.

'Something women use after child birth to stop them weeing their pants while doing star jumps.'

'What is a pelvic toner?'

After paying my bill and leaving Evie to go back to annoying her parents, I walked down the steps to the beach, where I was met by a smiling Argos.

'That was so good,' he said, beaming a beautiful, white-toothed smile at me.

Once again, I flushed crimson. He'd been watching me!

'Hello there,' I said, pushing the machine back into my handbag and closing the zip. 'I thought you'd be having an early night after today's events.'

He smiled and peered down at my handbag which I was furtively pushing behind my back. 'What is that thing?' he asked.

'Oh that? Just a little mini karaoke machine – a child's toy really. I like to practise my . . . erm . . . breathing techniques.'

'Ah. Well, it was lovely. How are you, lovely Binnie?'

At last, he had learned my name. Which to him wasn't

'Mrs David Dando', it was 'Lovely Binnie.' Nice. I liked 'Lovely Binnie.'

'Oh, fine,' I said. 'I had a lovely dinner and I think I'm just going to head back now.'

He frowned. 'That is a shame, because a few of the local people go to a cove for swimming at night. I thought you might like to come too?'

'Oh, I'd love to, but I didn't bring my costume and as I said, I have to make a phone call.'

And I'm not swimming in my poo-brown Spanx.

'That's alright. You don't need a costume and it's just for a leetle while. Come on.'

He took my arm and, ignoring my protests, walked me uphill towards his moped which was parked at the quayside.

Chapter Thirteen

A romantic meal for two under the stars. And
oooh, Italy just scored!

I stood in the small clearing and updated my Facebook status while Argos went over to chat to some friends as they were leaving. There were sounds of music, whooping and laughter from somewhere below us. Finally, he waved the group off and beckoned me to follow him.

I grabbed my bag from the moped's basket and ran behind him as he led me to a rocky ledge. There we found a single rope to climb down to the tiny, hidden cove below.

As we scrambled down to the dimly lit beach, I could make out glistening, wet, naked bodies everywhere, diving in and out of the water. My stomach turned over. Despite the fact that in a few days' time I was due to meet my toughest challenge yet – a nudist beach – I couldn't rip off my dress in front of Argos! Before I was able to think about it a moment longer, he was running past me in all his naked glory and diving headlong into the moonlit sea, only to be surrounded by a group of giggling girls.

Ignoring all of them, he beckoned to me, 'Are you going to come in?'

I could feel my support underwear almost creaking from the strain of redistributing my belly fat to my back and boobs and waved him away with a 'Hah, what me? Nooo!' and planted my backside firmly in the sand to watch him. Behind us, a guitarist sat beside a small bonfire, fingerpicking the most alluring music. Despite all the splashing and flashing of young bodies under the light of a new moon, it was quite romantic. I wasn't going to spoil the atmosphere by producing my own, extremely full moon, spilling out of a way-too-tight pair of beige support knickers. One thing was certain, if I took the thing off my body would show every stitch and seam like I was still wearing it.

As I watched all the splashing and commotion, without being able to make out anybody's faces, I heard a familiar voice shout out.

'Hughie, are ye coming in tae swim or are you just going to stand there ogling everything?'

I didn't turn around. Naked Hughie was not something I needed to see.

'Binnie! Please come for a swim!' Argos was standing waist-deep in the sea now and walking back in to the shore towards me.

'I'm okay,' I told him quietly, with a shake of my head. I wasn't sure how close I was to Hughie but I didn't want to attract his attention.

'Why?' he said. 'You are so lovely for me.'

Bless him. He's lost his contacts in the water.

'Thank you,' I said.

'Binnie,' he continued. 'If you won't come in the water then let me sing to you.'

'Sing?' I said. 'What on earth would make you want to do that?'

'Because I want to,' he said, gesturing towards the nearby guitarist, who was just starting to play a new song. 'Do you know this tune?'

I listened to the gentle plinkety-plink of the first few finger-picked bars. 'I don't, no,' I confessed.

'We were born before the wind,' Argos sang, whereby I recognised a much loved Van Morrison tune. 'Also younger than the sun. And the bonnie boat was won, as we sailed into the mystic!'

Bless him. I was born before the wind. He probably turned up around about when Bryan Adams was at No. 1 for a hundred weeks with '*Everything I Do.*' Turning to look back at the musician, I spotted Greta and Hughie's bare backsides walking away in the other direction. So they hadn't seen me. *We bring you another exciting episode of Naked Old People You Know in 3D next month.*

'Come on, Binnie,' Argos called. 'Come in the water!'

I hunched up, bowing my head towards my lap, trying to make myself smaller; invisible.

'*What's wrong with me? Why aren't you turned on?*'

David rolled back onto his side of the bed and sighed. 'It's not you, Binnie,' he said. 'It's me.'

'Well, just tell me what to do to help and I'll do it. What turns you on?'

He paused, before turning his face to the bedside table. 'You know what turns me on,' he said. 'It never fails.'

His words stung and my heart ached, but I knew what he wanted. And, I knew he was right.

'We don't have to if you don't want to,' he added quickly. 'It's horrible. I won't say it again.'

'No,' I said, sitting up to face him. 'If it's what you need, let's do it. I don't mind.'

I lay back down on my back, waiting as he picked up his mobile phone.

'I'll just be a minute,' he said. 'Just got to find the right thing. Are you sure you don't mind?'

I shook my head, swallowed hard and stared up at the ceiling. And there I remained, with my eyes closed tightly shut, as he finally found what he wanted, placed the phone on the pillow above my head and climbed on top of me. I heard a dog barking outside; a distant ice-cream van playing the theme from The Archers. I heard the squeals and moans of lithe, young women, the bed rocking and his breath now coming thick and fast. And when finally he collapsed on to my body, whispering his thanks into my ear, I was glad to be invisible.

'Let me use your microphone.'

Argos's shout brought me back to the present. I blinked back tears and stood up.

'Look,' I said. 'I really should go . . .'

'No, wait!' he cried, making his way out of the water. I turned my face away, realising I was about to get a full frontal. 'Just one song for you, Binnie. Please.'

'B . . .b . . . but it's broken,' I stammered, covering my eyes with my handbag. 'And I really have to get back now, I promised to phone my sister tonight.'

As I peeped out from behind my bag, I saw his pubic area began to appear above the water. Lowering my bag now, my mouth fell open and I fiddled furiously with the zip. 'Alright, alright! Just stay there and you can have it!'

Laughing, he sank his lower body back down into the sea, keeping his manhood covered. He held out his hand for the probe.

'Take it! Take it!' I said, thrusting it at him.

He grasped the bulb to his mouth and, seeing me still holding the unit asked, 'are you recording me?'

'Argos, I told you, it's broken,' I said, pretending to press the buttons to demonstrate the machines inefficiency. At least – I thought I was pretending. Until he opened his mouth to sing, swung his head and yanked the unit out of my hands – knocking it into the water – where it fizzled in front of his pelvic region.

'Arghyaggghhhyaaaaggghhh!'

He did a quick, violent judder at the waist which astonished me. He was a way better dancer the other night. 'Waaarrrrgggggghhhh hah hahaaa haaaaaa!' he cried out. He was a way better singer a second ago too.

'Okay, it's not quite *The Lady in Red*-style serenade I was expecting,' I said, trying my best to be tactful. All at once, he dropped the bulb into the water. It sank like a stone.

'Oh, no!' I yelped. 'My Kegel . . . er . . . Karaoke thingy!' It was only then that I realised he had fallen to his knees, looking like he was about to pass out.

'Oh, Argos, are you alright?'

As he began to flop forward, I waded in just in time to stop him dropping face first into the sea.

'Oh, help!' I cried.

I tried to heave him up out of the water, made easier as he began to find his legs again.

'Upsadaisy, there you go,' I said, guiding him to the beach and forgetting he was naked. Which was just as well, because I sounded like I was his mum and about to put a plaster on his ickle knee. Then it hit me. Well, not *hit* me exactly. Just boinged off my leg.

'Argos! Oh my . . .' I started, peering down at what was a very impressive erection.

Still dazed, Argos scratched his head in wonderment, and with a weird, stupefied smile on his face. I grabbed his towel from a rock to cloak him in, just as a very drunk young guy appeared from nowhere, wearing nothing but a pair of shoes and a cap.

'Hey, man,' he said, staggering and hiccupping all the way. 'Which way to the rope ladder? I need to get out of here.'

Argos turned towards him, still stunned and fully erect, and opened his mouth to speak. But no words would come. Before I could offer a response myself, the man donned his cap, said 'Thanks man!' and staggered off in the direction Argos's very prominent member was pointing to.

Chapter Fourteen

Late night - wine and skinny-dipping. Sun's
down, bottoms up!

As I posted a photo of a sun-kissed, pert bottom that
everyone would know wasn't mine to Facebook, my
face flushed pink at the memory of Argos's electric-shock
induced erection, which had poked me in the back as I had
driven him home on his moped the night before. My wet
clothes lay strewn on the floor somewhere, after I'd dived
onto the bed, shattered from my calamitous day. Still, it
wasn't *all* bad. It was ages since anyone had poked me in
the back with their erection.

'I love you today, Mr Dando.'
    'I love you *every* day, Mrs Dando.'
    'I'm going to love you every day, I just haven't had
them all yet.'
    It was the morning after our wedding and we were
lying, arms and legs entwined, under a thin, cotton sheet

on the hotel room floor. My idea that we should try a very quiet quickie on the private balcony for a bit of 'al fresco' variety that morning had only served to make David more anxious and unable to perform. I'd reassured him everything was fine, the euphoria of waking up as his wife filling and comforting me like warm, mulled wine. We had the rest of our lives to get it right.

'Hey, honey,' he'd said, touching me under my chin, which I immediately dipped to stop him brushing the early morning she-beardiness. 'Why don't you go get us a paper while I jump in the shower?'

'Sure,' I said, grinning from ear to ear. 'It's the least a wife can do for her husband.'

Oh the memories. That morning after marriage romance. That morning after marriage euphoria. That morning after marriage stroll to the newsagents while he has a wank in the shower . . .

With some satisfaction, I wondered if David was reading my updates, perhaps wondering who I was skinny-dipping with. He might know there was no other man I could love right now, but he couldn't know I was being faithful and I wasn't going to help him to this conclusion.

I remembered an email counselling session I'd taken two years earlier without telling David. I'd written: *'It isn't just when I'm out with David that I feel so bad. I've been avoiding going out with friends too. My last night out was a couple of weeks ago with two colleagues and all I did was spend the entire time staring at the pretty, slim young things on the dance floor, feeling like a fat, old hag. I couldn't wait to get back home and hide. The truth is, I've begun to wonder where I've gone.'*

My head had been swimming in David's problems; I

knew that now. That was where I had gone. The therapist had advised me to do one thing a day that made me feel better about myself – something I'd only begun to try now – on my honeymoon, with the five steps to a new me. Sure, I'd strayed from this new path of righteousness a couple of times, but I badly wanted to feel as free as a woman should feel of all these doubts and, for heaven's sake, have some fun. I knew my battered heart wasn't ready to stop loving David yet. Even knowing that at least *some* of the bad thoughts and feelings I had about myself had been fostered from memories of how he – and Michael – had treated me. When would I ever feel good enough?

'Michael, are you planning on bringing *that* girl to your cousin's wedding?'

'Yes, of course.'

'Oh. Wonderful.'

Michael seemed not to notice the sarcasm in his mother's tone as he pushed his bedroom door closed and bounced gleefully back into bed beside me, laughing.

'At least we know she doesn't realise you stayed last night,' he said.

'That girl?' I said, aghast and hurt. 'What does she mean, *"that girl"*?'

'Oh, you know Mother,' he replied. 'She's just a terrible snob.'

I wondered why he hadn't defended me. Why he hadn't said, 'Actually, that girl is here and I love her and we're going to have a baby.' I wondered why, two months into my pregnancy and as delighted as a child with a new toy that he seemed to be, he hadn't told either of his parents yet.

'I'll tell them when the time is right,' he'd said coyly.

139

'Just not now. We've only been going out a couple of months so it's going to be a shock. Besides, it's their silver wedding anniversary this month and I don't want to spoil it for them by giving them something to worry about.'

'Worry about?' I roared. 'I'm nineteen and you're twenty one next month. We're grown-ups for heaven's sake! Why are we hiding our relationship? Our sleeping together? *Our baby*?'

I thought I was ready to tackle the world at nineteen, that my unanticipated new family would be much better than my old one. That Michael was going to be the loving, supportive parent I never had. That my child would never have to feel like he or she was a perpetual disappointment to him.

'You're WHAT?'

'Pregnant, Dad. I'm going to have a baby.'

My father stared back at me, open-mouthed. Smother had rushed to put an arm around his shoulder to soothe him.

'What did I tell you about using contraception?' she scolded. My father visibly shrank at the mention of the word 'contraception'. He always looked as though he needed to leave the room whenever any references to sex were made in his company.

'It wasn't planned, of course, but Michael and I couldn't be happier,' I'd said, unable to comprehend why everyone wasn't as over the moon as Michael was.

As *Michael* was.

Only as an older, wiser woman had I acknowledged that the proud, smiling teenager telling everyone, including Michael, that this was the beginning of the rest of her life and that she couldn't be happier, had been cloaking her fear and bewilderment in false joy. All the while my tummy had felt weird. Like there was something there, questioning the reason for the new life inside it.

'Hey, you up there! How the hell did this happen? Do you even love this guy?'

My father had died from a stroke just two months before Sal was born. I felt sure the disappointment had killed him, a belief my mother helped exacerbate in a series of heavily cloaked digs. As I'd walked down the aisle with her giving me away later that year, I looked to the heavens and silently asked him if he was proud of me now. I was to have a new husband, rich in-laws and already had a beautiful baby girl.

'How do I look, Mum?'

'You'll do. Don't be getting too attached to that dress though, you'll want to sell it on afterwards. What do you think of my hat?'

'You are a very pretty lady, Binnie.'

Argos had said this last night, before the electrocution by pelvic toner thing. Sinking further into my bed, I allowed the words of this gorgeous, young twenty-whatever-he-was to marinate. Somebody desired me! How long had I had to wait for that wonderful feeling? But then, all he saw was the covered up, Spanx wearing version of me. What if, heaven forbid, he actually saw my body? Would we need to try pelvic toner intervention again?

'Wait, wait, wait . . .'

ZAAAAAAPPPPPPPPPPPPPPPP!

'Okay, GO!'

As the memory of his enormous erection boinging off my leg came back to mind, all at once it occurred to me that every single intimate encounter I'd ever had with David had been lukewarm rather than sizzling hot. I'd accepted his faults and his awkwardness in bed. I'd listened to the counsellor, doing everything she advised to make things better for him. But in the process, I'd lost what was important to me. I needed to feel desired. I needed intimacy. And David had given me neither of those things.

I started to let myself imagine what sex with Argos would be like. He was a gorgeous distraction from all my problems right now, and of course I wanted him. But the truth was it was an attraction based entirely on lust. There was no connection, like that first moment I'd met my husband. And it was hardly surprising, given that I hadn't had sex in such a long time, that I was pretty much desperate for some. But I wasn't ready to put a 'finished' stamp on my marriage by sleeping with someone else. I couldn't do that, even knowing how easy it would be to ensure David never found out.

The clock on the bedside table buzzed a wake up alarm. *Come on Bernice, don't you have enough complications to worry about? So you fancy this guy a little, fine! But you're not going to mourn the loss of your youth by getting yourself another one.*

A text alert flashed up on my phone.

Weren't you going to call me? Is everything okay?

Suzy. I still hadn't phoned her, because I was dreading the conversation. I really needed to confide in her, but I still felt so, *so* embarrassed.

Today was scuba day. *Cancelled* scuba day, which was

why the alarm had been set. Putting aside my mobile I resolved to call her later (again) and turned over to flick the button on the clock off, when my hands touched something cold, wet and slimy.

'Ew!'

I looked to see what it was. And if God had needed an alarm call too, he was getting one today.

'YARGHHHHHHHHHHHHHHHHHHHHHHHHH!'

A black, slimy monster of a giant spider was covering the clock on the bedside table. In seconds, Chris was hammering at my door.

'Binnie! Are you okay? Let me in!'

I jumped up and fiddled with the key in the door which sprung open, almost knocking me backwards as Chris burst in wielding a small trowel.

'Oh, thank God,' I said. 'It's Supergardener!'

'What is it? Where?' he gasped, puffing from what must have been an effortful burst of running from one of the oleander patches.

As the day's light filled the room through the open door, I turned and pointed to the monster alarm-clock-eating spi . . .

Bunch of seaweed.

'What? What is it?' Chris stabbed the air with his trowel, poised to weed the monster to death.

Awakening is a wonderful thing. No sooner had I realised my assassin was more 'kelp' than 'help!' I realised I was standing in nothing but my knickers and made a quick grab for the sheet to cover my modesty. Chris, thank God, turned from the 'monster' to looking back at my face.

'Sorry, it was the . . . er . . .' I pointed. 'Seaweed,' I said, feeling like a prat and not for the third time this week.

A moment ago, Chris had been a dashing hero racing to help a damsel in distress. Now, he was alone in a bedroom with a crazy half-naked woman. There was a horrible, gaping, great awkward silence. And we all know what I do whenever there's one of those.

'Did you see my tits?'

BLURRRRRRRRRRRRRRRT.

Chris began backing out of the room. 'Have you, erm . . . lost them?' he asked.

At last, I'd found my blurting twin.

I half-laughed and another, momentary awkward silence fell before Chris bumbled on for me.

Ignoring the 'did you see my tits' thing, he said, 'You can't beat the old *phikeia* in the dark monster trick. Fallen for that myself a few times. I've . . . er . . . left coffee on upstairs. Got to go.'

As my ears heard '*phikea*' and my brain processed it as 'thick,' (*had he just called me thick?*) he bolted out of the door faster than a sheet-stealing goat; before I even had chance to ask him where he stood on the big, natural boobs are best/not-best debate.

'Oh Godddddd!' I fell back onto the bed with an almighty moan and clasped my hands to my head. My boobs hid under my armpits – I would say in embarrassment, but the truth is they always do this when I'm horizontal.

Chapter Fifteen

My mobile phone keeps telling me it's unable
to perform operations. What a relief! I
wouldn't want it to start one on me when I'm
not expecting it.

After cheering myself up with a silly Facebook status, I threw on a swimming costume and sarong and headed upstairs to see Chris. This was too bad. I needed to get our next meeting over with now so that I didn't spend the last few days avoiding him.

He smiled as I walked towards him and handed me a cup of coffee.

'Going swimming today then?' he asked. I couldn't be happier to follow his lead by not referring to the flashing incident at all.

'It's a free day today, nothing planned,' I said. 'So after breakfast I thought I'd check out the little private cove down the lane you told me about, for a spot of sunbathing.' *Like I hadn't been there last night with all the naked folk.*

'Well, that's a fine idea,' he remarked. 'I have a free day too. Well, there may be a client later this evening, but all day I'm free, so I was going to go out in my kayak before lunchtime.'

'So what exactly *is* a kayak?'

'It's a lot like a canoe. Very easy to steer,' he explained. 'I try to go out every day. Exercise for the body and soul.'

Being alone all day didn't appeal too much. Linda was still loved-up with Eydis, who in turn was busy in rehearsals with Gelle. A day with Chris would be nice. Maybe we could start to be friends again, just like old times.

'Well, okay then. I'm not doing anything else. Why not?' I said.

He looked confused. 'Excuse me?'

'Oh! You weren't inviting me to come watch you on your kayak thingy then?' I said, knowing full well he hadn't meant to invite me.

He paused, scratching his chin. I could see he was trying to think of an excuse not to spend any more time with me than he had to and it hurt.

'I really hate being by myself,' I said, trying my best to look pathetic.

'Well, I suppose it might be fun,' he said at last. 'There's room for two. I could take you out on it if you like? Oh, but you hate deep water, don't you?'

'I'm sure I'll cope,' I said. 'Divide and conquer as they say. Although, I was always rubbish at maths, so I'll just try the conquering thing for today.'

Chris's kayak was stored at one of the many pretty, secluded coves only a stone's throw from the villa. There was a small taverna at its heart, which Chris told me was run by Stefano. Stefano greeted his old friend warmly.

'Cristos, you want *Mythos*?'

'Oh good God, no,' Chris laughed, 'save that shit for the tourists.'

Stefano threw back his head and gave a hearty laugh, before taking his *Mythos* loaded tray to a table, with I assumed, two waiting tourists, not far from where we were. David loved *Mythos*; maybe now was not the time to mention this.

As we dragged the kayak and oars over to the beachside, my eyes took in the gorgeous, twinkling turquoise expanse before me. Every time I came to Greece, the prospect of staying forever in this Aegean paradise of hot sunshine and clear blue seas seemed even more inviting. No wonder Chris stayed here for six months a year. Lucky him.

'We'll park it here and go have a little drink first, okay?' he said.

He pointed to a line of chairs with parasols in front of the tavern, looking out to sea – a place I could have sat happily all day without physical exercise. Today the temperature was a searing 32 degrees, a burning heat that was hopefully shielded from my all too willing to burn, peel, then drop off skin, by factor 50 sun lotion.

'You know, Stefano told me yesterday that Priscilla Hart and Kurt Davies moored a boat up here and came by for a drink the other day. How cool is that?'

'The movie stars? Very cool,' I agreed.

Directing me to a couple of seats in the shade, overlooking the beach, he asked, 'What would you like?'

'Well, I do love Priscilla Hart,' I said, taking my chair. 'What did she drink? I'll have some of that.' I was feeling adventurous.

A couple of minutes later, as Stefano delivered my glass of iced water, '*Gee, er . . . thanks*,' we noticed a fishing boat beginning to get closer, as if making its way to shore. Chris heaved a heavy sigh.

'Great! Now we'll need to wait a while longer to go out,' he said, annoyed. Stefano, however, looked pleased.

'Why?'

The boat dropped anchor and its occupants began hopping off its side onto the jetty.

'Because this beach is about to get crowded for about an hour,' Chris said.

As Stefano took off to prepare for an unexpected burst of business, Chris told me about his life on the island.

'It's been a wonderful few years,' he said. 'So much has happened. My art has improved no end with all this lovely nature to paint.'

Recalling some of the wonderful, framed prints on the wall of my apartment, I said, 'Yes, your work is remarkable.'

'Thank you.' Chris's voice faltered a little as he gazed across the water. He was watching what looked like a line of about twenty or so tourists making their way to the beach. Clearing his throat, in what I imagined was irritation, he added, 'I love it here. There was nothing to keep me in England. I'm thinking I may move out permanently.'

'Really?'

'Really,' he said flatly.

His clear blue eyes misted and he took a long swig of water before wiping his mouth and turning back to me. 'I go back to touch base when it's winter here. But you know what? I don't really want to.'

'I can understand that,' I said, 'but I . . . we missed your friendship. David was sad we never saw you much. That's why he persuaded me to come here on our honeymoon.'

A young, slender, tiny-bikini-clad woman and an older, more portly man began to lay towels down in front of where we were sitting. Seemingly not even noticing us, the woman turned to face Chris, beckoning to her partner to loosen the clasp on her bikini top.

'Yes, I know I've been guilty of being a bit of a loner,' Chris said, staring at his glass and not noticing the young lady who, *Oop, yep there it went*, was released from her bikini top to reveal pert bosoms thanks to the deft hand of her fella, right in front of us. Without understanding why, I felt uneasy. I looked at Chris, who was still gazing at his glass of beer thoughtfully. He took another long gulp from his drink and turned to me. 'There was nothing for me in England. Nothing but misery.'

The woman began smearing sun lotion generously all over her breasts. My eyes flicked back and forth from her boobs to Chris's face. I felt so uncomfortable; Lord knows why I couldn't just stop staring at her. Chris remained oblivious.

'I've never looked back. It's been wonderful,' he continued. My eyes pinged from him to the breasts. Then back to him. Then the breasts. And the smearing. *Oh, God, the smearing!* It's customary, I'm sure, to avoid staring at people undressing on a beach – the most natural thing in the world – yet I was embarrassed.

'What about you then?' he asked, looking at me, still oblivious to the goings on behind him, as I flushed more hotly than the sun. 'Are you going to tell me what happened with David?'

I wondered, not for the first time, if Chris had been calling him. Letting him know where I was and providing updates on me, as only a good friend would.

'We had . . . issues.'

Thank God the half-naked, sun-lotion-daubing goddess was now making to lie down. I sucked in the sit-down spillage again and hugged myself, suddenly feeling the familiar sting of body-consciousness.

'That you don't want to talk about? That I can

understand,' he said. 'What I don't get is him leaving you alone here without a fight.'

'Hah!' I laughed. 'Why would he bother?'

Chris looked at me and smiled. 'You women,' he said. 'Why do you do that?'

'Do what?'

'Put yourselves down all the while,' he answered, frowning. 'It's ludicrous really.'

I pulled my wrap tighter around my shoulders. Gazing beyond Chris again, I noticed more topless women sunbathing without a care for who might be watching them. I had never sunbathed topless in my life, even as a younger, slimmer woman. I dreaded the sight of them all before every sunshine holiday yet, secretly, I was in envy of their blithe uninhibitedness. It was a matter of my own confidence, not prudishness. My problem, not theirs. It was only now, with Chris not giving them a second glance that I realised David's inexorable gawping at every opportunity probably hadn't helped me. Who here now was gawping? *Me*. Judging myself, not them. Who would give two flying fucks if I decided to release my second pair of flip-flops on the world today?

Taking a long sip of ice-cold water, I looked beyond the topless sunbathers to the calm ocean beyond.

'This is what my life should be like,' I said, almost to myself.

'What?'

'When I look out to sea,' I explained. 'I think of the horizon as a place that's far away from all my worries, my insecurities and all the confinements of imagining what people are thinking of me. And the thing is, no matter how far you sail, you never really reach the horizon, do you? Yet just for that moment, while I'm looking out there, I'm at peace with myself for one exquisite second in time.'

'Is that what you do all the time?' Chris asked. 'Worry what people think of you?'

'Isn't that what everyone worries about?'

'Er . . . no.'

'They don't?'

'Can you imagine a life without all that, Bernice?' He said. 'What would you miss? Some important and accurate information about yourself? The joy in accepting everyone else's opinion as your own? What do you suppose will happen if just one person decides they don't like you?'

'Oh, I don't know . . . guilt. Shame. Hours and hours of wondering what the hell I did wrong.'

'Exactly.'

I looked away from the horizon now and turned to face him, blinking back tears. How could one man speak to my heart so well?

'Actually,' I said. 'I *can* imagine it. I can imagine it because once upon a time that is what my life was like. Way back when I was a young woman. I was funny, flirty and downright – well – *sassy* to be honest. I do remember not caring what anyone thought of me then.'

'I think you just described the woman you are now,' Chris remarked, staring hard into his beer and not looking up.

I felt surprised. *That* was how he saw me?

'Chris,' I said. 'Why did we stop talking?'

He looked up now. 'What?'

'I mean, before you came out here. We got on so well and then, I don't know why, but we seemed to just stop being friends.'

'I don't know what you're talking about,' he replied,

shifting uncomfortably in his seat. 'We were fine weren't we?' He sat up straight and waved at Stefano for another round of drinks, before deciding all too soon to change the subject. 'Hopefully, that bloody boat will be going again soon and we can get out for some fun on the kayak.'

The moment was gone, brushed aside. Chris didn't want to talk about whatever it was. Maybe he just didn't like me and that was that. But then, why would he give me so much thoughtful advice?

'Yes, it'll be great,' I agreed.

'And for the record, whether they know it or not, most men are naturally drawn to curves,' he went on. 'Be grateful for your God-given shape.'

'*Most* men? Give me a break!' I said sadly. 'Not my David.'

I felt tears well up in my eyes and withdrew from Chris's stare to sip my water.

'Whatever David did or didn't do, it's obvious you have a really skewed view of yourself Bernice,' he said.

'I'm sorry, Chris. This is such a bloody awkward conversation under the circumstances. I'm going to shut up now.'

'Look,' he said, seriously. 'Of course, I don't know what has happened between you and as I keep saying, I'm not going to pry. But, if it's so bad that you end up having to cut all ties . . . I know about heartbreak and all I can tell you is it gets easier over time. Not easy, but easier.'

'You know about heartbreak?' I said, not able to stop myself sounding surprised. As far as I knew, Chris hadn't had a relationship with anyone for years. Was it clog-woman, or a more recent liaison, here on the island? *Was he in love with Ginger?*

'Yes, I know a lot about heartbreak,' he said with an air of indifference. 'Now where is that drink?'

Stefano appeared on cue with a tray and I cursed myself for not ordering a glass of wine – or even beer – as he delivered another tumbler of iced water à la Priscilla Hart. With the help of a little Dutch courage, I could have more easily delved deeper into this very interesting new side of Chris. And I could ask him about Ginger.

'Do you remember the night at Julian's wedding?' I asked him instead. 'When everyone was whispering about some woman called Clarissa that they hoped I wouldn't bump in to?'

'You heard all that?' he said, looking surprised.

'Yes I did. I wondered who she was, but never got up the courage to ask David.'

'And now you're asking me?'

'Yes, I think I am.'

He put down his glass and stared out to sea again. 'Why on earth are you asking me that now? It was maybe six years ago.'

'Because I need to know if he was cheating on me.'

'Well, as I'm his best friend, you probably wouldn't believe me if I said no.'

He was wrong. Somehow, I'd always felt I could trust Chris not to lie to me. Avoid the question perhaps, but not lie.

'Is that what you're saying?' I asked. My heart was in my mouth because at that moment I was afraid of the answer.

'That's what I am saying,' he replied. 'Clarissa was – is – Julian's cousin. David and she had a one night stand way before you came along.'

'Is that it?'

'That's it,' he confirmed. 'Who on earth was saying that though?'

'Oh, I just overheard some of the wives talking. And as for David, well, he didn't take his eyes off her all night.'

'Clarissa? Hah!' he laughed, but seeing my sorrowful face, he turned serious again. 'Well, he never said anything to me. Why are you asking me now?'

'I wondered if she was someone who the group felt was better for him than me,' I replied.

At this, Chris frowned. 'Why on earth would you think that?' he asked.

I flushed red again. *Because I always wonder if I'm good enough.*

'Just because I've always felt like some of his friends looked down their noses at me, that's all. Not *you* of course.' I added.

'We're all just an ordinary bunch of people, you know,' Chris said. 'Heavens, there was more than one fling with Clarissa among the group although I'm not naming names of course. Better than you? Give me a break. We all thought you were the best thing that ever happened to David.'

'You did?'

He shook his head and laughed again. 'Bernice, you really don't like yourself very much, do you? I can't imagine how on earth that happened.'

'Mum, Mum! MUUUUUUM!' I shouted, my voice hoarse from exertion. I had run all the way home from primary school without stopping.

My mother came out of the bathroom and stood, hands on hips and cigarette in mouth, peering down at me. 'What on earth have you done now?' she said.

I leaned on the wall to catch my breath, scratching idly at my knee with my other hand. Tiny nettle bumps were radiating angrily all over my legs from where I'd taken a short cut through a field in my race to get home.

'Guess what!' I said. 'You'll never guess.'

'What? Just tell me and make it quick!' she snapped. 'I'm soaking a duvet in the bath and your dad will be home soon, expecting his tea.'

'I just had an English test,' I told her happily.

'Well, that is good news,' she said, going back to dragging on her cigarette, unable to hide her disinterest. 'I'll call the Education Authority first thing tomorrow and thank them.'

'But, Mum,' I continued, feeling so excited and tired from running, I thought my heart would leap out of my chest. 'I got ninety nine out of a hundred!'

I waited for the joy on her face, the pride. The scooping me up into her arms and running around the block with me on her shoulders, screaming 'My child is brilliant!' at the neighbours. My reward was an outward breath of tiny wisps of stinking cigarette smoke as she spoke into my face.

'Really? Ninety nine, eh?' She pulled back to suck on her cigarette again and almost smiled. I fancied it was the short rush of nicotine pleasure rather than pride that had pleased her. As she turned on her heels and headed back into the bathroom with a chortle, her final words on the matter bounced off the echoey walls within. 'So,' she called back at me. 'If you could get ninety-nine, why the hell couldn't you get a hundred?'

In just under an hour, the tourists were gathering up their things and Stefano handed Chris our life jackets.

'Okay, Miss Funny, Flirty, Sassy,' Chris said, pulling me to my feet. 'Time to kayak!'

Chapter Sixteen

I am kayaking! Well, Queen.

After a shaky start getting into the tiny vessel, when I leaned so heavily on Chris I thought I'd end up injuring him to the point of having to row myself, we left the shore, pushing our oars through the waters in unison. Feeling like a floating Weeble, the oh-so-tight life jacket crushed my chest like a Victorian girdle. I mused over Chris's words, and wondered at my ability to let almost every experience I had this holiday involve an inner conversation with myself about my body. New Bernice Plan, rule number two, was soooo sunk.

'You have to do exactly as I do, to get a momentum going,' Chris told me, offering a welcome break from my illegal, self-deprecating thoughts. At least I was adhering to the New Bernice Plan rule number one.

At first I was nervous. As much as the sea always looked so inviting from the safety of a boat, deep water terrifies me – the reason scuba lessons had been thrown into the fez. Every dark patch of seaweed and rocks had *Jaws* potential as far as I was concerned. That damn film was set to ruin my seafaring life.

'Gorgeous isn't it?' Chris called back to me.

'Yes.' I was still peering into the waters below. 'Spectacular.'

Yet as we began to pick up speed, venturing further away from the safety of the shoreline, I wanted to forget my inner, critical dialogue and just let myself be. Allowing Chris to lead, I paused and closed my eyes, really allowing my senses to imbibe the gentle cooling of the sea breeze fluttering across my hot face; letting myself hear the soft, schlooping sound of oars cutting through the water. It was so peaceful and warm. When I opened my eyes again I saw, not a deep, terrifying dark blue ocean of lurking monsters, but a sea sparkling like a million tiny sapphires under a clear Grecian sky. I felt a serene sense of escape. I did love being out here on the water, making my way to that place, beyond worries, beyond self-doubt. Why had I forgotten that?

I began to chuckle, remembering Linda's advice on the Greek night, spoken in fluent Sean Connery, 'You really should shttop a while and shmell the dahlias.'

She was so right. I had forgotten every delightful, intoxicating scent under my nose in recent years. When I'd told myself the only thing I'd done with my life to be proud of was having my daughters, it was because I'd been trudging through life without looking outwards. It was no wonder that up until now, all I'd noticed were the ditches I'd fallen into. For one thing, my mother had gone to great pains to point them all out to me, again and again, so that I could never forget or be in any doubt about how much of a failure I was.

I began to row again, making Chris jump at the sudden picking up of speed. So, this was what freedom felt like.

'Hey,' he called out. 'Good to have you on board at last.'

Binnie the Magnificent takes off to the open seas, captainess of a two man – no – two *person* vessel. She laughs in the face of dark, shadowy, underwater thingies.

'Steady on there, we don't want to go too far out on your first go!' Chris shouted, sounding a little alarmed now.

'This is actually quite cool!' I cried, chuckling. It was as though I was, metaphorically, finally leaving the safe shore; a sort of inner release. It was strange yet intoxicating.

'Where can we go now?' I asked.

'I thought you might want to head back in shortly. Aren't you anxious about going out in deep water or something?'

'Well, that's what I thought, but I'm really enjoying myself,' I said.

I really was. Where was the big white shark now?

Chris laughed heartily.

'I'm throwing off the bowlines,' I sang out, borrowing the infamous words of Mark Twain. 'I'm sailing away from the safe harbour. I'm catching the trade winds in my sails!'

I was either delirious or Priscilla Hart's 'iced water' had actually been a miraculous, tasteless gin.

'Bloody hell, a kayaking convert,' Chris said.

'This holiday seems to be converting me to a lot of things,' I enthused. 'No wonder you do this every day. It's wonderful.'

'Yes, it's very relaxing . . . usually,' he replied, with a hint of irony as he fought to pick up my pace. 'We can try just a little further out now, if you're sure?' He stopped rowing for a second and pointed to the rocks that signalled the end of the cove we were in. 'But not that way. Better turn left.'

'Why not?'

'Because there are a lot of private beaches around there. The villas belong to some very rich folk who don't appreciate strangers cutting across their privacy,' he explained. 'It's nicer the other way anyway . . . I think.'

'So you've never been that way?' I said.

'Never.'

'Oh, come on, who cares?' I was having far more fun than I'd expected to and was still pushing on single-handedly with my oars.

'Well . . .' Chris began to row again, but his trepidation was obvious.

'Aren't we allowed round there?' I asked.

'Yes, of course we're *allowed*. It's just not the done thing – it's awkward, you know? Feeling like you're interrupting people's privacy.'

'Hah! There's nothing I like more than annoying toffs. Let's do it!'

As we turned the kayak to head across the right hand peninsula, the coastline revealed a series of small, secluded coves. We passed several private beaches, with steps up the rock face to the most luxurious villas. To me, it looked like a stairway to another life.

'I think we should turn back,' Chris said shortly. 'It's coming to the hottest part of the day and we'll fry.'

'Can't we just check one more beach out? Just one?' I pleaded.

I was aware we were rocking more than normal and looked up to see a ferry making its way across the water some way away from us.

'Oh shit, the ferry is passing!' Chris exclaimed. 'You have to watch now; the swell will knock us sideways. We'd better row away from the rocks.'

'But it's miles away!'

'That's as maybe, but you wait and see what happens.'

'Alright,' I said. 'But let's just see if we can make it for a quick look round this last corner.'

'No really Binnie, we need to . . .'

Chris had stopped rowing now, but I was pressing ahead, giggling like a wayward teenager.

'Come on, where's your sense of adventure. Oh . . .'

As the next beach came into view, it was clear this one was not deserted. A couple lay on the sand in a close embrace.

'Whoopsie . . .' I said.

'Binnie, we need to get away from these rocks.' Chris's voice sounded more urgent now, as the kayak began to bob more precariously in the water, over a series of small, choppy waves.

'Okay,' I agreed, straining my eyes to try and make out whether the couple had noticed us yet. They hadn't and carried on with their canoodling, the man on top and, as the kayak floated nearer, propelled by the rising swell now, a mortifying realisation hit me. They were having sex.

'Ooh, maybe now we should try to reverse a bit,' I said.

'Oh Jesus! We are way too close!' Chris cried out.

The waves were getting bigger and I could feel the kayak being dragged out and then sucked back towards the shore.

'Shit!' Chris shouted, seconds before another huge wave hit us, turning the kayak over and spilling us both out into the sea. I flailed around, trying to keep my face above water and felt myself being carried towards land. Before long we were beached, just a few feet away from the couple, who were now hastily dressing. Unable to get a footing as the tide pulled me out again, I rolled around in the sea. Chris, however, had managed to scramble ably to his feet.

'Bernice, are you okay?'

With what seemed to me to be the most extraordinary strength and stamina in the circumstances, he was at my side, tugging me back towards the beach and up to a sitting position with one arm, whilst dragging the kayak to safety with the other. I was dumbfounded; feeling as though I'd just watched a fireman save a woman from a burning building by throwing her over his shoulder and climbing down the ladder with her on his back.

'Yes . . . fine . . .' I replied, not able to catch my breath enough to stand.

'Well,' Chris said, grinning and letting go of my arm at last. 'That was some ride! I never did that before.'

Just as I opened my mouth to say something else, another wave crashed into me, slamming over the back of my head and pushing me further up the beach on my bottom. Chris threw his head back and laughed out loud.

'Pah,' was all I could say.

'Ahem!'

We both turned together to see a tall, slender and very beautiful woman, hand on hips, glaring at us. It was the woman we'd seen in a compromising position on the beach only a few minutes earlier. I felt I'd also seen her somewhere else before. As a flash of recognition came to me only moments later, so did another wave.

'Wow,' I said dizzily, spitting out salt water and rubbing my eyes. 'It's Priscilla Hart!'

Chapter Seventeen

Fraternising with celebs now. You know, I'm not
one to brag about my press exposure but yes,
it's true what they're saying in my local paper.
I am selling my couch.

I fought the urge to ask for an autograph as I stood in front of the apartment watching one of the world's biggest movie stars help Chris lift his kayak off the back of his pickup truck. One, because it felt a bit pushy, and two, because I'd just interrupted him and his wife having a romp on their private beach by sailing arse-first almost into the middle of them. *No, perhaps I'd better not.*

Within a matter of minutes, Chris was crunching up the driveway to join me.

'How did you get on?'

'All sorted,' he replied. 'I think I finally convinced him we're not paparazzi.'

'Well that's good news,' I replied, adding, 'I am so sorry, you know. I should have listened to you when you said to go back.'

'Nonsense,' he said, without a hint of cynicism, 'look at the afternoon we ended up having. You don't get to have a beer with Kurt Davis and Priscilla Hart every day.'

'True, although I don't think Priscilla could wait to see the back of us.'

'I think she saw the back, front and derrière of you, to be fair,' he joked.

'Same here with her, which is probably why she couldn't wait for us to go home. Anyway, that's enough excitement for one day. Do you fancy a glass of wine on the balcony?'

He looked at his watch. 'You know what,' he said. 'It's been a pretty long day. I think I'm just going to head on up for an early night.'

'Oh, come on, it's early yet,' I coaxed. 'Just a little one?'

'No, really, I *am* pretty tired,' he said, patting me on the arm. 'There's someone I promised to call anyway. Night!' He headed for the stairs and I watched him, feeling a little disappointed.

'Well, okay. Me too, as it happens,' I said. 'But, oh wait, there was something I wanted to ask you.'

He stopped and pivoted around. 'Yes?'

'I wondered if you'd like to join me on the sunset horse ride tomorrow? If you're free, I mean. It'll be long after any classes you might have?' He looked hesitant. 'My treat?' I added.

'Treat?' he said. 'What for?'

'You know, a thank you gift,' I replied, giving him my brightest smile. 'Just in case you haven't had enough of me already.'

'You don't have to thank me Bernice, really,' he said.

'Yes I do.'

'For what?'

'For the day. For letting me stay. For being my friend right now when I need one.'

He exhaled loudly and leaned on the wall. 'You're *paying* me for the stay.'

'I know,' I answered, affording him a mischievous grin. 'Oh, come on, Chris,' I said. 'It'll be fun. Do you ride?'

'Well, I have done a little,' he replied. 'Michaela is an excellent instructor.'

'Michaela?' I said. 'Cookery instructor Michaela?'

'The very same,' he said. 'She owns the stables. A fine horsewoman, she is.'

'Well, that's great news. I really like her.'

'Me too,' he said.

'That's settled then,' I declared. 'If I can't tempt you with my own company, which can be fraught with incident, admittedly, come and see *her*.'

He hesitated for a moment, opening his mouth to say something but appearing to change his mind. 'Hmm, I don't know,' was all he said.

'Please?' I said, fluttering my eyelashes for extra puppy dog eyes effect. 'We did have fun today, didn't we?'

'Yes,' he admitted, smiling at the memory. 'Well, maybe I will. I'll let you know tomorrow.'

I moseyed towards the patio set in front of the apartment, pulling my phone out of my pocket. Suzy's last text was still showing in the notification window. Time to make that call to the one person who knew my grief, my person, my life better than I did. But first, to open that bottle of white I had cooling in the fridge.

The storm raged on as I watched Suzy stare out of the kitchen at me, sobbing. Through my own tears and the lashing rain, I could see her pleading with Mum to let me

164

back in. Rubbing snot from my face with the now-opaque, soaking wet sleeve of my school blouse I shivered, coatless in the cold, but it wasn't the icy, nipping cold that was hurting me. It was my own shame.

'Did you take my bar of chocolate, Bernice? DID YOU?' she had boomed.

I could still taste the sweet, swirly milkiness on my gums, only now it was tinged with a bitter, guilt-induced aftertaste. There was no sense in trying to lie, she knew. She *always* knew.

'Yes.'

'Where is the wrapper?'

What? I wasn't expecting this line of questioning after giving up the truth so soon. A smack, yes. Early bed, a week's grounding? Most likely. But where's the wrapper? Didn't she believe I'd taken it? I didn't dare offer any other lies, Mother's shouting was enough to terrify me into early submission.

'I threw it in the garden.'

The wind howled as if in agreement as she turned to look out of the window, maybe expecting to see the wrapper flutter past it. If only it had.

'Get out there and find it!' She hissed, dragging me by the shoulder to the back door and flinging me outside.

'But . . . Mum, it was ages ago . . .'

'AND DON'T THINK OF COMING BACK IN HERE UNTIL YOU HAVE!'

Suzy had always been Smother's favourite. She was the golden child, the one who went to university – the brains of the family. She had taken an ordinary degree, worked for ten years as a youth counsellor before, recently, taking up an Open University course in her insatiable quest for knowledge. I often wondered if our rather different childhoods had fed her need to counsel young people as an adult.

Smother would use her successes to push me to having some of my own. 'Suzy's doing so well now, using all those brains she got from me, naturally. You'd do well to take a leaf out of her book and go back to college.'

It was enough to make me hate or at least be envious of her, but I didn't. I adored my kid sister.

'Hello, Suzy, are you there?'

There were a series of crackles and then nothing as the phone signal came and went. The death of a line. I dialled again.

'Hello?'

'At last, I've got you,' I said, feeling a tinge of regret that I didn't have an excuse to put this conversation off for another night.

'Oh, hi, Bernice, how are you doing?'

With my free hand, I refilled my wine glass, took a big drink and sat back in my chair and began to cry. 'Well,' I sniffed. 'It's a bit of a long story. And one I perhaps should have told you about a long while ago, sis.'

'So, you think I'm overreacting because I'm co-dependent? Isn't that something to do with Alcoholics Anonymous?'

Suzy's psychobabble often left me confused. Had I gone to university too, maybe I could understand some of it.

'No, I didn't say you were overreacting, Bernice, and it's nothing to do with Alcoholics Anonymous. As it happens, I agree with you. If Graham was doing that to me, I'd be furious. It's virtual adultery.'

'Thank you, I'm so glad it's not just me,' I said, with a huge sigh of relief. Virtual adultery. It had a name. Something that sounded officially placed in the category of complete wrongness.

'It isn't, really it isn't,' she continued. 'You have every right to determine what trust means to you in your relationship. But you say he's done this before?'

I sighed. Now it was time to let my sister know once and for all what a complete, gullible plank I was.

'Yes,' I admitted. 'I thought he had stopped though.'

'Damn, bloody, bloody co-dependency,' she sighed.

'What does *that* mean?'

'Why did you marry him, Bernice? What made you do it?'

'I thought . . . I thought . . .' I was stammering through sobs and snivels now – faltering behind the humiliation of shame. For some bizarre reason, I was thinking of her gorgeous, new dress for the wedding, of the suit she'd bought for Graham and the beautiful, yellow flowers on her granddaughter's dress, paid for by my niece. I'd let everyone down.

'You thought you could change him.'

'Yes.'

That was exactly it, except there was more; I thought I *had* changed him.

I heard her pause on the line to take a deep breath. Maybe she was crying too. There was a sniffle before she spoke again.

'You're co-dependent, just like I've been. A people pleaser.'

'I don't understand. Is this some paper you've been working on for uni or something?'

'No. Well, yes, it's kind of a study but not for uni. For me.'

I sat forward in my chair and put down my wine glass. 'Go on,' I said into the phone.

She sighed again and I knew for definite now, she was crying too.

'I wish you were here right now, Bernice. There's so much we need to talk through together. Why don't you come home?'

With my free arm I hugged my belly and gazed out over Chris's garden, to the moonlit, shimmering sea beyond. I allowed this now-familiar view to mesmerize me again; feeling the warm, fragrant, Grecian air brush my sun-kissed skin, my ears attune to the chirping of a million crickets. I was alone, but never more alive.

'Because I'm not ready to,' I told her truthfully. 'Not yet.'

Chapter Eighteen

'This love triangle is waaaaay too complicated'
- Pythagoras's other woman.

The following afternoon I finished poking fun at one of Greece's most famous mathematicians, waved to Chris as he sat with a new tutor group on the veranda and headed off on my moped alone for some sightseeing. At half past four I returned to find a note pinned to my door:

Sorry, something came up. Enjoy the ride.

That beautiful. balmy evening, when I made my way to the gate in front of the stables, I was met by Linda, Eydis and Greta.

'Are you really going to get up on a horse, Greta?' I asked.

'Fir sure lassie!' she said cheerily. After her evening of skinny-dipping, I should have guessed she was up for any adventure. At seventy-seven, she was putting me to shame.

'Is this it, then?' I asked. 'Just the four of us?'

'Looks that way, honey,' Linda replied.

'I thought Ginger wis coming?' said Eydis.

'Ach, I chapped her room earlier an' she said she has a wee bit o' sunstroke. An' the guys are daein' an archery thing,' Greta explained.

'So it's just us ladies then?' I said, ignoring a tug of sadness, as I guessed exactly where Ginger might be at this moment.

'And Linda,' Eydis joked.

'Hi, ladies, come through!' came a shout from beyond the gates. It was Michaela's cheery voice.

'Have you never ridden before, Binnie?' Michaela asked, as she introduced me to my horse, a creamy-white, agreeable-looking beauty named Shyla. The others had already mounted, but I was hesitant, having not ridden a horse since a series of riding lessons I'd had as a girl, going through what Smother had called 'another of your fancies and phases that died a death.'

'Yes,' I replied. 'Although I must warn you, it's been about thirty years. And . . .' I whispered so that Shyla couldn't hear. 'I kind of crashed a kayak yesterday.'

'Oh, you will be fine,' Michaela said, smiling assuredly at me. I wondered at her not demanding more information on the kayak-crashing thing and the fact that she believed in me. Such trust. 'It's like riding a bike,' she continued. 'You never forget.'

Shyla had begun to nibble my right shoulder. I patted her nose and nudged her off.

'That tickles,' I told her. 'Stop it.'

'She likes you,' said Michaela. 'Now, are you ready to climb up?'

Shyla was nibbling my shoulder again. 'What are you doing that for?' I asked, half laughing, half, well, a bit scared really.

The horse pawed the ground with a clod, clod, clod.

'She says three!' Eydis declared.

'I can tell you what she says,' remarked Michaela, as Shyla went back to nibbling and nudging my shoulder. 'She says, "I have got your back, Binnie".'

'Eh?'

'I think she's tryin' tae tell ye to ride her oan the right side o' the road,' Greta declared, beaming at me.

'She is helping you,' Michaela said. 'Horses are emotive creatures. They can sense your deepest thoughts and feelings.'

Shyla continued to nuzzle my shoulder and I tried with no success to hold her off again. 'Can she sense I don't like being tickled?' I asked.

Shyla stomped the floor again.

'Today is not going to be just a ride through the waves for all of you ,' Michaela said. 'Use this time to look away from whatever is troubling you and go back into yourself. Tune in.'

'Tune in?'

'Aye, tune in,' Greta said, leaning forward to twiddle her horse's ears as if trying to get a radio signal.

Michaela continued seriously, 'Horses can make an important connection with you. Let them in. I promise you will be surprised and amazed.'

'They're horsey healers,' said Linda.

'Indeed,' Michaela replied. 'When I came to work here four years ago, I had just lost my husband.' There was a collective 'Ahh,' from the other women.

'Oh, I'm so sorry,' I said. 'But you're so young. How old was he?'

'Twenty seven,' she replied. 'It was very unexpected; a heart condition. The horses helped me through what was the toughest time of my life.'

'The trouble with the world is that it just keeps on turning,' said Eydis.

'That is very, very true,' I said, adding. 'I'm sure your husband would want you to go on with your life and be happy.'

'I tell you what,' Michaela said, smiling again and patting Shyla's back, inviting me again to climb up. 'I will if you will.'

I turned Shyla's face to mine and looked her in the eye. 'What is with my shoulder?' I asked her, as she nudged it again. 'It's not hurting.'

'I wonder what you are carrying on it?' Michaela said. 'Climb up. All will become clear.'

Chapter Nineteen

Enjoying equine holistic therapy in the
company of some formidable women. I don't
recommend the shoulder massage.

'I wish *I* was one.' The comment was to myself really, but heard by all.

'One what?' Linda asked.

We were on the beach enjoying a salad of feta and figs, washed down with sweet, icy peach juice from a flask, while the horses rolled around in the warm, soft sand. Everyone else's horses that is. Shyla was at my side, back to nudging and chewing on my shoulder as I updated Facebook for the second time that day. I'd given up trying to stop her. Unfortunately, she didn't fall for the 'Here, have a fig horsey' distraction method.

'I was just thinking how great it would be to be a horse,' I lied.

Shyla stamped the ground.

'A horse?'

I had of course been wishing I was 'a formidable woman', but didn't want to admit it.

'Yes, a horse. Imagine this life in the sun, rolling around the sand and occasionally carrying the odd human along the shoreline. No worries in the world except who's buying the hay. I could do that.'

Shyla stamped the ground again, gently pushing my head with her nose.

'Why does she keep doing that?' I asked.

'Whatever it is you're holding on to,' Michaela said. 'I think Shyla just wants to help you to let it go.'

The horse nudged my head again.

'I wish I had your courage,' I blurted out. The statement was to Michaela.

'*My* courage?'

'Yes. And Greta's courage.'

Greta blinked at me. 'Me? Whit did I dae?'

'And Eydis. And you, Linda. All of you really. I wish I was as strong as all of you.'

'In what way?' Michaela asked.

I breathed in. Shyla nudged me again. 'Well, you, Michaela; you have such a passion for life and your work. You've been widowed so young, yet you're getting on with your life, doing what you love in a place you love. Doing absolutely *everything* with *meraki*. I want some of that!' Michaela nodded in understanding.

I continued. 'Whereas I don't even know what it is I love – work-wise anyway – and I don't know where my place is. Where I 'fit' exactly.' There was a lot pouring out and I didn't quite understand where it was coming from. *Was there vodka in this peach juice?*

Shyla pawed the ground some more, but had stopped nudging me.

'And Greta,' I went on. 'I know you won't mind my mentioning that I found you and Hughie walking up and down a beach at midnight, nude amongst twenty or so young folk, after an evening of skinny-dipping the other night.'

'Greta?' Linda said, astonishment in her voice. Eydis and Michaela looked surprised too.

'Aye weel,' she laughed. 'Ye only live wance.'

'And what were *you* doing there?' Linda asked me.

'I was sat on a rock, fully clothed, hugging my handbag to my belly and thinking about a bunch of sad times I'd really rather forget.'

Linda laughed. 'Didn't I tell you to . . . ?'

'Wake up and smell the dahlias?' I finished for her. 'Yes, you did, but I completely suck at it. Look, I'm going to be brutally honest now, Greta, and tell you that at the time I was horrified to find you there,' I admitted.

'Well, I was a wee bit horrified to fun' masel' there tae,' she said, chuckling at the memory. 'It was Hughie's idea, the ol' bampot.'

'Hughie made you go to a nudist beach?' Linda cut in, sounding incredulous.

'No, he didnae *make* me go,' she replied.

'And it wasn't a nudist beach,' I added.

'Aye, it was just a place where young 'uns gather at night wae their clathes off.'

'And then there's you, Linda. And Eydis. Two openly gay women in a world that's still so full of bigotry and intolerance; there's still such a long way to go, sadly. I can't imagine what that must be like and I can't imagine my being able to do it. I'd rather chicken out, than stand out. Do you know what I mean?'

'Sure,' said Linda. 'I think I do.'

'The point is, living that kind of authentic life takes a hell of a lot of courage actually. It shouldn't, of course, but it does.'

'I have a brother who hasn't spoken to me since I came out,' Eydis admitted.

'I haven't lived authentically,' Linda said. 'I've never told anyone I'm a lesbian.' I turned to look at her, expecting to see sadness in her eyes, but she just looked thoughtful.

'I've never come out to anyone back home,' she continued. 'Finding Eydis online was the first time in my life, ever, that I've had the courage to explore my sexuality.'

'I didn't know that!' I said.

Eydis hugged her. 'It's not easy for everyone.'

'Especially when you teach children in a small town in the back of beyond,' Linda added. 'They hunt you down if you are in any way different. Hell, what if their babies catch gay off you?'

'I had no idea,' I said. 'Now I can understand what you said about all those years of being alone.'

'Like you say,' she replied. 'It takes courage to live – what did you call it – authentically? A lot of courage in some cases.'

'*That's* what I wish I had. Courage.'

'You had the courage to leave your rat of a husband, didn't you?'

The words 'rat of a husband' stung a little. *Was David really a rat?*

'Oh, God! I'm sorry, Binnie. It wasn't my place to spit that out to everyone,' Linda said, clasping a hand to her mouth.

Shyla snorted into my ear, making me start.

'Oh, I don't mind,' I told her. 'It had to come out at some point. Although I didn't *leave* him yet. Technically, we are on a break.' Everyone fell silent. Shyla began nibbling my shoulder again.

'Oh, okay Mrs Wise-Ass Horsey!' I cried, pushing her face away. 'And I'm not sure he is one.'

'Wan whit?' said Greta, now leaning forward with interest.

'A rat,' I answered.

'Why?' asked Linda.

I hesitated.

'I just don't know . . .'

'You dinnae hae to talk aboot it, lass, if ye dinnae want to,' Greta interrupted, leaning in to put a hand on my shoulder.

Michaela patted my back too, adding, 'Not a strong woman? Well, for someone that survived a fish explosion . . .'

'Not to mention a volcanic eruption,' Eydis said.

'And ye snowboarded doon it too,' Greta chipped in.

The three other women laughed, but Michaela looked astonished.

'You snowboarded down a volcano?' she said. Somehow this was more astonishing news to her than my newly estranged husband.

'I don't feel brave,' I went on. 'Or strong. I feel very weak actually.' At least while I was talking, Shyla stopped eating my shoulder. 'I didn't send him home for cheating,' I said.

'You sent him home?' Eydis gasped. 'You mean, he was here with you?'

'Yes, he was here and yes, I sent him home. It was because he was using porn. All the time. I found him doing it in our hotel room.' My last words opened the floodgates. 'He was using porn instead of making love to me.'

I waited for the 'You did what?' the 'How weak is

that?' and the 'Why didn't you just join in?' There was a moment's silence – presumably for the loss of my dignity. It was all so embarrassing. Greta spoke first. 'Haw, that's why my Hughie and me dinnae hae internet.'

'What?' I said.

'We don't have internet,' she accentuated. 'That dirty auld bugger.'

'Really? You too?'

'Aye.'

'Me three,' said Michaela.

I was stunned. 'You?'

'Yes, me too. I hated it,' Michaela said truthfully. 'But I lived with it. I thought, at least he wasn't having a real affair.'

'But, what if that's just something we tell ourselves to make it seem normal. A permission-giving belief?' I said.

'What does it matter if he's doing it?' she answered. 'Porn, half naked women . . . temptation is everywhere and men just can't help themselves. How can they?'

'You see,' I said. 'I've been so stupid. I ended my five-day-old marriage because . . .'

'Five days?!' said Greta.

'Yep. Five days,' I said. All eyes were on me and all looked astounded at this latest newsflash.

'You're on your honeymoon?' said Linda.

'Yes,' I admitted. 'And yes, I'm weak, because I don't think I can live with that thing that men 'just do' and stupid, because I married him thinking he'd stopped.'

'I have to admit,' said Eydis, 'five days is a pretty short time to give up on someone for doing something you knew they'd done before. Not that I want to bash you when you're down, or anything.'

'No, you're right,' I agreed. 'It sounds awful doesn't it?

But he has a problem. An addiction, if you like. We went to counselling and there had been nothing for a whole year. Marriage seemed the right thing to do. I thought I'd saved him from himself and we were happy.'

'Why were you worried about the porn?' Michaela asked. 'It's not about you.'

'That's what he always says,' I admitted. 'But I don't know, it just hurts me. I feel betrayed. Why can't I be allowed to have all these feelings?'

'You can,' said Linda.

'Of course ye can,' Greta added. 'He's your guy an' it's your marriage. Dinnae think twice aboot it.'

'I have to admit though,' Eydis added. 'It sounds to me like maybe you married him for all the wrong reasons. You shouldn't marry a guy for *his* sake, you should marry him for yours. Because it's what you want. If it isn't right for you, then what's it all for?'

'You can't save someone by marrying them.' Linda said.

'But I do love him!'

Michaela shook her head. 'I just think you should try to save your marriage. He's just being a man.'

'Bull crap,' said Greta. 'Sorry, Michaela, but I don't think it's right tae tell a girlie tae put up and shut up. She's unhappy an' she's hurting. That's nae life for aw'body.'

'Deep in your heart, Binnie, did you think he'd really changed when you married him?' asked Linda. 'Or did you just hope? Because hope ain't a big enough cradle to hold something like the rest of your life's happiness.'

'I really, truly believed he'd stopped. I mean, there were times when we used it together, but I hated it, I admitted. 'Maybe I'm the one to blame though. Michaela has a point. Millions of women must live with the porn thing and don't see any problem with it. Maybe I'm just weak and pathetic.'

'I think Linda and Greta are right,' Eydis said. 'If it hurts you, it's not acceptable.'

'You're right, what you say, Bernice.' Linda added. 'It sure is hard to admit it makes you feel like you're not enough for him. Of course there will be folks thinking that's weak.'

'Bugger 'em,' said Greta.

'Why the heck should you feel weak or less than a woman?' Eydis cut in. 'It was his problem, not yours.'

'There was more to it,' I admitted. 'We never had sex and I'm sure that his porn was the reason. It was like I just wasn't enough for him. But, still, it doesn't feel like a valid reason to leave someone.'

'Are you kidding? If it hurts you and he knows it does . . .' Eydis started.

'He knows it does and he's supposed to love you. And yet he kept on doing it?' Linda continued. 'He should have loved you enough to want to make you love you enough. Every damn day.'

'You know, he may have been numbed by it,' Michaela said thoughtfully.

'Yes, that's very true,' agreed Eydis. 'People get desensitized by it.'

'But other women manage to live with it,' I argued. 'Michaela managed to live it.'

'I wonder about that, to be honest,' said Linda. 'Not you, Michaela, but women in general. Are they just giving their permission because it's easier than admitting it hurts? I wonder how many marriages have ended because of the husband – or wife's – porn use and the wronged spouse has just made up some other reason for the split?'

'It is a shame, really,' Eydis said. 'There is so much of it everywhere, no wonder women are so down on themselves. We are becoming a society that just *accepts* it.'

'That is it exactly,' I said. 'Don't I have the right to make a stand about the things I'm prepared to accept? What kind of life will I have if I just continue to live with it, pretending it is okay, when it is not?'

'Not an honest one,' said Eydis. Linda and Michaela nodded in agreement now.

'Women just need tae be theresels,' said Greta, adding, without a hint of malice, 'even the big, gay wans.' We all laughed.

'You teach people how to treat you,' Eydis carried on.

'Listen, lady,' Greta said, giving me a cuddle. 'If you keep accepting what yir getting', you just get more o' the same. If someone gies ye cream cheese crackers at a party, and you hate cream cheese, but you eat them anyway, the next time you go tae their party, what do ye get?'

'Cream cheese crackers!' Linda, Eydis and Michaela all said together.

'Isn't it nice?' Michaela remarked. 'This isn't equine therapy; it's all girls together therapy. I should get the company to employ you all.'

'That's okay,' Linda replied. 'But I'm not staying in a stable with the horses.'

'I just cannae believe a pretty young thing like you was worried you werenae enough for oanyone,' Greta said. 'My Hughie hinks yer hot stuff.'

'It's not even my first marriage I'm messing up,' I admitted sadly.

'You messed up?' Linda said sharply. 'Oh, no, no, no. It sounds to me like you showed your man the boundaries and he strolled right across them.'

'But, Linda, my first husband didn't think I was good enough for him either. He had a six year long affair. Maybe it's all related. Maybe it has everything to do with me.'

'Dear God, Binnie,' Eydis remarked. 'It's like you think you need to live up to everyone's standards but your own! Your first husband cheats on you – you weren't enough for him. Your second husband betrays you – you weren't enough for him. Have you ever considered the possibility that they weren't enough for you?'

'No,' I admitted.

'Weel,' said Greta. 'Think oan that for a wee while, 'cos it's true.'

'You know, I was sat on the beach with Chris yesterday and this beautiful, young woman stood right in front of us, whipped off her top and started smearing sun cream on. I don't know why but I felt so uncomfortable! And I found myself just watching her all the time, like some pervert. But Chris was with me. You know, the painter?'

Michaela nodded.

'And he didn't seem to notice at all.'

'Were you and Chris talking at the time?' Linda asked.

'Yes, why?'

'Because I guess he was enjoying that wonderful, funny personality of yours,' she said. 'Because Binnie, the truth is women aren't two-dimensional. The people that truly fall for us are attracted to what's inside of us. The rest is just gift wrap.'

'Do you know, I've been considering telling people I cheated,' I admitted. 'Just to make it all sound more *normal*.'

'What? Are you insane? This isn't your fault!' said Linda.

'And what's more normal than asking your husband to be faithful to you?' Eydis added.

'Well, it's just going to look like I'm the one with the problem if I do call it quits,' I explained. 'Because I hate my body so much, I can't take any competition.'

'You hate your body?' Linda gasped. 'Why?'

'Because it's old,' I sighed.

'Wummin are supposed tae look like they're supposed tae look,' Greta added. 'Thin, medium, curvy, voluptuous, old, young – it's all womanly whatever shape or age ye are.'

'I know, you're right,' I said. 'I've been looking at my body and feeling like I can't compete with the women David looks at. What if I'm too old? Too fat? Too unsexy. The young me isn't coming back. What if the rare time he comes to me for sex he's just doing me a favour? I just got tired of all the agonising over it. I really, really don't want to live like that anymore.'

'I'm sure he isn't just doing you a favour,' Linda assured me, rubbing my hand in sympathy.

'We're aww gorgeous creatures, ye know,' Greta laughed. 'Me, you, Michaela, Eydis, Linda. We're bloody stunners, that's whit we are.'

Tears prickled my eyes again and I turned to her. 'I couldn't even take off my clothes the other night when it was dark and everyone around me was naked. I don't even feel comfortable wearing bikinis.'

'Dae ye never go topless? Ah dae it a' the while!'

'Greta,' I said seriously. 'I've never gone topless on a beach in my entire life.'

'Who do you suppose is looking at you?' Eydis asked. 'Have you ever noticed that on the beach? No-one is really looking at *you*, it sounds to me like it's you, looking at them, comparing yourself to everyone around while they're busy just getting on with enjoying the sun.'

'The answer is tae get yer baps oot no matter who's lookin'!' said Greta.

'Metaphorically speaking,' Michaela said.

'And knowing we're all as gorgeous as the next woman,' said Linda. 'No matter what shape or size we are. We're women. We're *all* shaped like women.'

'You can be out and proud like us,' Eydis said, pointing at herself then Linda, while starting to lift her top off over her head. 'Do you know what the perfect body is, Binnie?'

'What on earth . . . ?' I began.

'The perfect body protects its owner from disease, gives birth to amazing new people and stops your bones from falling out. The end.' And with that, Eydis threw her top in the air to whoops from the rest of the women.

'Yeah, drop 'em out. You too, Binnie!' Linda yelled, getting her own top off.

'Go topless? That's a great way to make a stand against "Page Three" mentality.'

'Why the hell not?'

'Lady Godiva stripped naked and rode a horse through Coventry to protest at rising taxes,' Eydis said.

'Ooh, yes, I like that. Shall we ride naked through the sea to protest at the porn industry?' I joked. 'Would that work, in a kind of contradictory way?'

'Binnie!' Linda announced, 'We shall do a Godiva this very evening. All of us!'

'Will the cuddies get worried if we jump oan 'em starkers?' Greta's question was to Michaela, who frowned.

'Cuddies?'

'Aye, the horses,' Greta explained. 'Can we ride 'em in the buff?'

'Oh, I don't think . . .' Michaela began to protest.

'There's no-one around,' said Eydis.

'Okay then, just topless!' Greta sang out.

'A half Godiva!' Linda added, chuckling.

'Can we burn wur bras?' Greta asked.

To my amazement, she followed up the question by ripping off her t-shirt and bra. Everyone, even Michaela, cheered. And then fell silent, as our eyes couldn't help but take in the surgical scar where her right breast used to be. On the floor beside her lay a discarded prosthetic breast, still inside her bikini top. We were, all of us, speechless. Except our bonnie Greta.

'Whit's wrang?' she asked. 'Huv yae never seen a half boobless old lady before? Get yer tits oot girls while you still can. I can dae it in half the time!' And with that she clambered on to her horse. 'Remember whit I telt ye, Binnie? Whatever shape yir in, thin, curvy, boobless, legless. Yir a woman for heaven's sake. Ye' huv a lot to be proud of and grateful for. Dinnae hide yersel' away.'

In that moment I wanted to cry, I felt so deeply ashamed. Turning to Linda I could see her biting her lip, fighting back sadness too as she stared across at Eydis. Nobody knew what to say, yet Greta was already off, galloping through the waves on the back of her horse, laughing and cheering; looking for all the world like she didn't have a care.

'Well, I wasn't sure I could do this, but . . .' I started, fighting back tears of sympathy and shame I somehow knew Greta wouldn't want.

'Michaela, you don't mind if we alter this evening's lesson slightly do you?' Eydis asked.

Michaela looked from Greta to me and announced, 'Binnie, in the words of Sylvia Pankhurst – the moment of greatest humiliation is the moment when the spirit is proudest.'

To my astonishment and another round of cheers, Michaela whipped off her bikini top too.

Greta turned back and began to charge back towards us again.

'Are ye ready, ladies?' she called out, her face flushed with exuberant life and happiness.

I suddenly felt inspired, and had it not been for the fact that Eydis had shaken off her initial shock and begun to pull my vest top over my head, I'd have done it myself and hang it all. In a twinkling we were all giggling like schoolgirls.

'Linda, your woman is undressing me!' I cried out through fits of laughter, but as I turned towards her, she whipped off her bra too and threw it in my face, singing out, 'To the horses, sisters!'

Everyone had their boobs out except me, still standing like an uneasy wallflower in my bra. Even the beautiful and courageous Greta. How had I wasted so much time wrapped up in my small, pathetic body confidence issues? She was amazing. And all the while as she listened to my woes she hadn't said a thing to suggest she had any of her own. All at once, I knew that was what they were doing on the beach late at night, walking about and swimming naked with the youngsters. It wasn't so that Hughie could ogle the young girls; he and his wife were roaming, free to do whatever they liked in spite of their age and their differences. I was beginning to see them both in a whole, new light.

What the hell? In an actual flash, I pinged open my bra, whipped them out for the sisterhood and climbed onto Shyla, who I felt sure would approve. Hugging the reins, I closed my eyes and breathed in, as though filling my lungs with sunlight. For what I was sure was the first time in my life, I felt the sun and sea breeze on my naked breasts. And it was exquisite.

'Feel ready for a gallop through the waves?' Michaela shouted, clambering onto her horse.

'Well, my floppies aren't as springy as they used to be,' Linda laughed. 'Can we just make it a slow canter?'

'Aye weel,' said Greta, who had pulled back around to hurry us up. 'You'll excuse me for no haeing those kind of worries oanymore.' And with that she galloped away into the lead again with a 'Woo hoo!'

Within moments, I had flung my bra over my shoulder and raced after her with a whoop.

As the sun set over a glorious, Greek horizon, five women on five horses splashed through the sea with the wind in their hair and their bosoms. I couldn't remember the last time I'd felt so free and so inspired, and all because of this small collection of courageous and dignified women, brought together by chance on a tiny Greek island. And all at once, I knew what I had to do about David.

'Titty Ho!' yelled Greta, before diving off her horse and crashing into the sea with a whoop.

As I said. Dignified.

Chapter Twenty

A bareback horse ride in the sea at sunset!
Best. Day. Ever!

'MOTHER,' Sal's comment below my photo of the backs of four proud women, riding topless through the waves posted to Facebook, was in shouty cap locks. 'ARE YOU WEARING CLOTHES FOR ANY OF YOUR HOLIDAY?'

I laughed aloud to myself, to a puzzled look from the barman loading a tray with the three cocktails I'd just ordered from him. I pushed my phone back into my pocket.

'Sorry, I was just laughing at . . .' His blank, not amused look told me a full Facebook comment explanation would be pointless. 'Oh, anyway, thank you. These look lovely.'

He nodded and passed me the tray, which I carried back to the low, candlelit table, where Greta and Michaela sat on huge, squashy cushions on the floor. Linda and Eydis had left us to go for a romantic meal for two and we three had decided to come to the Taverna Nereids to enjoy a quiet drink. On such a low seat, Greta reminded me again of an old, kindly and tiny Mrs Pepperpot. Even though just a few hours earlier she had charged through the sea on the back of a horse like Lady Godiva on speed.

'What a beautiful setting for a wee drink after wur dinner,' said Greta, taking in the view of the sea from our beachside table, which winked back a glinting reflection of the moon.

'Yes, what a great idea for a stop off, Michaela. It's a lovely place,' I replied. 'Here's to a wonderful day, in the company of lovely new friends.' I raised my glass to theirs. 'Yammas!'

'It's a little-known haven where all the expats gather for drinks. I thought you'd like it,' Michaela told me.

Greta took a huge sigh and staring out to sea. 'Aye, we hae beautiful beaches where Hughie and I stay, but ye rarely get tae sit oot in weather like this.'

'Beaches? I thought you lived in Glasgow?'

'No. We come fae Glasgow but when Hughie retired we moved tae the Isle o' Harris.'

'How lovely!' I exclaimed. 'I've only ever seen it in pictures but I'd love to go one day.'

'Aye it's lovely, but a wee bit cut aff fae folk. That's no always a guid thing when you're no weel.'

The reminder of her battle with cancer made me feel guilty. How could I have complained about my body woes in front of her?

'When did it all happen then, Greta?' Michaela asked. 'If you don't mind talking about it?'

'Och naw, I dinnae mind at all, hen,' she said, smiling broadly and patting her on the hand. 'It's been a year since ma surgery noo. But I've no given masel' time tae dwell oan it. Me an' Hughie huv been living life tae the full ever since.'

'Yes, I can see that you like to enjoy yourselves,' I laughed, thinking of their previous evening's naked stroll on the beach. 'Still, I had no idea you'd been through so much Greta. It must have been so hard. And the mastectomy! Such a difficult decision.'

'Och no!' she answered, shaking her head before taking a big swig from her Pina Colada. 'It was that or die. That's no a difficult decision at a'. Oanyways, I've still got two tits left.'

'Eh?'

'Aye,' she laughed. 'The left one an' Hughie!'

Michaela and I looked at each other and laughed, a little guiltily. 'Oh Greta, you are a wonderful lady,' I told her. 'I don't know how you've coped. Or how you listened to my insignificant moanings earlier. I feel such a shit.'

'Dinnae be daft, hen,' she said. 'We've all got wur problems tae face. I could hae died but I didnae. What you need to dae noo is listen to yer ain heart, dear, and take notice o' what is sent tae ye. They say everything happens fir a reason and I believe that, Binnie, I do. Maybe ye met me to show ye that life is bigger than ye've been making it.'

'What do you mean?'

'Well, tak that man o' yours fir one. And even the bampot before him,' she continued. 'It sounds tae me like you're wan o' they people pleasers. Ayeways daein things for others and no thinking o' yerself.'

'That's just what my sister said.'

'She's right, you know,' Michaela added.

'I do try hard to keep everyone happy,' I admitted. 'Linda was right about that altruism thing.'

'Exactly,' Greta went on. 'Whit did ye dae when you fun oot ye were preggers wae a guy ye'd only just met at, what was it ye said, nineteen?'

'Married him immediately, of course,' I answered sadly.

'Aye. And who was that for?'

'I thought it was for me at the time,' I said.

'But it wisnae, wis it?' she said. 'It was tae save face. Tae huv a family. Tae make a happy life for the wee bairn, and naebody can blame ye for that, ma dear, naebody.' She put down her glass and grabbed my hand. 'But what your life should aw be aboot to you, is you.'

'Always it's you,' said Michaela. 'No feeling guilty. No thinking what if nobody likes me if I don't go along with everyone else. I've been guilty of that myself, but I've changed.'

'But it sounds so selfish,' I said. 'Too many people go around thinking "What can I get in life?" when they should be thinking, "What can I give?"'

'That is true,' Michaela replied. 'But think of your own needs first, Binnie. How can you give your best to the world when you haven't given your best to yourself yet?'

'An' the least ye can do is marry for love and your ain happiness,' Greta added.

'I thought I loved my first husband, Michael,' I sighed, staring off into the horizon. 'But with hindsight, you're right. I was trying to make the best of things, but deep down in my heart there was a nagging doubt that I was taking the wrong road.'

'An' wae David?' Greta asked.

I looked back at her before taking another long sip of my drink. She gave me a knowing smile and I wondered how I hadn't noticed all of her understanding and wisdom before. How many times might somebody so kind and perfect for answering your life's questions be right in front of you and yet you make on the spot assumptions about them, blink and miss all they have to impart. Somebody sent, just as she said.

'Same?' she asked, bringing me back to her question.

I nodded. 'I'm beginning to think so.'

She let go of my hand and leaned back, looking satisfied with herself. 'Ah'm a wise ol' duck, me,' she said.

'Indeed you are, Mrs McAteer.'

'I'm Greta to ma friends,' she told me. 'Just Greta. Ah didnae marry ma man just tae forget that. I didnae lose ma self, Binnie, and neither should you.'

'It's funny isn't it, the old Mrs Hughie McAteer or Mrs David Dando thing? I changed my Facebook name to that an hour after the ceremony, did I tell you that?'

'No, ye didnae,' she replied. 'It's the done thing tae take yir husband's name though.'

'What about his whole identity?' I asked her.

'Come again?'

'You mean, forgetting who you are and materialising into a version of him?' Michaela said.

'Ach, that would be awfy silly, Binnie,' Greta chuckled. 'Ah'd hae tae go aboot chasing all the wummin.'

'Greta,' I said. 'You're right. It is awfully silly. And do you want to know a secret? My name is Bernice. I hate the name Binnie. It was David that started calling me that.'

'Well, it's affy guid tae meet ye, Bernice,' she said, shaking my hand.

'You look beautiful tonight, Mrs Dando.'

David and I had taken the floor for our first waltz at the wedding, surrounded by our family and friends. Our taxi was collecting us in thirty minutes to take us to the airport, when the party would continue merrily on in our absence.

'Thank you,' I said, hugging his neck tightly and closing my eyes so that it was just him and me in a world of our very own.

'Marilyn Monroe though?' David laughed into my ear. 'Seriously?'

For months, I'd tried to choose a song for our first dance, settling on *Baby, Baby, Blue* from one of my favourite films,– a song David thought was hideously cheesy. Having him dance with me to it and cringing with embarrassment, I told myself, had been my just-for-fun addition to the evening. In truth, it was because *Baby, Baby, Blue* had accompanied one of the most romantic moments in cinema history for me; a final scene when the star had written a song for his love and had it played it for her in his hospital bed, seconds before his untimely death. I'd cried buckets, thinking of what my life would be like without David. He had tutted and raised his eyebrows throughout the film. I doubted he even remembered where it was from on our wedding day.

'I thought we'd agreed on The Stone Roses?' he said seriously. '*This Is The One*? You said you loved it.'

'You know I do,' I replied, grinning from ear to ear. 'But I changed my mind. This is funny!'

My love of old films had become buried after David and I had moved in together and he found me watching one.

'What on earth is this shit?' he'd said mockingly.

I wanted him to love me, not think I was ridiculous. Thereafter began six years of watching old reruns of *Miami Vice* and episodes of *Top Gear*, pretending they were the best thing since sliced bread because that was what *he* liked.

As we sat putting my world to rights, I resigned myself to calling David at last, later tonight. It was time to tell him what I was going to do. Before I could think on it any further though, there was a commotion at the bar and we turned around to see Hughie making his way towards us, almost tripping over a young woman on a cushion at a table nearby.

'Helloho, ladies,' he said, his nose purple from what looked like it could have been a full afternoon's boozing. 'Whit are ye's aw daein' on the floor?'

'Ach, Hughie, yir pissed again,' Greta chided, standing up to catch him as he stumbled towards her.

'Ah'm no' pissed,' he argued, looking aggrieved. 'I'm merry.'

'I'd say ye were more than merry,' Greta replied, cuffing him across the head playfully. 'I'd say ye were delighted.'

'I may have had a wee skelp,' he agreed, before turning back to bellow across to the bar at the top of his lungs, 'WAITER!'

The peaceful ambience was shattered, people began tutting and shaking their heads in disgust.

'It's not waiter service here, Hughie,' I told him, myself and Michaela standing to help Greta hold him up. 'And anyway, I think you may have had enough.'

'Aye,' Greta agreed. 'I think we'd better get ye a taxi.'

'Oh, Greta, I was going to ask you and Michaela to come with me to Gelle's show tonight. They should be ready to go on about now and it's a special one tonight – in celebration of National Orgasm Day,' I said, feeling exactly how the day would make me feel every year – hugely disappointed.

'There's a National Orgasm Day?' Michaela said, almost letting Hughie drop in her surprise and I sensed, a bit of embarrassment.

'The strippers? I thought ye were against all that porny stuff,' said Greta.

'Exotic dancers,' I corrected her. 'They don't take everything off and we're not going to ogle, we're going to be supportive to our friends.' I looked at Michaela's bright pink face and added. 'Absolutely no orgasms necessary. Or on the menu, for us anyway. It's a gay club.'

Hughie was about to say something, most likely rude, but Greta cut in.

'You call it what you like,' she said. 'Ah'm coming tae ogle. But let's get this saft auld bugger hame first. Then we can go party like it's nineteen ninety-two.'

I giggled. 'You mean, nineteen ninety-nine?'

'Och no,' she replied. 'Ah'm ayeways way ahead o' the crowd when it comes tae partying.'

Chapter Twenty-One

Seeking fun tonight. Yeehaaa! PS: This is
not a Craiglist personals ad. (Well, it was
meant to be but I started typing in the wrong
window . . .)

'The Merocca Lounge? Are you sure?' The taxi driver gazed disbelievingly at the two middle-aged and one elderly lady in his back seat, asking to be taken to the island's only gay club.

'For sure!' I said.

'But, you know what the Merocca Lounge eez?' he asked with a frown.

'Aye, we do,' replied Greta. 'Aboot eight euros, am I right?'

The three of us giggled but the less-than-amused taxi driver shrugged and released the handbrake.

'Whatever you want,' he grunted, before turning the car away from the staid safety of the harbour, where he clearly thought women of a certain age should remain in the evenings.

'You know, I've never been to this club,' Michaela said, a little shyly.

'Don't you work for the tour company that promises first time, worthwhile experiences?' I joked. 'Because this is one for me. I've never been out for a night at any gay club in my entire life.'

'I'm not sure they'd let me put this on the itinerary,' she laughed.

'How no?' Said Greta. 'It's ma first time too. We're like gay club virgins.'

In ten minutes we were there and our gruff taxi driver had grabbed his money and spun the car back round before anyone coming out of the club could wave him down.

'There was a definite air of disapproval and bigotry about that guy,' I commented.

'Yes, it is normal here,' Michaela replied. 'It is a very small island and a lot of the local people don't approve of this club. There were some serious objections when the plans were released.'

'Then they're living in the dark ages,' I said.

'Well, it is a little . . .' Michaela began.

'Seedy?' I finished for her. 'Is that what you think? Why? Not that I've been in a gay club before, but I imagine it's the same as all the other clubs on the island.'

'It's not the club that's seedy,' she went on, looking even more uncomfortable as the three of us walked towards the entrance. 'It's the strippers.'

'They don't completely strip off,' I explained. 'They dance, they entertain. That's all.'

'They dinnae get aw their claithes aff?' Greta said. 'That's no' fair.'

'Well, I have seen them rehearse a bit,' I admitted. 'And it's quite raunchy, but you're not going to see anything seedy. You told me it was time I began embracing the naked form.'

'Dae I get a wee peek at Dominik's bum?' Greta asked, with a mischievous grin.

I winked at her. 'Maybe a tiny bit.'

'Bullseye!' she cheered, throwing both hands in the air like Scotland had scored a goal.

'I think I'm going to need a very big drink,' said Michaela, clutching my arm.

'Greta,' I said earnestly. 'You're a married woman. You know I don't approve of such things.'

'Och away!' she chided. 'That man has eyes fir everything. Ah reckon it's well and truly ma turn.'

As we entered the club, the first thing that we saw was a woman dancing on the stage in a gold, sparkly bikini.

'Nice,' Michaela remarked, as the woman turned her back to the crowd and proceeded to bend forward, displaying her derriere to a baying crowd.

'Take a seat here,' I told her and Greta. 'I'll just go and find Linda.'

Weaving my way through tables full of men and women, all watching the show, I couldn't see Linda or Eydis anywhere, so decided to head for the side of the stage. As I got nearer, I strained my eyes to make out faces through the dim light and finally saw Linda and Eydis at a table with a beautiful woman I'd never seen before.

'Linda!' I called, rushing forwards. However, my way became suddenly blocked. By a glittery, gold encrusted cleavage.

'You like?' asked the stripper, who had climbed off the stage to join me in the crowd.

Before I could say anything, she had whipped off her top and was jiggling her breasts with her hands and pushing them into my face.

'Gah!' I protested, closing my eyes and putting my arm up to get her jugs off me and finding someone else's hand instead.

'Binnie! I'm so glad you came!'

It was Linda. She waved the woman away, who immediately turned her attentions to another more willing onlooker at a nearby table.

'Have you come alone?' she asked me. 'I didn't think you'd show.'

'No,' I replied, turning to wave at Michaela and Greta, who'd begun to make their way forwards via the far right aisle – as far away from the stripper as they could get. I understood, feeling desperately uncomfortable myself now we were here.

Thankfully, the Miss Jiggly Boobs act was coming to an end now and she bounded back onto the stage to a round of cheers from the audience.

'You know, Linda,' I said. 'This really is everything I've come to hate if I'm honest.'

'You're right,' she agreed. 'It's not really what Eydis was expecting either, but the guys came all this way to do a show.'

Just as we all began to sit down with Eydis and her companion, Linda pulled me back up again.

'No, no, no,' she said. 'There's dancing to do! Let's at least enjoy the night. Christie, order Tequila Sunrises all round, on me, please.' Her request was to the exotic-looking beauty at the table, who nodded and smiled before summoning a waiter over.

'Mario,' she called out, in a very deep, masculine voice. 'Six Tequila Sunrises over here, please. On Linda's tab.'

'Linda,' I said, into her ear. 'Is Christie . . . ?'

'A man?' she finished for me. 'Indeedy, darlin'. Beautiful, ain't she?'

I nodded and smiled. Indeed she was. And with a figure I'd have died for.

'I'll just sit here wae yous for a wee while,' said Greta, taking a seat at the table.

As Michaela looked around her not knowing quite what to do, I grabbed her arm and we made our way to the dance floor, which was already packed.

'I thought we'd be the only women in here,' Michaela shouted across.

Linda laughed. 'No, there's always a good mix of folk.'

'What, even with the strippers coming on?' Michaela asked.

'Especially with the *dancers* coming on,' Linda replied.

As I strutted around the floor doing my worst middle-aged mum dancing impression, I felt a crunch underfoot and looked down to find my heel had snapped clean off.

'Oh, no!' I cried, reaching down to take off my stiletto. 'Not again! Bloody cheap shoes.'

Seeing my predicament, Michaela and Linda stopped dancing and followed me back to the table.

'Oh, darling,' said Christie, looking as concerned as if I'd sprained my ankle when she spied the broken shoe in my hand. 'We'd better fix those gorgeous shoes. Come with me.'

'Gorgeous shoes, my ass,' I complained. 'This is the second time the damn heel has broken off. I just glued it back on a few days ago. I think they're finally done.'

She took my arm and led me towards the bar. 'But you need them for tonight, my darling. Follow me. The owner, Giannis, has something to fix everything.'

In no time at all, after a brief trip to the bathroom, I was back at the table with my friends, offending, cheapie shoe fixed.

'Wow,' said Eydis. 'That was quick. What did you do?'

Christie winked at her. 'Superglue,' she said, with a smile. 'Giannis always keeps it behind the bar in case one of us girls needs a repair.'

'Great!' Linda said. 'We can get back to the dance floor now.'

'Oh, no,' I said quickly. 'Better let it dry properly first.'

'Anyway,' Eydis cut in. 'The boys will be on in about five minutes.'

As she finished speaking the lights went up and the music faded, as a man in a top hat and tails came out onto the stage.

'Hello girls and girls!' he shouted out, to rapturous applause and whistles. 'How are you enjoying your night?'

We all cheered, including Michaela who, having swallowed down her first Tequila Sunrise quickly was now reaching for her second and looking much more comfortable.

'Good, good,' the compere continued. 'Now, are you ready to sexy things up tonight?'

'YEAAAAHHHHHHHSSSSSS!' The crowd, including our table roared.

'Okay then, time to partay with a little booty. Give it up everybody for my favourite arty boys . . . GELLE!'

The house lights went down and the stage lights came on just as millions of silvery streamers burst from the stage into the crowd in time to the opening notes of ZZ Top's *Sharp Dressed Man*. Greta looked fit to burst as the guys, including her favourite, Dominik, came on stage dressed in smart suits and began peeling off their jackets.

A waiter arrived with the third round of drinks, and Michaela downed the final half of her second Tequila Sunrise in one go.

'Woohoo!' she shouted out. 'Over here! Over here!'

I lined up my third Tequila Sunrise behind number two, which I was still sipping. I'd had enough hangovers this holiday to know all about drinking too quickly. Greta and Linda, however, were matching Michaela drink for drink.

The boys gave a fantastic performance, peeling off one item of clothing after another to the screaming and clapping audience. I caught Dominik winking at Greta and within moments they began to make their way off the stage and into the crowds, he was heading our way in nothing but a pair of shorts.

'Oooooohhhh!' Greta cried, jumping up and down in excitement. 'He's coming over here!'

Dominik strutted and shimmied through the crowds until he came to our table, whereby he turned and began shaking his bottom in front of Greta, who promptly spanked him with a, 'Woooohooo!'

He turned back and smiled at her, pointing to the front of his shorts. Taking his lead she pulled the strings to release him from the shorts which fell down about his ankles to reveal his muscular bottom in nothing but a small, black thong. Then, he looked over to me.

'Oh no,' I cried. 'Just you stay where you are!'

With a mischievous grin he walked up to my chair, pushed it back slightly and, turning around, stood over me and began to writhe and shake his bottom in front of my face.

'Oh, no,' I laughed. 'Gerroff!'

I kicked out my leg to push him away, feeling mortified, but he swung round and grabbed my ankle. Before I knew it, he had begun rubbing my legs, pressing his crotch against my foot whilst writhing suggestively.

'Oh, God!' I cried, covering my face with my hands.

'Make it stop!'

With a final pelvic thrust, he released my ankle and turned to Michaela who was next in line for a show. All at once, I realised I had lost my shoe. Thinking it had fallen off, I bent down, and as I searched the floor with my hands there was a burst of laughter from the table.

'That is dynamite!' I heard Eydis say.

I looked up in time to see Dominik, with this back to me and his hands behind his back, performing a sexy dance in front of Michaela. To my astonishment, from where I was sitting, it looked as though she was touching his crotch! *For heaven's sake! How drunk is she?* Even more incredible was the fact that everyone at our table and the tables round about us was watching and laughing hysterically.

Eydis and Greta stood up at the same time and reached over together, both going for Dominik's crotch too. He turned back towards us and it was then I saw what all the commotion was about. I had found my shoe.

It was jigging and bouncing around, held fast by the heel, hanging from the front of Dominik's thong.

In the wee, small hours, heading back to the apartment in a taxi, full of remorse for having enjoyed a strip show, I had sent a single, drunken text to David:

It's time we talked.

Chapter Twenty-Two

We're having a party for National Orgasm Day. Who's coming?

I almost brought the three Tequila Sunrises from the previous night back up when I read 'me!' underneath my status from Smother. I closed the Facebook app on my phone and saw a mass of notifications.

You have ten voicemails.

You have twenty seven missed calls.

There are fourteen text messages.

You took four photos of the inside of your pocket and fifteen screen shots whilst out riding yesterday.

I really should learn how to lock my phone. I did a perfunctory flick through the voicemails to ensure there were no panics from home, pressing the required key for instant deletion of each pleading message.

'Hello Binnie, I need to tal . . .'

I pressed three.

'Please talk to me. I love y . . .'

Three.

'Baby, I mis . . .'

Three.

'Hi, it's Mum, I hate to bug you on your honeymoon but I'm worried about this massive verruca looking thing on my . . .'

Three. Three. THREE!

There was a knock at the door. Reaching down to my bedside to pick up my ruined stilettos and throw them in the bin, I looked at the clock. It was eleven o'clock. I couldn't remember the last time I had slept so late. Or why I had unblocked David's calls.

'Hi, Binnie are you in there? I just wanted to make sure you were alright?'

Jumping up and into my shorts and pushing the phone deep into the pocket, I pulled on a t-shirt and opened the door.

'Hi, Chris, of course I'm alright.' His deep, blue eyes looked almost sorrowful and I felt a flutter of concern. 'Are *you*?'

'Yes, oh, it's alright,' he said. 'Just, well, you didn't come home last night and . . . of course . . . it's none of my business . . .'

'I see, oh!' There was something behind his eyes; something unusual in his discomfort. He thought I was *with* someone. Perhaps David had been calling him too. I casually opened the door wider to let him see that I was alone.

His eyes briefly flicked to the bed and then back to me. 'I was worried, that's all,' he explained. 'This is a tiny island and we don't see a lot of bother, but, well, you never know.'

'No, you don't. Thank you for your concern, but I'm fine. We had a proper girls' night after the horse ride. I went up to get some food with Greta and then later took Michaela to watch Gelle. It was a brilliant night. You were right about her, she is lovely.'

'Oh, well, that's good,' he said, looking instantly happier. 'Only I thought you hadn't come home. I must have fallen asleep before you got back.'

'Well, no, actually we ended up embroiled in girl talk till the wee small hours. I slept on Linda's sofa. I actually got home a short while ago.'

He paused and swallowed hard. I wondered if he was trying to work out if I was lying. If, in fact, I had spent the night with a man.

'That's alright then,' he said finally. 'As long as you haven't been arrested for driving that bloody moped on the wrong side of the road again.'

'Have you got any coffee on upstairs?' I asked, swiftly changing the subject.

'I do, as it happens, but I've got an art class in fifty minutes, so Mita and I were just beginning to get set up.'

'Oh, okay. Well, I'll come and watch.'

'You mean help?' he said. 'Great!'

We walked together to the pergola where I'd had my first art class with him only days earlier, although now it seemed an age away. Some of his paintings were stacked in a box on a chair and I began idly sifting through them.

'Oh,' he said quickly, moving the chair with the box on it away from me. 'Don't bother with them. That's just a lot of really old stuff.'

'Oh, no, please, let me see?' I said, pulling it back.

His faced flushed hotly as I fingered through the canvasses. 'Honestly,' he said. 'It's a lot of tripe. The things in here are just examples I sometimes use for showing classes the different styles of painting or differing subjects. There are none of my finest hours in there.'

I stopped and caught my breath as I came to the last but one canvas in the pile. It was a very intricate oil painting of a woman's face. The detail was exquisite, the colours, vibrant and alive. It was like looking in a mirror at myself – eight years ago.

'It's me!' I exclaimed.

Chris grabbed the painting. 'You? No, I don't think so.' He inspected it briefly before throwing it back into the box which he picked up.. 'It's just something I did ages ago, but you're right. There is a resemblance, isn't there?'

I stared at him in puzzlement. *Why would he paint me?*

'Did David ask you to do that?' I asked.

'You know, I think that might have been it,' he answered. 'It was so long ago now, I hardly remember.'

I sighed inwardly, feeling a stab of pain. The painting was of a slightly younger me, during a much younger relationship. It was most likely from a time when David still found me attractive and wanted to have a portrait of me. Then he'd changed his mind, or had forgotten to ask Chris about it again. I guessed Chris was trying to spare my feelings by showing it to me or speaking about it, because it had ended up thrown in a box, only coming out as an example of a portrait for his daily classes.

'These are all very beautiful though, Chris,' I said, fighting back bitter tears. 'You really have an amazing talent. It must take a lot of patience and hard work to produce something like this.'

As my eyes met his, I saw so much sorrow I could hardly bear it. I didn't want his sympathy, but he was definitely regretting that I'd seen the painting. 'Thank you,' he replied. 'But doing what you love never feels like hard work really, does it?'

He smiled and right then, I envied him.

'I don't know,' I answered truthfully.

Doing something you love. I wished I could say I did. I thought it must be the best feeling in the world to be in a job you know in your heart was made for you; embodying all of your God-given gifts. Not like toiling behind a desk in an office in the grey, wet city. Not like photocopying forty-seven forms while the whole world – and a well overdue and deserved promotion – just passes you by. *Life really is too damn short.* I thought of another person who had given up the rat race to do what she loved.

'Michaela was lovely, really inspirational,' I said. 'I've learned so much more from her than how to cook and ride a horse through the waves. So much more.'

Placing a pot of brushes in the middle of the table, Chris paused for a second to idle with them and then smiled.

'Yes, she is quite an extraordinary lady. Very resilient. Particularly after her . . . er . . . after she . . .'

'Lost her husband?' I finished.

'Ah,' he said. 'She told you then.'

'Yes. And I don't think I've ever had the privilege to meet a person who has turned such a negative into a wholly positive thing. She really loves and appreciates life, it's so infectious.'

'Yes, she is a beautiful person,' he said.

'Do you know who else is amazing?' I added.

'Besides me?' he chuckled.

'Greta. She's a breast cancer survivor, did you know that? She calls herself an NHS high flyer.'

'No, I did not,' Chris said, looking very surprised. 'She and Hughie are a really upbeat, funny couple. Who'd have thought it?'

'That's the thing,' I told him. 'She isn't at all gloomy about it. She says that after the operation to remove her breast, that's when her life truly began. Can you believe that? She said she realised that at the end of the day death is always there, waiting in the wings for you. Better give him some light entertainment while he's got nothing else to do.' I chuckled at the memory of her words.

'Well, I don't know what to say to that,' Chris replied, looking wistful. Then, he began to smile. 'Except,' he continued, 'how on earth does she cope with him flirting with you like he does?'

'Oh, it's just harmless banter,' I laughed. 'I guess when you make it to forty-odd years of marriage, you know each other better than you know yourself.'

At that moment Mita breezed by me, placing water jugs on the table. Spilling out of an extremely low cut top like a busty bar wench again, I thought she looked about ready to place another set of jugs on the table. Yesterday I'd have eyed her enviously – today I couldn't be happier for her right to do so.

'Good morning, Mita, how lovely to see you again,' I answered, smiling at her. She smiled a 'hello' back and continued quietly with her work. 'Well, I better get out of your way,' I said. 'It looks like another scorcher and there's sunbathing to be done, after all.'

'Aren't you parascending this afternoon?' Chris asked.

'Yes, but not 'til 4 o'clock. Why?'

'Well, my class finishes at noon and then I have an exhibition on at the museum – you know the building that you walk past to get down to the beach?'

'Yes, the one that has the balcony overlooking the sea?'

'That's the one. When you're done whizzing over the sea, why don't you drop in?'

'No prior engagements tonight then?' I asked.

'None at all. And if you're good I might even buy you dinner.'

The phone in my pocket began to ring out loudly. *Damn, I forgot to turn it to silent.* It was a ring tone I'd downloaded for David to cheer myself up which announced loudly:

'WANKER ALERT! WANKER ALERT!'

Chris and Mita both stopped to watch me. I fumbled around in my pocket, cursing myself for having had a wine-fuelled weak moment and unblocking him, attempting to buy time for it to stop ringing by pretending it was just out of my grasp. Thankfully, it fell silent – just as I retrieved it.

'What eez a wanker?' Mita asked Chris, who stared back at her wordlessly.

'Ah, well, they'll maybe call back later . . .'

It started again. 'WANKER ALERT! WANKER ALERT!'

'Sorry, I'd better, erm . . . just take this over here.' Pressing the reject button and putting it to my ear this time to look as if I was taking the call, I rushed back towards my apartment, arriving at the patio just as a text alert buzzed my ear. *What on earth was making David so insistent today?* I opened it and read the message:

I'm back at the hotel. Where are you?

It was no use pretending I'd gone home. The one thing that would have alerted everyone at home to the fact that something was wrong would have been deleting David from my Facebook friends list. 'Mrs David Dando is now single' would have caused some concern. He knew I was still here in Greece and still going through the list which meant he probably knew where I was going to be this afternoon. On this small island, if he wanted to find me he would very likely succeed. The best thing to do was avoid him having to come look for me, because the one thing I didn't want was him showing up in front of any of my new friends. Way too complicated. Everyone knew we were recently separated but not everyone knew just how recently – or that I was on our honeymoon. Quick thinking was required. I'd have to agree to a meeting.

> I've moved into an apartment elsewhere on the island. I'll meet you but please, give me a little space. I'm not ready to face you right this minute.

The response was immediate. He called me and I rejected it before sending another message:

> Please David. I can't speak to you right now.

It was true; the lump in my throat and stinging in my eyes told me that one word with him and the floodgates would open and my power would once again be given over to him. Not now David. Not now. His reply was another text:

> Then meet me tonight. Please, I beg you xxx

It was David who had chosen the parascending experience so I knew that if I said no to a meeting there was every chance he would just turn up. He'd booked the lesson himself.

'We'll start with the honeymoon, then after that it's one thing a week that scares us. We'll both do it. You get one shot at life, Binnie. Just one! Let's take it and all its experiences by the balls. We are going to be so happy from this day forward, just you wait and see.'

That was our wedding day. I waited. I saw. And it was all complete and utter bollocks. I answered him with another text:

```
We can meet up later this evening, okay?
I'll let you know where this afternoon.
```

At that moment Chris appeared behind me. 'Everything okay?' he asked.

'Yes, fine. It's Linda calling me, I promised to meet up with Eydis and Linda tonight to watch a bit of a last night rehearsal thing with the dance troupe. She's just chasing me up about it.'

'Does she know you think she's a wanker?' he said, sardonically. It was clear he had guessed it was David calling me. I wasn't going to talk about it.

'Yes, it's a private joke between us,' I lied.

'Fine, well, what about the exhibition later?' he asked.

'Sure. I'll drop in before I go out,' I promised.

He stood staring at me for a moment, as if he wanted to ask me something else. I guessed what he really wanted to know was whether I was going to speak to David.

Finally, he asked, 'How long have you got left till you go home now?'

'Not long, sadly.' I sighed and felt a knot in my stomach but couldn't decide whether it was the thought of leaving or meeting David later. I was going to miss the island and my new friends; and I realised that it was likely I would never see Chris again once I'd gone back to England. I wondered if his question meant he realised too.

'Binnie, I'd like to have that dinner, I really would. There are things to say before you go . . .' his voice trailed away, but his words had already surprised me.

The goat bell at the gate sounded out, signalling the arrival of his first pupil for the morning. With a 'We'll talk later,' he rushed off. And then a thought occurred to me. Maybe he was going to spend an afternoon trying to talk me into taking David back. Suddenly, I remembered what I had been thinking in my Tequila-fuelled haze last night, and the text I'd sent to David. Dammit. That's why he was calling me! And he had probably been calling Chris too.

I flopped back into my chair, shielded from Chris's pergola by the patio curtain, and my mind spun − thinking of David, the love of my life, my new husband. Shouldn't I go to him? But then, life was so much different, better, easier here in Greece with my new friends and not all of them were going home this coming weekend. My life was to return to normal on Saturday when I went home to my two grown daughters, who both rushed around living fearless lives of their own the way I'd made sure I raised them. I didn't want them to rely on anyone or have all the insecurities I'd grown up with. And they didn't. What else did I have to rush back to? A super dull job. Real life back home in England was one relentless bloody drag.

And here was Chris; creative, affluent, not unattractive, and with not one but two homes. His life had two seasons – winter in England and summer in Greece. So he might be a bit of a cad who was having an affair with a married woman. Or was he? I didn't actually have any evidence except a tiny, nagging hunch and a couple of coincidences. Anyway, what business was it of mine? Why should I care? But I liked him; a lot. That's why I cared.

My thoughts turned from Chris to the bronzed, fit body of Argos, who, at twenty whatever-it-was called me 'beautiful Binnie.' And, after giving him a lift home on the back of my moped the other evening, I knew my pelvic toner had magical properties that could give him an erection that lasted over an hour. I must get a new one of those.

It was Argos who would be giving me my parascending session on the beach. How many jobs the guy had, I didn't know. Everyone out here seemed to have so much going on.

I'd done so much thinking since I got here, after having had almost no time to spend with myself in many, many years. This island honeymoon had changed me, I could feel it. Why should I feel bad about going to a strip club after the way David had humiliated me? Did I want to go and meet him? Could I let Chris talk me into taking him back? Why? When I was beginning to consider the possibility that I had found myself right here in Greece after being lost for a very long time.

Husband number one hadn't deserved the real me. Maybe David didn't deserve the real me either. Maybe I did. All that was needed was for me to make a start on taking my power – and my sexy − back. A delicious idea was forming in my head – an exuberant peach of a thought.

I sent two texts – one to Linda and one to David.

Chapter Twenty-Three

It's 32 degrees here today! Doncha
wish your girlfriend was hot like me?
- Joan of Arc, 1431.

'Now, you just count to three, walk forward a few steps and then run.'

As Argos strapped me into the harness, feeling around my backside to fasten it, I prayed to the God whose living room I thought I might be about to fly into.

The shorts I'd chosen for the day pinched my tummy; made too tight by a week's worth of scrummy feta cheese and olive oil. But hey, they'd had some healthy tomatoes for company.

'Okay. Hold the reins . . .' I repeated. 'Count to three . . .'

Argos laughed. 'Reins? It is not a horse like yesterday, Binnie!'

'Wait. What? You saw me?' *With my tits out?*

Argos waved to the boat, "It's okay, go, go!' he shouted, then turned back to me. He was grinning like the cat that got the view of my boobs. 'Are you ready?'

'You saw me riding the horse yesterday? On the beach?'
The boat's engine roared.

'Count to three, Binnie!'

I took two steps forward. 'One, two . . .'

'SHIIIIIIIIIITTTTTTTT!!!'

There was no three. And no run. More of a sitting glide across the water as I was yanked forward. Finally, I was lifted high into the air. As I felt the wind in my hair, I found peace and solitude again. Not for the first time on this holiday, I felt like I was really living.

'Georgio,' Chris barked.

A short, stout man with a large, bushy moustache appeared, carrying a clipboard. I'd gone to Chris's art gallery as arranged, to find him more than willing to escape for a welcome break.

'Could you take over for a bit?' Chris asked him. 'I'm taking my friend to lunch.'

The man nodded.

'Well, that'll be lovely,' I said. 'But Linda is expecting me at her place soon, so we'll have to make it a very short one.'

'I've been hoping to get a proper chance to speak with you,' Chris began, as we sipped wine and shared a huge, Greek salad and fresh bread.

We were sitting at an outside table in one of the tiny restaurants that lined the bustling, cobbled side streets. At this time of day there were always tour boats flooding the island for a brief time with additional custom it was no doubt grateful to receive.

I looked up from my plate and frowned. This was it. My lecture about taking David back. Only he didn't know it was way too late.

'Really?' I said, bracing myself for his speech.

'Yes, really,' he said.

I sighed loudly. 'Look, Chris, I know what you're going to say,' I started.

'It's about that thing you brought up the other day,' he cut in.

'Oh,' I said, feigning understanding, then immediately realising how pointless that was. 'What thing?'

'You asked me why I stopped talking to you.'

'Oh, that,' I said. 'But you said we were okay?'

'We were. We are.' He stopped and looked away for a moment, as if carefully contemplating his next sentence. 'No,' he said at last. 'We weren't alright. I was lying. There was something else.'

'Was it something I said or did?'

'No.'

'David?'

'No. Well . . . yes.'

'It was something David did?'

'Oh dear, wait,' he sighed. 'This is all very difficult for me to explain. David is my best friend.' He pulled a napkin out of the holder on the table and mopped his brow. 'But yes, in a nutshell, it was because of him that I stopped talking to you.'

'What did he do?' I asked. 'Or was it something he said?'

'Nothing. No, it's not that,' he began. 'You and I always got on so well, always laughing together. I think I sometimes took you away from him.'

'I know,' I said. 'I thought we were becoming friends. And then it all stopped. You took your friendship away and didn't tell me why.'

'I liked you a lot. I still like you a lot.' He lifted his

glass and took a huge mouthful of wine. 'This isn't an easy thing to tell you,' he said. 'I couldn't be your friend because of David.'

All at once, the light in my head came on. I stood up, pushing my chair back angrily and the buzz of conversation that had been around us from other diners ceased. 'He told you to stay away from me, didn't he?' I said.

'What?'

'He told you to back off from his woman, didn't he,' I stormed. 'What a jerk!'

'No, that's not what happened . . .'

I was already making to leave, my meeting later with David now more urgent than ever.

'Bernice,' Chris pleaded, reaching for my arm. 'Please sit down. You're getting the wrong end of the stick . . .'

'Don't you try protecting him anymore,' I said. 'He's not worth your loyalty!' I reached into my purse and threw ten euros on the table. 'Here's my half for lunch.'

'Wait,' Chris said, standing up now too. 'Bernice, it's not that, honestly. Could you please just sit down?'

Tears welled in my eyes and glancing around, I could see everyone in the restaurant had stopped what they were doing to watch the show. I felt mortified.

'I'm sorry,' I told Chris solemnly. 'I have to go.'

Chapter Twenty-Four

Parascending = awesome! But can someone tell
my arse my legs are still attached to it?

Posting a 'haha' status to Facebook felt harder than usual today, but I knew my girls would be expecting news of our parascending adventure. I clicked 'send' and flopped back into the chair in Linda's apartment. The only person left to arrive was David. I hoped that around about now Linda was down at the fish restaurant leaving him some crumbs.

The plan was for her to apologise for my being unavoidably detained. She'd been told to tell him 'something had come up,' and then offer to have a drink with him to discuss 'Binnie and her problems.' At the end of their little chat, Linda would come over very sympathetic and reveal that she knew where I was staying. Then, the stinger. The suggestion that he came to see me to try and patch things up. What harm could it do? Linda was my friend. She only had my best interests at heart.

If only he'd hurry up! The tiny thong I was wearing,

under a flowery, pink, baby doll nightie, was continually riding up my backside and however much I'd tried to stay upset that afternoon, the dance troupe had fussed around, plying me with margaritas. I gulped them back gratefully, waiting for the gradual numbing sensation they'd bring that would protect me from all my pain and anger as well as the embarrassment of frolicking around in front of virtual strangers in sexy lingerie. In no time at all, I was dancing around with Gelle to *The Birdie Song*, my head all a-fuzz.

They did not disappoint. As the guys writhed and jiggled in front of me in nothing but tiny gold thongs, Roman poured oil over his chest and arms before turning around to smooth some over his tight, tanned bottom. The margaritas had helped to tear down my inhibitions and all at once, I was no longer a spurned woman in emotional turmoil, I was simply loving the show. Roman had slapped my hand at least seventy-seven times as I pawed his thong while he danced to the sound of The Tweets.

'We haven't started yet, lady!' he laughed saucily, smacking his own backside at me and making me scream with laughter.

All of my anger seemed to have melted. By the time Eydis came running in to tell us the buzzer was ringing, I'd almost forgotten David was coming.

'He's here! He's here!' she shouted. 'Change the music, quickly!'

Dominik raced to the CD player to change the disc and I jumped into a seat trying to look unfazed and busy.

A peel of church bells boomed out of the stereo.

'Sheeeettt!' Roman shouted. 'It is the wrong song!'

Dominik reached forward to quickly switch to another disc, but instead, fast forwarded the current one. Now canon fire boomed out. Everyone looked alarmed, not knowing what the hell was happening or what to do next and knowing that David, as planned., could appear anytime. Evidently they had never done an erotic dance rehearsal to Tchaikovsky's *1812 Overture* and, until now, I had never seen one either.

As the door to the room burst open, Roman jumped over me on the sofa, putting one leg on the arm and his crotch near my face, and began thrusting in time to each boom of gunfire. The guys behind him all followed suit, arms on the man in front's shoulder and thrusting in time to each 'BOOM!', all the while maintaining their serious, 'aren't you turned on by my body' faces like true, sexy dance professionals. As David entered the room, Roman turned to wiggle his arse in my face and I all-too-enthusiastically twanged his thong, which promptly came off in my hand. I had forgotten an earlier warning about the stripper Velcro.

'What the FUCK is going on here!'

David's face was nearly purple. I'd never seen him so angry.

As Tchaikovsky's canon-fire-filled concerto played on, Roman stopped dancing, stooped to cover his modesty with his cupped hands and trotted away with the rest of the group in hot pursuit. I turned back to look from David's face to Eydis right behind him. I couldn't make out who was more surprised.

'What the hell are you wearing?' David shouted.

Realising she needed to be out of the way too, Eydis stepped in, grabbed Roman's thong out of my hand, clicked off the stereo and bolted.

My fuddled, giggly, drunken brain wanted me to say, 'David, could you go out and come back in again in, say, twenty minutes?'

Instead, I went all out for the 'best surprised look in sexy underwear' Oscar.

'David!' I exclaimed. 'How on earth did you find me?'

'Binnie, how could you do this? I don't understand . . .' To my surprise, I saw that he was almost in tears and for a second, my conscience pricked me.

'Er, David you shouldn't have seen that. I'm sorry.'

'What on earth were you doing?' he demanded.

'Oh, that little show? It was nothing David. Just a little warm-up for us. I was only enjoying myself a little. Getting myself revved up for you.'

'WHAT?'

I continued with the script in my head, the one I'd read twelve months earlier on a website for people whose partners were addicted to porn.

'It's just, well, our sex life hasn't really been that . . . you know . . . racy. I wanted to hot things up to help us start over again. So I've been spending some time with these guys.'

'Spending time with these guys? You mean, this isn't the first time? Shit Binnie, is THIS what you've been doing while I've been breaking my heart over us? Cheating on me? And us being only a WEEK married?'

This was working better than I'd bargained for. Despite the hurt look in his eyes, I couldn't help smirking at the irony of it all and he caught me.

'This is funny to you?'

'Oh, David, relax!' I said, putting an arm on his shoulder. 'I'm not cheating. Just watching. You know, like you do. It's nothing.'

'You don't think this is cheating? I never once, not once, had any other woman in my room! I never touched another woman.'

'Well, I didn't touch anyone either and no-one touched me. I was just looking. Like you do.'

'And doing what?'

'Well, I might touch myself a little bit. Like you do. Hey, maybe we can do it while we watch them?'

'Oh, Jesus Christ, I'm going to be sick,' he said, pushing away my arm.

With each 'like you do,' the pain of remembering everything I'd ever caught him doing behind my back came rushing back stronger than before. It was almost as though David was an antidote to the male strippers and margaritas. I pointed to the open toilet door. 'The lavatory is that way.'

He made a bolt for it and I followed him. As he knelt before the bowl, making what sounded like contrived heaving noises, I pulled my wedding and engagement ring from my pocket and tossed them into the toilet. They landed in the water right in front of him with a spla-clunk.

'What did you do that for?' he screamed.

'So that this time, when you're shitting all over our relationship, you'll know it,' I said, turning on my heels and strutting away.

'This is nothing like what I did to you!' he shouted from the bathroom. 'You were in a room full of men half my age, slobbering all over them. You're killing me, Binnie!'

I heard the chain flush, although he obviously hadn't been sick at all, and he appeared in the doorway, ruddy-eyed and looking pathetic. I almost caved, especially as I spied him turning the retrieved rings over in his hand.

'I love you, Binnie. I do,' he sobbed. 'But all this has changed things. I don't know who you are anymore.' He put the rings in his pocket, adding, 'I just don't know how we can move on from this.'

'You're right, David.' Tears welled in *my* eyes now. 'How can anyone stay in a marriage where the other person is lusting over something else? Something more exciting? Getting their sexual gratification outside of their intimate relationship with another person? It can't work, can it?'

'You were in a room with a bunch of other men!' he bellowed, angrily. 'I never went that far. I wasn't with anyone!'

'Yes you were,' I cried. 'On a website. In front of a TV screen. On your mobile. You were with lots of other women! Perfectly sculpted, young, sexy, plastically and digitally enhanced women. So much so that when I wanted you to make love to me, you had nothing left to give. You make me sick. Worse than that, you made me sick – inside. I hated myself when I was with you.'

'Is that what this was about? Revenge?' he screamed, 'Well, you got it. You win, Binnie.' He turned and walked over to the door through which the guys had left – and from the distinct sound of scuffling behind it, I knew they'd been leaning against it to listen and were scurrying away, probably falling over each other in the rush.

'I'm beat,' he continued, opening the door to leave. 'There's no coming back from this.'

As I looked into his hurt, angry and what I knew were unforgiving eyes, it all became suddenly clear. I loved him more than my own life, but he could never make me feel like I was his priority, as any truly loved women should be. He was never going to stop because he just didn't get it and I wasn't going to be the one to make him. Even after all of this. Even long after I was gone, he'd never understand.

'That's all I wanted to hear,' I said coldly, 'close the door behind you'.

Chapter Twenty-Five

I'm drunk not. Hello phone. Or is this
Facebook? Can you send a taxi to number one,
oh I don't know, I'm somewhere in Greece?

As the sun rose on the penultimate day of my holiday, I slept the deep, untroubled sleep of someone still drunk from the night before. It was the sound of voices and crunching on the gravel path outside that finally brought me round, and I checked my mobile. It said 1.30pm and alerted me to fourteen voicemails . . . and seventeen texts. I guessed all were from David, but wasn't in the mood for checking right now. Need. Coffee. And. Pee.

Passing the window en route to the toilet, I peered through the shutters to see Chris and Ginger taking off through the gate towards her car. Again, there was no sign of Edvard. I watched as she shook his hand and walked away. Surely if they were in the throes of an affair, there would be more than the shaking of hands? I sighed. My numb heart couldn't feel anger at their deceit right now, I was just thinking I could definitely live the life Chris had:

six months in Greece, six months in a country cottage in Worcester and zero emotional baggage. If it was a choice between that and spending all my time in four-weeks-of-sun-a year-if-we're-lucky England, working in a job I hate, with a cheating, lying husband, it was no contest. Maybe Ginger had it all worked out. Get them before they get you.

The girls were both grown up and no longer so reliant on my being around. One thing I knew for sure was that they would love all the free holidays if I stayed. Rubbing my head and remembering my night's excesses – and the triumph of giving David a sizeable kick to the kerb – brought about a heady mixture of elation and nausea.

Definitely need coffee.

Still, I wondered what on earth Chris was doing with Ginger. He seemed like such a nice person; not at all like David, and this new side of him just didn't fit with the Chris I thought I knew. Should I just come out and ask him? I put the kettle on and opened the door to let the sunshine pour in. It was another clear, blistery-hot day. Could I ever get tired of this?

I threw on a Saress and my sunglasses and took my coffee outside to the patio where I sat in its leafy shade thinking of the time, almost twelve months earlier, when I'd been called to a meeting with my boss's PA, Cilla, after asking for a pay rise. The bastard hadn't even faced me himself.

'Bernice, the company is very grateful to you for your hard work and enthusiasm,' she'd said. 'You are a phenomenal asset to the company. Well done.' The 'phenomenal asset' part being the £18,000 I'd saved the company in just under twelve months, by introducing some radical new administrative changes. 'But, whilst we appreciate all your hard work,' Cilla went on, 'we can't agree a pay rise. I know this will be a disappointing blow for you, but all the extra work you've taken on isn't within the pay grade for your post. We are grateful of course, but, well, we didn't ask you to do it.'

She was right; they hadn't asked me to do it. I had just seen the solution to some major problems that my boss had missed and gone about doing something about them of my own accord. In some business circles this might be called 'using your initiative'. It might be encouraged, nurtured − even rewarded. But I was being held firmly in my place; the bottom rung of the corporate ladder and one thing I knew for sure was that Cilla loved helping to keep me there. I imagined she had savoured the opportunity to give me the news that no pay rise would be forthcoming. It was clear she hated me. She even called me on her way into work some days, just to ask me to water her plants. On her way in! It was her way of letting me know, that no matter how hard I worked to shine, she had me at her disposal and I was going nowhere. I found out, entirely by accident, that Cilla's plants didn't thrive well on the boss's gin. But that's another story . . .

I picked up my mobile phone and flicked through the text messages. As I'd suspected, all were indeed from David. Somehow, he seemed more forgiving today and had gone back to begging me to talk to him. Pushing thoughts of him from my mind, I opened my email and typed in my boss's address.

By the time I'd finished my first cup of coffee of the day I had resigned. To do what? Who cares? It was time to find out what Bernice Dando could do for herself. I was giving myself permission to get a life. It had just been an all-too-short fortnight's holiday, but my head was now bursting at the seams with endless possibilities.

*

'Mum! Dad! I've got a weekend job!'

It was the first job I'd ever had and I'd raced in to find him fiddling with a picture frame, looking as though he was struggling to get the back off it with his one, useful hand.

'Burughh trurdummm at.' My dad was looking angrily at me, dribble leaking out of the right side of his mouth as he tried to make me understand him. He hit the picture frame hard with his forefinger. 'Burgggh urtttttt.'

It didn't do to show you couldn't understand what Dad was trying to say when he spoke, it always annoyed him. Sometimes pure frustration would make him throw cups across the room – not at anyone in particular – just through the sheer anger he felt at having his speech stolen from him by the stroke. I took the frame from him and saw that it was the photo of my sonogram that I'd given him the previous week.

I looked around desperately for my mother, but she was nowhere to be found.

'Oh, Dad,' I continued, trying to sound upbeat. Not at all like I couldn't understand him. 'Did you hear what I said? I got a job!'

He sighed heavily, still looking at the picture frame and nodded.

'At Bernie's, the fast food restaurant in Mansell Street.'

I perfectly understood Dad's next communication though. He started to cry. As I rushed forwards to hug him, my mouth brushed the tears. They tasted of disappointment.

'Oh, Dad,' I sobbed. 'I know it's not the best job in the world but Michael and I need some extra money coming in right now with the baby coming and all.'

He pulled away from me and pointed to the picture frame again. 'BABY!' he shouted, his face almost purple with fury.

'Yes, it's for the baby, Dad,' I replied, crying myself now and looking down at the five month old bump in my tummy where she lived. 'I can still work for a little while longer.'

He tried to speak again, but when nothing would come, he made an angry grab for the picture frame. I instinctively pulled it away, fearing he would smash it in temper.

'What are you trying to do anyway,' I asked him. 'Get the back off? Don't you want to have a picture of your grandchild? Are you ashamed of me because I'm pregnant? Dad, I gave this to you, please don't throw it back at me.'

He huffed and turned away from me, reminding me of the moment I'd told them just before he had his stroke. Remembering the way he had been unable to hide his disappointment. Even such a debilitating illness hadn't mellowed him.

Just one week later, he had another stroke and died.

It took three attempts to sign into Facebook, but finally the signal came through, offering me a brief window to rid myself of some of my more restrictive baggage. There was a long conversation to be had with Beth and Sal later, I knew; but for today, my only job was to unfriend and block Caroline and their father. The pretence was over; I was not their friend, extended family member or otherwise, and our relationship wasn't even 'complicated'. I avoided accompanying my 'unfriend' with the message I'd like to have sent:

Dear Caroline, you shagged my husband for
thirteen years, I wonder if you'd mind
awfully just fucking off?
Bernice likes this.

As I stared out at the distant blue horizon, I picked up a swatter and batted away the four hundred bitey, irritating insects that were buzzing around my head; an action that bore a striking resemblance to the rest of my morning's activities. All I had to do now was today's planned activity, which was all of my own choosing. Today was my 'envelope day' and although I didn't have it – David did – I recalled the contents clearly:

'David, for what seems like a lifetime I have hated the sight of my own body. What I wouldn't give to be free of all that nonsense, the way naturists are. Let's get naked, in broad daylight, on the beach.'

Not the romantic prose he might have expected from me, but the sentiment was clear. *Dear David, it's show the world your arse day.* This day I'd planned to throw caution – along with my bra and pants – to the wind, (again, as it now transpired) by enduring an hour on a nudist beach. Even now I couldn't believe I'd been the one to dream that one up. Calling to mind the free, exhilarating loveliness of my topless horse ride, it didn't feel quite so daunting as before. Not quite.

Argos called me 'beautiful Binnie.' Michaela had told me, more or less, to look in the mirror and find the love of my life. Then there was dear, brave Greta who, just one year after a mastectomy, had led five middle-aged and topless women on a gorgeous, sunset horse ride through the sea yelling 'titty-ho' at the sky. She didn't have to ask me if she looked like the perfect woman. She was perfect in every way and I knew her bravery would inspire me for the rest of my days. My body was a shining, healthy gift that had given life to two beautiful young women; it was time to have my day in the sun.

Taking a couple of aspirin for my head, I packed a good, strong, nipple-saving sunscreen, my iPod and a towel before heading off to the nudist beach. I wasn't afraid anymore . . . until a series of angry beeps from other motorists in my path made me swerve onto the kerb again. *Curse this right hand side driving thing.*

The car park at the beach was full of cars and bikes and there was loud music coming from the beachside taverna. There was one thing to look forward to − some gorgeous, young Greek barmen – all of them naked.

I wanted to behave like a man would in this situation, faced with a naked woman waiting to serve him alcohol. *'You betcha I'll have a cocktail!'*

The music was loud and sounded a bit like hip hop – not exactly to my taste, so I dug out my headphones. As Britney Spears fittingly told me I was *Stronger than Yesterday* and I realised I'd brought Sal's iPod instead of my own, I stepped out onto the beach, treading carefully through a sea of naked sunbathers. Without looking at any of them, I threw down my towel, whipped off my Saress and lay down, nipples to the sky. I had no idea who was beside me . . . and for once in my entire life, I didn't care.

There was a tap on my foot and for a moment I thought it was the goats again. I opened one eye and the first thing I saw before me was a pair of smooth, shaved bollocks.

Wait! What? Opening both eyes, I looked up into the smiling face of a bronzed, long-haired blonde guy who towered over me. He was the tallest man I'd ever seen naked.

'Oh, hi there,' I said, reaching for my purse. 'I'll have a mojito, please.'

Staring nonplussed at me he opened his mouth to speak.

'Hit me baby one more time!'

As his lips moved out of synch, like a bad Japanese martial arts movie, I struggled to make sense of what was going on. And then I understood.

'Sorry?' I said, removing my headphones to get Britney out of my head.

'I said, you have a beeyouuutiful voice!' His voice boomed out all over the beach and I realised he was speaking into a cordless microphone.

I sat up and my heart stopped. Everyone in the vicinity was watching us. I started to pull my towel around me.

'What? How did you . . . ?' I started. *Oh, wait a minute.* 'I was singing aloud, wasn't I?'

He nodded and said, away from the microphone, 'A leetle bit, yes. You like the Britney Spears?'

Inconspicuous my arse! Which wasn't either, as it happened.

'No, of course not!' I protested. Yes, I did. But I was nearly forty-two and not admitting it to anyone.

'We can seeng a duet, no?' he continued.

'Er. No!'

Please go away. Please go away.

He wasn't going away. To my horror he began pulling me to my feet to cheers from the crowd around us.

'Ooh,' I said, trying to protest but losing to his incredible, Herculean strength. 'What the fuuu . . . ?'

'Come on, come on,' he urged, tugging me up towards the stage. This wasn't quite the inconspicuous nudist experience I'd hoped for today.

'Come on everreeybodee. Let's give the lady a big hand.'

Oh great. Something to cover up my arse.

As we made our way through clapping, cheering and whistling nudists to the stage, I spied the sign in front of the beach taverna.

Nudeoke today with Adonis Manikas

Nudeoke? They had to be joking, right?

Adonis handed me a microphone and whispered, 'What would you like to sing?'

'Err, far away?'

'I don't know theees far harway,' he mused, scratching his chin.

'I mean far away from here,' I whimpered, feeling all eyes on me. 'I really don't want to do this,' I whispered to him. My heart was in my mouth and pounding.

'Have you done the nude singing before?' he asked quietly, looking for all the world like he was going to think me weird if I said 'no'. Still, I shook my head.

'No?' he said.

'I've never even done nude before,' I admitted.

Adonis signalled to the barman, who rushed over with a tray of shots. He downed two to uproarious applause and signalled for me to do the same.

'A leetle help, perhaps?' he said.

'I don't like shots,' I protested.

'Oh, you want the cocktails?' He signalled to the barman again.

'No, no,' I said at last. 'The shots will do.' They would be short, sharp and quick. I peered down at the tray of drinks, catching sight of his monster of the sea at the same time, gulped and threw the first one back. I hadn't tried to sing in front of an audience since I was nine years old.

And that had ended in a way that remained in my memory to this day. But today, singing seemed like the teeniest, tiniest part of my worries. I was on a beach, naked . . . and all eyes were on me.

'Okay,' I said, gulping down the second shot.

'Do one thing a day that scares the bejesus out of you.'

I looked into Adonis's smiley, optimistic face and – weirdly for me – I felt a rush of adrenaline. 'Let's do this!'

'What do you want to sing?' he asked me.

'You choose.' Whatever it was, it was going to sound terrible anyway. I was petrified, only this time more about singing than my state of undress.

'Ah good. Krista!' he yelled at the DJ behind me, and, eyeing my ample bosom said, 'Islands In Thee Stream!'

Just great. *'Hey, I'm naked. Think of a song.'*

'I'm thinking of Dolly Parton.'

When the song finally ended, Adonis kissed my hand and passed me the biggest cocktail I'd ever seen in my life, which I took gratefully. But instead of my being booed off, as I'd anticipated, I was amazed to hear cheers, clapping and shouts of 'More, more!' *How much more could I possibly show?*

'That was wonderful,' Adonis gushed. 'Let us do another wan.'

'No, no, please. I really couldn't.' I pushed my way off the stage, glass in hand and walked straight into David, throwing ice-cold alcohol and juice all over his chest.

'Binnie, that was incredible!' he said, looking flushed and oblivious to the ice-cold drink I'd just spilled down his shirt. 'I didn't know you could sing!' he exclaimed.

I turned away from him, rushing over to get my things, and made my way to the car park, dressing as I went. 'My name is Bernice. B-E-R-N-I-C-E. And I don't want to talk to you, David!' I shouted behind me.

He ran to keep up with me. 'I knew you'd be here Binnie, do you know why?'

'Yeah. You opened my envelope.'

'Exactly,' he said, reaching out to hold my arm and stop me getting away. 'Did you open mine?'

'What? Why would I?'

'Did you? Tell me you did?'

Realising we were being watched by other people in the car park, I pulled away from his grasp, whispering sharply, 'No, and I don't intend to. Leave me alone!'

Saress and shoes now back on, I threw my stuff angrily into the basket on my moped, jumped on and began revving the engine.

David grabbed my arm again. 'Binnie,' he said.

'Bernice,' I corrected him.

'Bernice. You were amazing up there, I've never been so proud. You sounded beautiful. You looked beautiful. I thought about what you said last night and you were right. I'm sorry I hurt you. I thought I was helping us. I've been such a weak idiot.'

'Do you know why you had no idea I could sing, David? Because I only doubted myself when I was with you. And because I could never be myself when I was with you!'

'Don't say that. I love you.'

'I have to go now, David.'

'Binnie . . . I mean . . . Bernice, please don't give up on us. You're my wife. I haven't slept for a week, I need you! Please let me just explain . . .'

I pushed his arm away and began turning the moped towards the road.

'Okay, okay,' he said, looking panicked now. 'But just tell me one thing, why on earth did you think you couldn't be yourself with me? I don't understand. I thought we were happy.'

'You were happy!' I said scornfully. 'Not me. Do you know something David? I don't like The Stone Roses; I never have. You do. And I didn't choose *Baby, Baby, Blue* for our first dance just because it was funny. The truth is I've been keeping my love of what you'd call "cheesy films" to myself, just to be the way I thought you wanted me to be. I kept my love for that silly, funny song buried on our wedding day, just to be bloody agreeable. Yes, maybe it's silly and cheesy, but I bloody like it!'

He looked positively poleaxed. 'Baby, Baby, Blue?' he said, scratching his head. And I knew right there and then, he didn't even remember the song.

I revved the moped again and held the brake to let him know I was leaving.

'I don't get it,' he said quickly. 'But I want to. Please, we need to talk. Just stop for a second so I can speak to you.'

'I like old films. And I still adore Blondie no matter how old she is now! I love her; I think she's sexier today than she ever was. I like dancing round the kitchen, singing along to Atomic with a wooden spoon for a microphone, still pretending I'm her like I did when I was ten. I've found me, right here in Greece! Not the sad, downtrodden, people-pleasing me – the funny, sassy, flirty girl I was before, back when I didn't give a hoot who was watching. And I don't want to speak to you!'

As I pulled out of the car park, his voice rang out behind me.

'Open the envelope Binnie!' he shouted at my back. 'Please, just open it!'

Chapter Twenty-Six

To err is human. To find water, divine.

It had been a long and difficult night. Firstly, because it was the second last night of my holiday and I'd spent it in my apartment alone and, secondly, because I'd cried pretty much the whole way through it. Yet still, I posted my silly, isn't-it-great-being-on-honeymoon Facebook status. Keeping up the charade, knowing that very soon I'd have to reveal the truth to everyone.

Because my marriage was over. After only two weeks.

Linda had invited me to stay with her for the night but, knowing it was to be her last one with Eydis, who'd be catching the ferry with the boys around now, I'd said I couldn't ask her to sacrifice her relationship time just because mine had sunk into oblivion. I envied her. Today she would be saying 'see you later' to someone she loved. I would be saying 'goodbye' to somebody I really, really loved.

In the days before his stroke, my father would say,

'When you're at rock bottom, strap on a different pair of boots and start climbing.' I'd never known whether I ever made him proud, but he had certainly spent a lot of time pushing me to succeed when I was a girl.

Greta had called cancer one of life's bastards, and 'like aw bastards it has to be pushed awa' fae yer windaes so the light can come in.' In other words, don't concentrate too much on the problem, see past it. I loved the way she saw things. It was Greta's advice that seemed to ring truest to me. I was starting to believe that meeting her at this point in my life had been synchronicity in action. I had needed to realise life was passing me by; she was living proof that if I wasn't careful, it would. When Greta and Hughie had arrived in Greece, she told me she had the taxi from the airport stop by the first beach they came to.

'Ah stuck my toes in the Aegean,' she'd said. 'An' ah dae that everywhere I go, just in case ah never get tae feel it again. Ye have to take every chance ye get to experience the things ye love, Bernice. Dinnae waste a second o' it.'

She was right. How sad that it often took a brush with death for people to really open their eyes in life. The biggest hurdle I still had left to climb was telling everyone back home David and I were through. And give a reason for it.

'You don't have to tell anyone why,' Linda had said. 'Nobody needs to know the truth but you.'

'So, these "other" women of David's, you're saying they're not real? They live in the television, his laptop and mobile phone?' Yes. Like Eydis did for Linda up until last week. Now there was an interesting parallel.

'I promise to love and honour you, forsaking all others.'

Five days after saying this, David forgot about the forsaking bit. Little wonder my wedding song choice was

Baby, Baby, Blue, I was now. A promise had been broken, and yet I supposed society would expect me to overlook it for the sanctity of marriage. Did a woman have to forget her pride, her dignity, her own feelings and her own self to become the complete property of her man? On the day of our wedding, I'd changed my name on Facebook to present the newly married me as Mrs David Dando. As if Bernice Anderson had dissolved and her identity was now morphed into his.

I had been asking myself where I'd gone. The answer was simple; I'd dug myself a huge hole called David and buried myself in it – and not just with the simple act of a name change. I'd married a man who had helped derail my already damaged self-confidence, who, like the rest of society, was busy being old but chasing youth – the perpetual caricature made from every media presentation of a woman. Rub out the lines, age spots, every wrinkle, give her a youthful tuck here and there, then add the glossy shine of a sixteen-year-old to her hair. David wasn't the only one buying it, I was too. I had thought that inside of a marriage was the safest, neatest place for a forty-something woman like me to hide. Because I, Bernice Annabel Anderson, couldn't be alone. I had bought the idea that real women past the age of forty were on the shelf. I thought we may as well do what Blondie had said in a song, *Die Young, Stay Pretty*. Disappear. *Tell 'em you're dead, and wither away.*

I had done this to myself. And now it needed to be undone, without a care in the world for what anyone had to say about it. This is my life. If anybody wants to look in and offer a review, I'll file it under 'whatever'.

Taking David's still-sealed envelope from my suitcase, I turned it over and over in my hands. Whatever it said, it didn't matter now. My phone buzzed, interrupting my thoughts. It was a text from Linda.

```
Eydis just left. Could do with a friend right
now.
```

Texting Linda back to arrange a meeting I bolted out of the door, tossing David's envelope into my bag and leaving Chris a note pinned to the rail on his staircase:

Sorry about yesterday. Meet me tonight at the street party?

I scribbled my phone number underneath and headed to Linda's apartment. She greeted me at the door. 'Hi there,' she said, beckoning me in. Her eyes were as ruddy and wet as mine. She'd been crying too.

'Saying goodbye was a toughie, eh?' I said, hugging her.

'Yes,' she sniffed. 'And more permanent than we'd planned.'

'Permanent?'

'Yes. We've decided not to communicate anymore, it's too tough. She travels all round the world and I kind of love making roots in a place. It just can't work. Silly, really. We both should have known this all along. I love her Bernice, I really do. But I'm too old to live everywhere.'

'But if you love each other?'

'It could work, but only if everything else fell into place. I know if I made her stop travelling, she'd be unhappy. She knows if she made me traipse around the world with her, I'd be unhappy. No matter what Hollywood says, love doesn't conquer all, Bernice. I need to be able to be myself.'

'Well, I'm really sorry,' I said. 'But I do understand.'

'You've been crying too?' she asked.

'Yes, well, for the record, I'm ending my honeymoon tomorrow and heading home to see about an annulment. Now that's being different.'

'Annulment? Really?'

I sighed. 'David and I got married a fortnight ago. This was to be our adventure-laden honeymoon, for a marriage that was never consummated. And one of our first-time-for-everything honeymoon adventures turned out to be splitting up for good.'

Linda stared at me with her mouth agape. 'I don't know what to say,' she replied.

'What is there to say?' I said, sadly.

'Don't you love him?'

'Of course I love him, that's why I married him. But I can't live with his deceit and, well, the lack of sex thing.'

She sat straightening the hem on her trousers, looking deep in thought.

Finally, she spoke. 'Bernice, to be honest I felt a bit guilty the other day once I got speaking to the guy. He seemed an okay kind of fella and he really, really loves you. Are you sure this is what you want?'

'He cheated on me. Alright, not in the complete sense of the word but he was getting off on other women and not me. What kind of marriage is that?'

'You're right, he shouldn't look elsewhere for his kicks but at least it wasn't a real woman he was with.'

'How can you of all people say that? You said you loved Eydis, yet you'd never met her?'

She looked stung at the reference back to the source of her own pain and for a second I felt very guilty. 'Oh, Linda I'm sorry. I didn't mean . . .'

'That's okay,' she assured me. 'Yes, I loved Eydis. But

that's because we talked every night, exchanged emails, learned each other's deepest, darkest secrets. We shared our hopes and dreams in regular conversations, getting to know each other just like on a date in person. We weren't simply "getting off" on each other – we were two people sharing thoughts and real feelings. It's not the same at all.'

'That's what this honeymoon was supposedly all about. Getting to know one another again, trying new experiences; a new start. All I found out, once and for all, is that he's a snivelling, weak-willed pig of a man and I HATE him!'

'Which, of course, is the universally recognised sign that you love him.'

'Yes, I fucking love him, okay? But I don't want to.'

'I know! Fucking man!'

'Fucking MEN!'

'And fucking women!' she yelled. Despite our misery we both laughed.

'I wish we weren't going home tomorrow,' I sighed. 'I am going to miss you and this place so much.'

'I know, not to mention all this hot sunshine, wine and great food.'

'The worst thing is – I know I won't see Chris again.'

'Why the hell not?'

'Because he's David's best friend. He's not going to want to know me when I've gone home and everyone realises the marriage is through,' I answered. 'The sad thing is I really like Chris, even though he might be having an affair. We used to get on so well.'

'Wait, wait, wait,' Linda cut in. 'He's having a what?'

'I think Ginger and Chris might be having an affair,' I confessed.

'What on earth makes you think that?'

'I'm not sure . . . Ginger keeps taking off. Chris keeps meeting mystery women and won't tell me who they are.'

'Jeez, is that all you've got?' Linda said. 'Because I have to tell you, it's a bit thin.'

'She's been at the villa at least twice since the painting class, you know. The first night I stayed with him, she turned up at ten o'clock at night,' I continued. 'And she clearly didn't expect to find me there.'

'No, she can't be. That lovely man just lost his mother too!' Linda shook her head gloomily.

'He did?' I asked, surprised.

'Yes. He adored her,' she explained. 'He was telling me at the Greek night before you arrived. His father died when he was a boy and he was an only child. His momma was all he had. Golly, he even cried when he was telling me about it.'

'That's just awful,' I agreed. Bloody hell, Ginger was a bigger cow than I'd given her credit for.

'Okay look, enough of this,' Linda said. 'It's the last day of my holiday and your honeymoon, what are we going to do?'

'Do you know what I'm supposed to be doing today?' I asked her.

'No?'

Wriggling free from our hug I unzipped my handbag and took out the envelope David had given me on our first day in Greece. 'This,' I said.

Linda took it from me and turned it over. 'Oh, it's sealed. What's in it?'

'My adventure for today. The programme of events for our last night together.'

'No! Aren't you going to open it then?' she asked.

'What's the point? It's all over.'

'It might be tickets? Deep sea diving,' she gushed. 'Or . . . oooh . . . sky diving.'

'I don't think so, David is afraid of heights. It was my idea to send us parascending.'

'Don't you want to see what it says?'

A part of me did wonder what it said. It would be easy just to throw it away but for some reason, I couldn't bring myself to.

'What the hell. If it's dinner for two at that posh restaurant in the hills we'll go together before the party tonight,' I told her, ripping open the envelope.

Chapter Twenty-Seven

To my darling wife,

For the few months leading up to our wedding I've taken it upon myself to abstain from sex, all in the hope that I can at last be the man you deserve. I want to have a full and proper sex life, with no outside help or influences. Just you and I. And I've never told you this but – I want to be a father. I love you more than life itself, Binnie. I want our child to be made out of that love. My ultimate holiday experience . . . is you.

David xxx

'What do you suppose he means about a full and proper sex life?'

I looked at Linda and sighed.

It was just a means to perk myself up, Binnie.

'He's telling me the porn use on our honeymoon was for me. For "us",' I said.

'Why?'

'Because when we had sex, he could rarely get to the finish line.'

She looked nonplussed.

'I mean, he never *came*. Unless he was watching porn during the event.'

'He watched porn during sex with you?' she asked. 'You mean, just him? Not you? Not sharing it?'

I nodded.

'Well now, are you thinking there's a chance this is just the greatest excuse for being caught out watching porn ever?'

I rubbed my forehead, trying to dull the ache that was beginning to take hold of my brain. It was a familiar pain; called, 'I've heard it all before.'

'Okay, maybe,' I agreed. 'But then, he wrote this before I caught him at the hotel.'

Linda looked thoughtful. 'What would he hope to achieve by watching it while you're on your honeymoon?'

Now this I knew.

'Getting in the mood,' I admitted, feeling embarrassed at what was still, undoubtedly something I was lacking. Something I had failed to give him. 'He was psyching himself up for one, big, last night.'

With the fat woman.

'But then he'd be all used up, surely?'

I remembered the tissues in the hotel room waste paper basket. I'd *thought* that was a little careless of him. Maybe he had had a bout of hay fever after all.

'He was watching porn without the happy ending part,' I said.

Linda's eyes widened. 'Christ,' she said. 'How do you know that?'

I laughed at the irony of her joke. 'I can never know for sure,' I continued after a moment. 'But that is what he means. Why else would he be so insistent I read this, like it held an answer for everything? It *has* to explain what he'd been doing.'

Linda exhaled loudly. 'So,' she said finally. 'What happens now?'

'I don't know,' I admitted. 'But, hell no! I'm not having any more babies!'

We both half-laughed, but inside me a mixture of emotions were stirring around. Shit! Trust him to complicate things just as I'd stopped questioning whether leaving him was the right thing to do. What he did hurt me, but it was what he needed. He was right. I'd promised to take him in sickness and health. This was his sickness. But then, it was his fault for doing it in the first place, wasn't it? *Arsehole! Gorgeous, oh God I do love him, git.*

'But you might reconsider the whole marriage annulment thing you were thinking of?'

'It doesn't matter now, it's over,' I told her.

'But Bernice,' she reasoned. 'He has a sickness; a sexual dysfunction. Doesn't that make it all a bit different?'

'Because we said in sickness and in health?' I said. 'Linda, I think the dysfunction was caused by his porn addiction. And you are forgetting one other detail.'

'Which is?'

'The way he had to ogle everything with a pair of breasts everywhere we went together. Really, Linda, I tried. We saw doctors, tried prescribed medication and did the whole counselling thing. In the end it was obvious this "dysfunction" was a product of his porn addiction. He did that to himself and he's proved time and again that he won't stop. There is only so much you can do for a person who isn't willing to help himself.'

As I said the words, my heart didn't believe them. He'd been trying to get better; maybe even using the porn on his phone to arouse himself for me. But then, he still needed to arouse *himself* for me! My phone buzzed, alerting me to a text message. I snatched it up to find a message from an unknown number.

```
Have lunch with me? I'm at Taverna Vasso's
at the harbour.
```

'Linda, I'm going to need to think about all of this,' I said. I felt sure the message was from David. Maybe he'd managed to get another number after I blocked his old one. Still, I did need to see him; that was for sure. 'Can we meet tonight at the village square for the shindig thingy? You're going to be alright aren't you?'

She nodded, 'I'm going to be just fine. I'd booked a massage this afternoon anyway. Hopefully, she'll be hot.'

I hugged her again and smiled.

'Off to meet someone?' she said. I stood up and checked my hair in the mirror over her mantelpiece. 'Yes,' I answered. 'I'll tell you how it all goes later.'

There was just time for me to hand in the keys to the moped to the centre before heading to the taverna for lunch with David. It had been a while but the young boy recognised me immediately.

'Thank you,' he said, snatching the keys and backing into the office. 'Have a nice day.'

'Aren't you going to check it or something?' I asked, passing him the helmet.

'No, no. It's fine Mrs Dando, thank-you-very-much-bye.'

'Ok, erm, do you know which taverna Vassos is?'

I asked, turning to point down the seafront beside the harbour. He closed the door with a bang.

'Right-o,' I said. 'Helpful, thanks.'

There were five or six tavernas along the harbour side, but luckily I spied Argos sitting at a table in the first one.

'Hello, beautiful Binnie,' he smiled, showing a string of pearly whites. God he was beautiful. But so, so young.

'Hi Argos,' I said. 'Do you know where Taverna Vassos is?'

He looked perplexed, and then started to smile.

'You are always a funny lady.' Snapping his fingers to the barman, he shouted out, 'Vassos! Ouzo!'

'This is Taverna Vassos?' I said, feeling panic rise in my throat. *David was going to find me having a drink with Argos!*

'Yes, of course!' he answered.

'Well, er, actually,' I stammered, scanning nearby tables for David and not finding him. *Phew!* 'I'm supposed to be meeting someone here,' I started to explain, but Vassos was already bringing the drinks and a basket of bread to the table.

'*Tsipouro* for two,' he said cheerily.

'You are here to meet me,' Argos said.

My heart sank. 'Oh, it was you that texted me?'

'Of course!' he said, positively beaming from ear to ear.

'Sorry, I had no idea. How on earth did you get my number?'

'You gave it to me for the parascending. In case the weather changed and you couldn't go, remember?'

'Ah, yes, I do. Very sorry about all that. Hope the chute I left on that tree was okay and . . . well, I didn't get chance to say sorry about that night at the beach. I hope your . . . er . . . thingy is okay?'

'My thingy?' He looked perplexed.

'Yes, your, erm' I pointed downstairs. The light came on.

'Ah, yes, yes,' he said, grimacing. 'Everything is working good.'

'Good.'

'Please, Binnie,' Argos continued. 'What would you like to eat?'

'What?'

'For the lunch?' he explained.

'Argos, I . . .' I started, but he was already preparing to make a speech of his own.

'Binnie,' he said. 'I know you are going to England tomorrow and that makes me very sad. You are very pretty and a very special lady for me.'

'Thank you,' I answered, taking a huge gulp from my drink. 'That's very kind but . . .'

'And so today I want to be together with you.'

'Together with me?'

'Yes, together.' He leaned forward and placed a hand on my knee, which made me jump, spilling *Tsipouro* down my top.

'I want to give you what you asked me for on the very first day I saw you,' he said, reaching for a napkin to rub at my blouse. 'Because I like you,' he finished.

'And I like you, Argos,' I said, taking the napkin off him. 'You are a very, very handsome young man and I'm extremely flattered.' Oh, dear God, I was sounding like his mother again.

'You are flattened?' He looked confused.

'Flattered. Happy that you like me,' I explained. 'And I do fancy you. Who wouldn't? You're gorgeous! But I'm not what you need and you are not what *I* need.' His poor, confused face made me ache to laugh, which was terrible. But the truth was, I fancied him but I wasn't attracted to all of him. Just his body. Just the young, carefree, raw monkey-sex he might be able to give me. *Wait . . . am I talking myself into this or out of it?*

'Now Argos,' I said firmly, pulling myself together. 'Can you just remind me? What was it again that I asked you for the first time we met?'

He grinned and pointed to his crotch. *'Psoli.'*

I downed the rest of the *Tsipouro* and stood up. There it was − that male, twenty-year-old cockiness. That's why I wasn't attracted to him. For all his flirting, compliments and apparent good manners, underneath he was just looking for what all young guys hope to get from visiting lady tourists. A leg over.

'I have to go now,' I told him. 'But thank you, Argos, for everything. You have made my holiday, you really have. I'm like a new woman.'

He leaned forward, grabbing my arm. 'I'm like a new woman too!' he said.

'You mean, *you'd* like a new woman. And I'm sure you will have one, Argos, very soon. But it's not going to be me.'

'But, I thought we could do the sex today?' he said.

'Do the sex today? Is that why you were going to buy me lunch?'

He looked shocked. 'Oh no, no, no!' he exclaimed. 'I am in love with you, my beautiful English Binnie. I want to give you the *psoli.*'

Something told me Argos had yet to find out what real love was.

'Thank you, Argos − and my name is Bernice, actually,' I said with a wry smile. 'You don't know what it means to a woman like me to have a young, attractive man like you throw himself at her. However, on reflection,' I took a piece of bread from the basket and bit into it. 'Hmm,' I said. 'The *psoli* here is certainly very good. But I'd really rather go dip my toes in the Aegean, if you don't mind.'

And with that I left him, speechless, at a table next to the sea. My young, randy, could-have-been-fun guy . . . who had told me I was beautiful.

It was a long walk back up to Villa Miranda now that I didn't have my little moped, but I suspected the island's motorists were all breathing a huge sigh of relief there wouldn't be a mad woman hurtling towards them on the wrong side of the road each day. When my tired legs had finally carried me up the hill, the first thing I saw was Ginger's hire car in the driveway. Shielding my eyes from the sun, I strained to see if they were visible out on the balcony. They weren't. Everything was still, and everyone was quite clearly, and on a roasting hot day too, indoors.

'It could be perfectly innocent,' I told myself, untying the bike lock on the gate and tiptoeing up the gravel path.

Nothing stirred. There was no-one in the garden either; but as I got closer to the house, I heard Ginger cry out from what must have been the balcony. She sounded like she was in ecstasy.

'Oh, Chrrrrisssss! That is so good!'

I covered my ears and hurried into the apartment so as not to be heard, feeling angry. So my suspicions had been right – even Chris was a rat. All men were rats! I wasn't sure why I cared, but I fell on the bed and cried.

Are you going to be at the square tonight?
Hope to see you there. Chris

The text woke me from a deep sleep and, checking the time, I jumped up to get dressed. It was almost six-thirty and dinner was in half an hour. *Shit!*

Throwing on a beautiful, turquoise-blue maxi dress that I'd been saving for a special occasion, I combed my hair, swiped on some mascara, grabbed my bag and raced out of the door. Shit! I didn't even have my moped to get me to the village square tonight. Ginger's car had gone too. Shame. I'd really wanted to shout up, 'Hey Ginger, have you finished shagging Chris now because I could really use a lift to the village square?'

Chris was coming down the stairs carrying what looked like a huge, covered canvas.

'Hey there,' he said, looking ever so slightly sheepish. 'Do you want a lift?'

'No, it's okay' I said, curtly.

'But I thought you invited me to the street party?' he said, looking confused.

He jumped off the last few steps, grabbed my arm and swept me towards his car. 'It's your last night, Bernice. Let's make it a good one. Plus,' he added, more seriously, 'I really need to finish our chat from the other day. I think, seeing as you are going home tomorrow, now is the time.'

What was the point in arguing? What was the point in asking none of my business questions like, 'What the hell were you doing with that married woman this afternoon?' None of it had anything to do with me.

'Okay,' I said. 'But let's do it here and now, before we leave.'

He breathed out. 'Right then,' he said. 'Come on, we'll take a seat under the pergola. And for heaven's sake, please will you let me do the talking this time?'

With the canvas stored in the car, Chris brought us two

iced teas and sat across from me at the huge table he used for his art classes.

'How did you get on with David the other day?' he asked.

'You knew I was going to meet him?' I said.

'Yes I did,' he replied. 'We spoke on the phone and then again yesterday, I went to meet him for a drink. He's a mess, Bernice.'

I felt a lump in my throat and willed myself not to cry. 'I know,' I said, taking a sip of the iced tea he'd given me before remembering I hated it. Note to self, stop drinking stuff you don't like because someone made it specially for you.

'But he says it's over, finished. He said you told him there was no chance of any reconciliation. Is that right?'

'Yes,' I lied. The truth was, I wasn't sure after reading the contents of his envelope. But I wasn't ready to tell anyone until I'd spoken to David.

'Well then, here is the thing,' he continued. 'I'd be a complete and utter liar if I said I was sorry about that . . . altogether.'

I was stunned. 'What do you mean?'

'Oh, Christ, Bernice, I'm just going to come out and say it. I did stop talking to you because of David, but not because he told me to. It was because I love you.' As he finished his speech, he looked away from my face and down at the ground.

I'd been waiting for the 'You should take David back' speech. This knocked me sideways.

'You . . . *love me*?' I stammered.

'Yes. I've loved you for as long as David has; maybe even longer.'

My face turned crimson. I could hardly believe my ears.

He swallowed hard, his own face getting redder by the minute. 'I'd fallen for you in a big way,' he went on, 'and David was my best friend! It was all so bloody hard.'

'Did he know? Did you tell him?' I asked.

'No. How could I tell him that? He'd think I was a right arsehole saying that to him – and he'd be right,' he replied.

'This is . . .' I started, 'a bit of a . . . shock. I don't know what to say.'

'You're the reason I came to Greece,' he went on. 'I had to get on with my life, away from you. Every time I saw you and David together, it killed me.'

'Really? But you hardly spoke to me towards the end,' I said.

'Bernice, I'm not talking about some schoolboy crush here, that would've been easy to cope with,' he explained. 'When I told you I'd had my heart broken in the past, it was true. It was you who broke it, without ever even knowing it.'

'But why on earth are you telling me now?' I asked. *After having just shagged Ginger,* I thought.

'Because now that you and David are over . . .'

'What, you thought you and I could just waltz away into the sunset?' I said, my initial shock starting to turn to rage.

'No, no. Jesus, no! David is my best friend,' he said. 'I'm telling you now because I know we're never going to see each other again after you go home. I just had to tell you. Not to give myself any hope of us being an item, I would never do that to David. He adores you. I just need you to know that I don't hate you. That in fact, I love you.'

I could hardly get my breath. It was all too much to take in. 'Chris,' I said, finally. 'I really like you; I always have. I wanted us to be friends and felt bereft when you drew your friendship back. That hurt.'

'I know,' he replied. 'And I could have gone on for the rest of my days never telling you all of this if I was safe in the knowledge that I would still see you sometimes. Ludicrous, I know. Why am I offloading this on you now? I don't know. I just had to tell you. Call it my parting shot if you like. The truth is it killed me to have you go away thinking that I hate you. I'm never going to see you again, because the only thing that connected us was David and I can't be your friend, because . . .' He stopped and put his head in his hands.

'You love me,' I finished for him.

To my surprise he began to sob. This was the real thing. I could hardly get my head around it.

'I'm so glad to have got that off my chest,' he cried. 'Because sometimes the truth can be bloody heavy. I've never met a more beautiful woman in my life that quite clearly has no idea she's beautiful. You're an amazing and lovely person, Bernice. Whatever David did, he's a bloody fool! But, God help me, there isn't a day that goes by when I don't wish that I had met you first.'

Yes, the truth is heavy, I thought. *Like having an affair with someone's wife.* I wanted to pity him; to thank him and put my arm around him and say everything would be alright. But, I had just heard him having sex with Edvard's wife. Suddenly, I hated the dishonesty that seemed to live in all men. *Why was he really telling me this now?*

'You got one thing wrong there, Chris,' I said icily, standing to go. 'But you can be forgiven because it was once true. Not anymore.'

'What's that?' he asked, looking up at me with red eyes and a hopeless expression.

'I know I'm beautiful,' I said. 'Now let's go to that party.'

*

We pulled up to the village square having not spoken for the entire journey. Chris looked mortified that he had opened his heart to me and I had simply swept him and his feelings aside. But I was so angry. He was a cad and worse than that, he had professed his love for his best friend's wife just as she prepared to split up with him. Once upon a time, I might have thanked him, given him a hug and told him that had I met him first I would certainly have dated him. There was no denying he was a bright, funny, good-looking guy and from the off we had got on famously. He appeared to be quite a catch and my love for and commitment to David hadn't prevented me from seeing that. Everyone who was wonderful deserved to be told so, I knew that much. Yet, all of a sudden, I realised I didn't know him at all.

The usually quiet cobbled streets were heaving with people. I'd never seen it so busy. Out in the open square a band was playing and the singer had a voice I recognised; (although I almost didn't recognise him with his clothes on) Adonis – belting out Madonna's *Holiday*. He waved to me as I ambled past, trying to hide myself amongst what seemed like a hundred dancing people. It was a last night fiesta.

Hughie and Greta were already up dancing the evening away, although Hughie did pause to eye up my cleavage as I passed and gave me his signature, dirty old man wink.

Chris led me to a table where Linda was sitting beside Michaela, Edvard and Ginger, who were all singing and clapping along to the music. I was none too pleased to see Ginger, although she embraced me excitedly as I approached her to say hello.

'Binnie, how lovely to see you, and also how sad it's our last night!' she gushed. Like the cat that got the cream.

She hugged Chris too – right there in front of Edvard, as though they hadn't been at it like rabbits all afternoon behind his back. She waved to Hughie and Greta to join us, flashing glasses of champagne for them and handing me one. 'And now we are all together,' she said. 'Edvard my darling, there is something Chris and I must tell you.'

Jesus, surely they weren't going to come out now, in front of us all?

Chris pushed the covered canvas he'd been carrying into her hands and she smiled at him. What a rotten cow!

Edvard looked puzzled. 'What have you done?' he asked.

I almost couldn't watch. *So, you love me do you, Chris?* I threw him an angry look and he peered back, seemingly perplexed.

'I had started this by myself,' she began, taking the cover off the huge canvas, 'because I wanted to do this for you. But time began to run out, as did my excuses for sneaking away,' she laughed, looking conspiringly at Chris. She unwrapped the canvas – and revealed a portrait of a rather regal-looking older woman. A lady that had Edvard's eyes. 'So,' she went on, 'Chris had to finish it off for me this afternoon. This is for you, my darling.'

'Oh, Chrrrrisssss! That is so good!' She had been looking at the painting!

Edvard stood up with tears in his eyes and pulled her to him. 'I can't believe it,' he cried, almost sobbing with joy. 'It's beautiful!'

Linda and I looked at each other guiltily as Edvard shook Chris's hand.

'This is wonderful, Chris,' he said. 'You've both captured my mother perfectly. I'm just . . . so . . . overcome. I don't know what to say. Thank you. Thank you!' he sobbed.

'You're welcome, my friend,' Chris said, patting his shoulder.

'It's incredible,' Edvard continued. 'And my wife painted it!'

'With Chris's help,' Ginger added.

'Och, it's braw,' Greta agreed.

'All I did was a few finishing touches,' Chris smiled. 'Ginger did a wonderful job. Although, of course, that had everything to do with your bloody marvellous teacher.'

'What a beautiful thing to do, Ginger,' said Michaela. 'Now I can almost forgive you for cancelling our riding session the other day.'

'You only missed getting your tits out,' Linda laughed.

'So that's whit ye were up to, Mrs McAteer!' said Hughie, poking his wife's ribs. 'Now,' he whispered to me, with a wink, 'where's the photies?'

As we laughed at Hughie, a waiter appeared at our table with four more bottles of champagne.

'These are compliments of my friend, Adonis,' he said, turning to point to the singer who was now gearing up for another song, looking straight at me.

Oh, holy hell, please God, not again.

But it wasn't me he was going to call up to sing.

'I have a request!' he announced, pointing directly at me. 'It is for a lady with a beeyoooutiful voice.'

Linda looked at me, stunned. 'How does he know about your singing?' she asked.

'I kind of sang the other day, on the beach with him,' I said.

'Him?' she replied, looking surprised. There was some commotion from behind Adonis as he waved somebody to the stage.

'The nudeoke guy?' Michaela said.

'The very same.'

'Go Bernice!' Greta shouted.

As I smiled broadly, my eyes met Chris's. He was grinning back at me but I thought I saw sadness behind his eyes. All of a sudden, I felt terrible.

'Bernice,' he called out to me. 'Look at the stage!'

I turned to look again at Adonis, who had stooped to offer his microphone to someone a fair bit shorter than he was. Before I could see who it was, a voice boomed out across the square. There was no accompanying music, but I recognised the song and the singer. It was David, reading the lyrics from a piece of paper.

> *I wrote these bars,*
> *For this song to be ours,*
> *Forever, always and a day,*
> *Even when your skies turn grey,*
> *Like the stars, you will shine,*
> *Always remember, you were mine,*
> *And live forever, Baby, Baby, Blue,*
>
> *Because eternity began from you,*
> *Baby, Baby, Blue,*
> *Forever, always and a day,*
> *In my soul, come what may,*
> *Your pretty smile filled my soul,*
> *Take my love, take it all,*
> *And live forever, Baby, Baby, Blue.*

It was cringe-making; and wonderful. As silence fell over the entire place, there were tears in my eyes and not all from rubbing them with disbelief at his terrible singing of my favourite movie classic. It was seeing before me the man I loved, only different, partaking in a moment of complete and utter cheese that the old David would have balked at.

Adonis and the band were all staring at each other wordlessly. I had no doubt they hadn't heard the song before and nor were they ever likely to hear it again on a party night! Perhaps only the fact that he spoke to me next saved David from being thrown from the stage and branded a drunk and a weirdo.

'Binnie,' he said into the microphone, looking right at me. '*Bernice*. I love you. Please be my wife.'

All of a sudden, seeing everyone gawping at him made me come over all protective. He was a weirdo. But he was my weirdo. I needn't have worried though. Thinking there had been a regular, first time proposal, the silence from the crowd was at last broken, as the whole square erupted into applause. They weren't to know we were married already.

'Aha!' Adonis cried, clasping his hands to his mouth before taking another microphone from the stand. 'Where is your lovely lady? Come here Bernice!'

I held my breath for a moment, my head telling me to save him but my feet staying planted on the spot. What should I do now? As everyone watched me, clapping in time; waiting to witness that magnificent, romantic movie moment when I screamed 'yes' and crowd surfed up to the stage, lifted by many hands to be at the side of my true love, I balked. Ugh.

Sod that.

But this was *David*. The actual love of my life, yes. But being with him meant having to be stronger; perhaps work harder at rebuilding my sense of worth – I knew that now. Should I give my marriage one more chance? If I rebuffed him in front of all these people, he would just be left looking stupid. I was in danger; danger of jumping to save another person when I should be protecting myself. Again.

Everywhere I looked people were smiling at me, waiting expectantly. I started to walk away and I wanted to walk towards him. My heart hurt. God, I'd missed him . . .

'Wait!' I shouted and turned my head to find Chris before pointing him out to all and sundry. 'Er,' I continued. 'I need to ask his friend something!'

There was a peal of laughter but the crowd carried on clapping and there was some whistling and cheering, everyone thinking this was all good, spirited fun and I would still say yes. Chris ran over to me, grinning like a Cheshire cat. At once, I knew David's being here had been arranged with his help. I felt disappointed. I thought he of all people understood. Chris expected me to fall back into David's arms now too.

'Aren't you going to go to him?' he asked. 'You can't leave the poor guy waiting.'

'Have you been sleeping with Ginger?' I shouted into his ear.

He stopped smiling and stared back at me, clearly astonished. 'No, of course not!'

'I heard you this afternoon. Ginger shouted out your name! I thought . . . I thought . . .' Tears rolled down my cheeks. I was so choked up with emotion and confusion, I could hardly breathe.

'You thought we were having sex?' he said, looking more perplexed than ever. 'Hah, that's almost funny.'

I turned back to see Adonis still frantically beckoning me forward and David smiling but looking decidedly agitated as he waited for me to make a decision.

'But why do you want to ask me at a time like this?' Chris went on.

I turned back to him. 'There's something I want to say.'

'What?'

The clapping was beginning to subside as the crowd seemed to consider the possibility of there being an unhappy outcome to the big proposal after all.

'Just thank you. Thank you for telling me you love me. That couldn't have been easy for you but I'm glad you did it. I'm a different, stronger woman now and it's all because I was here with you and,' I turned to point at my friends. '. . . and them. This has been an amazing ten days – life changing in fact. All of you, in very different ways, have taught me to really believe I'm someone to love.'

As I turned to make my way to the stage at last, he held my arm back. As I met his gaze once more, I saw sadness behind his smile. 'Why Bernice?' he begged. 'Why did you want to know about Ginger right now? I need to know.'

I opened my mouth to speak but before I could reply, Adonis called me again.

'Come on lovely lady. Come up to the stage!'

Taking in the faces around me once more, I saw Ginger and Edvard in a close embrace, the gift of a painting bonding them in shared memories of a lost mother. I saw Hughie and Greta, side by side, facing every day together with what looked for all the world like unending good humour, with years of marriage behind them and a battle against the ravages of the demon cancer before them; one fought with tenacity, bravery and togetherness. At last, I spied Linda – by herself again after a brief moment of joy amongst forty-two lonely years. It was a contest, this bloody little thing called love.

'I'm coming, I'm coming!' I called out. 'Just give me one more second!'

Hugging Chris to me, I whispered my answer in to his ear before feeling a tap on my shoulder. I turned around to see Michaela and Greta.

'I know you are nervous,' Michaela said. 'I know you've been afraid to be yourself. But if you are going to go back, it's time for change. Live your life your way. Remember what I told you about meraki? If nothing else, your own life should always be lived with one great, big helping of that.'

'She's deid right aboot that,' Greta added, coming forward to plant a huge kiss on my cheek.

I smiled at them both. 'Well, I'm not sure I've been as good at that as you two are,' I said. 'But I'm going to try from now on.'

Over a hundred faces watched me as I headed towards David, taking one last look back through the crowd again to find Linda, Hughie, Greta and Michaela all standing together and smiling at me. I read the words on Linda's lips:

'Are you sure?' she said.

I nodded, before leaping up to the stage and falling into David's open arms. I loved him and he was my husband, but I was a different woman to the one he had been forced to leave behind almost a fortnight ago. Somehow, we would make this work, but on my terms. I at least owed it to him to try.

'I love you, Mrs Dando,' he cried, hugging me tightly to him.

'And I love you, Mr Dando,' I replied, sinking into his embrace.

'She said yes!' Adonis shouted, somewhat prematurely.

And the crowd went crazy again.

'What took you so long?' David asked, looking puzzled.

'I just wanted to thank Chris for making this all happen,' I lied. 'He told you to come here, didn't he?'

Before he could reply, Adonis parted us by thrusting a microphone at me. 'A song! A song!'

'Yes, please, Bernice,' David said, stepping back to let me take the stage. 'I want to hear that beautiful voice every day, starting from now. The one you've been hiding from me all this time.' And then, quietly into my ear he said, 'I get it now, Bernice. I understand what you were trying to say the other night. I felt sick and, yes, cheated, seeing you surrounded by all those young guys. I know what you were trying to say and life is going to get better from now on, I promise.'

'David,' I said, giving him a look that I'd borrowed back from a younger, sassier, and flirtier me. 'I know it will, because I'm going to make it better. With or without you.'

He gazed at me, uncertainly, as though I was someone he didn't recognise. I smiled, kissed him on the cheek and took the microphone, remembering a ten-year-old girl who had stood on a stage in her local town hall to represent her school in a regional singing competition. A girl with the voice of an angel, but the confidence of a fawn just taking its first, tentative, wobbling steps. As the hall fell silent for the sweet tinkling of a piano, she had opened her mouth to sing. . .

'Why did you drag me all this way, paying a pound for the ticket too, to see you standing there with your mouth open and nothing coming out?'

My mother was laughing, not in a cruel, teasing way,

I thought, but in a trying to make light of a bad situation way. She couldn't hug me and tell me it was alright. I knew now it was because her own mother had never hugged her to tell her everything was alright.

'I'm sorry, I was really scared, Mum,' I said, wiping snot and tears from my face with my coat sleeve.

'You don't have to be sorry. We can't all be great singers like I was, can we George?'

Dad stayed silent. Yet, as he'd turned the key sternly in the car door to let me in to the back seat, his disappointment had seemed to me to be deafening.

Almost thirty-three years later, the same girl – now a married woman – had sung *Islands in the Stream* naked on a beach. Instead of feeling embarrassed and ashamed of her body, as she'd looked out at a crowd of nudists of every shape, size and age, and she had felt somehow, freer. Normal, yet extraordinary, like every person on the planet.

In amongst the sea of faces looking at me, I spied Chris, his face full of angst and I felt it too. It didn't feel like a good night for singing. I still wasn't sure if this was the right thing to do. David and I had a lot to discuss. Nevertheless, it was the night I was going to show the world I'd found my voice again.

'What shall you sing, lovely girl?' Adonis whispered into my ear.

'I am *not* a girl!' I said sharply.

On the last night of my holiday, in front of a live audience, I found my voice again, belting out what David would call another of those 'cheesy tunes', a Britney Spears song. It was about someone who was not a girl, and not yet a woman, even though I hadn't meant to request it and I was far too old to mean it. Or maybe . . . just maybe . . . I had only just grown. Maybe it was a good night for singing after all.

Chapter Twenty-Eight

They broke the mould when they made my
husband. Even back then, he wouldn't take a
bath.

The flight was supposed to leave Skiathos airport at
ten past one in the afternoon and Chris had promised
us a lift at eleven. But he was nowhere to be seen as I
sat on the patio, taking in a last, long look at the garden
and its incredible, distant blue view of Greece's glittering
Aegean Sea, where Greta had dipped her toes on the first
day just to enjoy its silky warmness and thank God she
was alive to feel it.

I was going home, but I wasn't sure how I was going to
live from this day on. I had no job and only the prospect
of the happy ending I was promised on the day David and
I said our vows, a fortnight ago, to hope for. Last night we
had all danced together under the stars and, as Chris made
his excuses and left early, David and I had ended our night
sitting on the beach under the stars talking everything
through. At the end of the night, after saying my tearful

goodbyes and exchanging contact details with all my new friends, I had gone back to my apartment alone to mull things over and David had staggered to his rented room in the town. I still wasn't sure what I wanted. But today we would fly home together to see if we could work it out.

As I'd hugged Greta one last time she had touched my chin affectionately. 'Remember what they say, Bernice, live to regret the things you do, not the things you don't do.'

Logging into Facebook to post a final status to England, I heard a car pull up to the gate. It was time to go. I could do it later.

I put the phone back in my pocket and stood up to take one last look inside Chris's apartment.

'Goodbye, beautiful little apartment,' I sighed, before catching my reflection in the mirror. 'Ah, there you are,' I said to my reflection. 'Beautiful Bernice.'

'Yes, there you are, Mrs Dando.'

I turned to see David standing in the doorway and my heart leapt. For after everything, he was still the love of my life. And still achingly gorgeous.

'Have you come to take me home?' I asked.

'You know it,' he said, sighing in contentment. 'Unless you want to stay of course?' he laughed, just as Chris walked in the door. 'You do owe me a honeymoon after all.'

'The apartment's free if you want it, mate,' Chris said. 'I haven't even begun to advertise it.' He passed the key I'd left on the drawer for him to David. 'Oh, and Hughie says thanks for the good times Bernice, but he has to go back to the wife now.'

David gave me a puzzled glance as Chris and I smiled knowingly at each other.

'It's a long story,' I said.

I was unable to shake a deep sense of remorse for Chris. I still hadn't had chance to apologise properly for my behaviour the previous evening when he had poured his heart out to me, and I needed to. Now that his feelings were out in the open, I knew this day couldn't be easy for him. But at least I knew, having told him my suspicions about Ginger, that he would understand why I'd been so horrible to him.

There was a tap at the door and Mita came in, carrying clean sheets for the room. As usual, her cleavage spilled over her top as she bent over in front of us to change the sheets. I thought I saw David's eyes steal a fleeting glance at her breasts but scolded myself for looking for it. Chris was watching me, with what I knew now was likely to be a partly forced smile. But today was a new day.

'It would be awesome to stay on,' I admitted. 'But the girls are expecting me back and there's the question of my finding a new job.'

'Well, there's no hurry for that,' David replied. 'I can keep us. There's more than enough for the two of us to live on, maybe even three?' He winked at me and I blushed. I would have to break the 'no baby' thing to him when we got home.

At quarter to two that afternoon, thirty-five minutes behind schedule, our plane home left the tarmac on its way to East Midlands Airport. It was a gloriously sunny, hot day and the let's-stand-together-and-drink-it-in-together-darling sea was especially glittery that afternoon. In spite of the new, yet uncertain life ahead of me, I felt sad to leave it all behind.

Chapter Twenty-Nine

I've just finished reading a book about narcissism. Absolutely nothing in it about me. What a waste of time that was!

'Viewing porn in a mutual way is different to using it alone.' The counsellor looked at me over brown-rimmed spectacles, tapping her temple with a pencil. 'It can be used as a bridge to bring a couple together, whereas lone use can build a wall that cuts one partner off, drawing sexual energy away from the marriage and widening the distance between you.'

'It's not that I think there's anything wrong with it,' I replied. 'It's just not my thing. And I do object to him doing it alone.'

'Do you have a particular thing you like, David?' she asked him.

'Well, er . . .' he began, tugging at the collar of his shirt and looking uncomfortable. 'I don't like hardcore porn and don't really get any kicks from watching men and women together.'

'So you only like to watch women?'

'That's about the size of it, yes.'

'So, just lesbian porn then?'

'Well, sometimes it can be just one woman. The thing is, watching straight sex doesn't really float my boat. That's not going to help.'

'You see?' I interrupted. 'He's conditioned himself to only like one sort of thing, what would be the point of me watching something I just don't get?'

'Well, maybe you could try acting out some of the fantasy things David likes watching together then?' the therapist said.

'Roll around in the mud you mean?' I replied, remembering a time when I had done exactly that.

'No, no,' David cut in quickly. 'I wouldn't want you to do that.'

'I know,' I said. 'Because it wouldn't be the same if it was your wife instead of some porn star.'

'No, that's not it . . .' David began.

'Listen, this anger, although understandable, Bernice, is getting you nowhere. You have to stop looking to the past. The only way to move forward is with forgiveness and trust.'

'Well,' I replied. 'If I'm honest, I'm not sure if I can.'

The therapist took off her glasses and rubbed her eyes. 'I see,' she said.

And without her glasses on, too. At least someone was cured today.

Something told me it was time to re-evaluate my life. A little while after the therapy session, I went to see Smother – the logical place to start.

'Mum, I need to talk to you. Can I come in?'

'Oh, I'm so glad you're here. I want you to come look at something for me.'

Smother stood back to let me into her house, before limping along ahead of me to the lounge.

'What on earth is the matter with you?' I asked, not really wanting to hear the twenty minute, all about her ailments answer.

'And the doctor says I have to put antiseptic ointment on them twice a day. But I have this frozen shoulder now, so I can't reach down there.'

I zoned back in at 'can't reach down there,' and shuddered. *Dear God, no.*

'You don't want me to . . . ?' I began, pointing to her nether regions.

'It's only for a couple of weeks,' she replied, looking unfazed. 'The pain is unbearable. I have to wear panty liners for all the leakage.'

'Boils?' I said, suppressing a sudden urge to run from the room and stick my head in the toilet. 'How on earth do you get so many of them down there?'

'It's my rich blood.'

'If this is what it is to be rich, I think I'll stick to abject poverty,' I said. 'But seriously, Mother, you need to get a nurse in. I'll do most things, but not that. Not on your life.'

'Charming,' she answered, beginning to get the familiar bitter look she always wore when I refused her anything. 'So, I have to have strangers messing about with me instead of my own daughter?'

'Yes, you do,' I said. 'Now, Mum, I need to tell you something. David and I have been having some problems.'

'Already?' she said, looking astonished. 'You've only been married a month.'

'I know. But things are a little, shall we say, difficult? And the truth is, they always have been, so I . . .'

'It'll be fine,' she cut in, pointing me towards a chair. 'Sit down. Hey, talking of weddings, have you heard I got invited to Jeremy Mathers' daughter's wedding?'

'Who on earth is Jeremy Mathers?' I asked.

'You know, the guy I speak to on the internet.'

'What guy? Oh, Mum!'

I was getting sucked into talking about her again. I took a deep breath and continued with the plan.

'Mum, I'm not sure if David and I are right for each other after all. There are some problems that I don't know if we can repair, but I want to try.'

'Oh, don't be silly,' she said, waving me away with her hand. 'Marriage takes hard work and commitment. You'll get there. Jeremy was just telling me the other night about his first wife . . .'

'Mum!' I cut in. 'Sod Jeremy bloody Mathers! Will you listen to me?'

'Well, that's nice isn't it?' she replied haughtily. 'Forget your old mum's life, let's talk about you.'

'Yes,' I said quickly. 'For once, let's.'

'Pah!' she laughed. *'For once!'*

'Mum, I need to ask you something,' I continued on determinedly. 'Was Dad ever proud of me?'

'Of course he was!' she snapped. 'He was proud of you and he told you enough times.'

'No, he didn't.'

'What?' she said, getting angrier by the minute. 'Of course he did. He told you all the time!'

'That's not how I remember it,' I replied sadly. 'The last time we spoke alone before he died, he was going on about Sal.'

'Sal wasn't born then.'

'I know that. I mean, he was throwing her scan picture back at me like he was ashamed or something.'

'He could hardly talk,' she said. 'How do you know that? Your dad was thrilled to be having a grandchild, actually.'

'He was?'

'Of course! Oh, dear, you have got your memories a little muddled.' She walked over to the wall cabinet and opened a drawer. 'I still have that picture in here somewhere,' she said, poking around inside.

'That's nice,' I said, still reeling from the idea my dad had been pleased I was pregnant. *Could it be true?*

'Here it is!' She pulled out the faded and tatty paper folder with the picture in it and waved it at me.

'So you kept it?' I said. 'That's funny, because the last thing Dad tried to do was give it back to me.'

As Smother waved the picture at me, a piece of paper fell out of it onto the floor. 'Ooh, what's that?' she said, stooping to pick it up.

'See,' I said dryly. 'He'd been trying to rip it up with his one good hand.'

'No,' she said, 'I had this out many times to look at it myself. I only took it out of the proper frame a while back, after it got broken in the house move.' She pulled the piece of paper closer to her face and squinted. 'This looks like your dad's handwriting.'

'Really?' I stood up and peered over her shoulder. It was indeed Dad's writing. Or at least, a scrawly, post-stroke version of it. 'It says "To Bernice."'

She handed me the letter and sat back down again. 'Probably some daft poem,' she said. 'He wrote a lot of silly things towards the end. It was like he knew he hadn't got long. Did I tell you Jeremy lost his wife to cancer? Poor man. Now *she* was a piece of work by all accounts.'

As Mum's continual chattering about 'Jeremy' faded away to a faraway place in my head, I opened the piece of paper properly and read the spidery writing in Dad's note.

To Bernice,

Now you're going to be a mum, share as much laughter, experience of life and joy in those moments with your child for as long as you can. We didn't do enough of that, you and me. Go on holidays, see as much of the world as you can cram in, go to the beach, share an ice cream on a sea wall after the spray gets all over it, row a boat out as far as the eye can see from shore (even if you might get soaked) and have picnics on a sunny hillside, somewhere remote. Laugh till your eyes run and you get hiccups. Be so silly sometimes that people stare at you in restaurants and shake their heads. Without the occasional nod of disapproval, your life is barren. Take trips – enjoy and savour each and every one. And when your children are old enough to stand on their own two feet and can do it without always having to look back for you, you will know you did the best job you could.

And wherever you go and whatever you do, let NONE of the experiences you share with your child be 'guilt trips.' I can give you plenty of postcards from there; it's not a fun place. But do go to the often quiet one called LOVE. Believe it or not, you can go there by yourself too. Because even when you believe it may have left you, real, unconditional love whispers in your mind rather than shouting in your ear while you're achieving your goals, at play and especially when things are going badly and you need to lean on it for a time. It watches you grow and is the voice in your head when you are gathering your thoughts. It stays quietly in the background, there to pick up whenever you need it. It envelops you, yet it helps you grow independently of it, confident, steady and knowing it's okay to step into scary, new places to be true to yourself.

Thank you, to you and Michael for making me proud, excited and desperate for February to get here! I can't wait to be a granddad XXX

'. . . and his daughter thinks I'm only after his money, but I told her . . .' My mum's voice jabbered on and on, as she chattered, oblivious to the tears that now spilled down my cheeks.

I wiped my eyes and hugged the twenty-two-year-old piece of paper to my chest, and my heart ached for my dad. He hadn't been trying to give me the picture back, he'd known he hadn't long to go and was trying to show me what he'd written. Knowing how proud he was and how hard he found it to speak from his heart, he'd most likely not had the courage to show me before he knew it was the end. Maybe he had never intended to show it to me. But one thing I knew for sure now, Dad had lived in Mum's shadow even more than I had.

'Oh, and you'll never guess what else? I think I might have to have an eye operation,' Mum went on, not stopping for a second to ask me what was in Dad's letter.

'Actually, Mum,' I said quickly. 'I've got an appointment in ten minutes, so I'm just going to shoot off. Do you mind if I keep this?'

'Oh, really? Okay,' she said, looking annoyed that I wasn't staying longer to listen to her stories about Jeremy. 'But didn't you want to tell me about you and David? Are there problems?'

I thought I detected a hint of a smile and right then I knew it was time to go.

'Oh, it's nothing really,' I told her. 'You're right, I was just being silly.'

'I thought so,' she said. 'But don't forget. I never see you that much anymore and I do need help with these medications, you know. Was it one of his daft poems then?'

'Yes,' I replied, stuffing the note into my pocket and heading for the door. Talking to Mum about anything was just useless, I knew that now. All I could do was mourn the mother I was never going to have and let life roll on. I had to take her as she was, and that was that. I kissed her on the cheek, not having ever known if she really loved me. Feeling like perhaps my mother could never really love anyone, except herself.

'I love you, Mum.' I told her – and left.

Chapter Thirty

Priscilla Hart says she keeps slim on the cucumber diet. I have a lot of that too and haven't lost a pound. I'm clearly inserting it wrong.

'Sal, why, oh, why are you weighing yourself?'

Beth and I were at the breakfast bar watching Sal step on and off the kitchen scales, removing articles of clothing each time to see if it made a difference.

'Oh, I don't know,' she replied, looking annoyed that the removal of her favourite scarf still hadn't shifted another pound on the scale. 'I just want to feel attractive.'

'But you are attractive,' I told her, stroking her back. 'It doesn't matter what the scales say, it's just a number.'

'I'm overweight, Mum,' she complained. 'And I want to look my best for all the gigs I'll be playing this year with the band. Kimberley at fat class says I should aim for two stone's loss at least.'

'Yes, and the company she works for will rely on you trying to reach that unattainable, unnatural you for the next

God-knows-how-many years – with a gap for gaining in between – that assures them a nice, even profit to the end of your days,' said Beth.

'Throw those cursed scales away,' I said. 'A healthy attitude is the most important thing. Be grateful for the body you have now. Don't spend years hating it, it's such a waste of precious time.'

I thought of Greta and sighed. I missed her wisdom and inspiration.

'Mum, you are so different since you came back from Greece,' Sal said, 'isn't she, Beth?'

Beth nodded. 'And you're looking good – revived. I hope I look half as good as you do now when I'm your age.'

'Oh, you'll both surpass anything I've got when that time comes,' I smiled proudly. 'I've raised two beautiful, confident and independent young career women. My work here is done. Now, how would you both feel if I told you we're thinking of going back there to live?'

David looked surprised. 'We are?'

'Don't worry, David,' Sal said, laughingly thrusting the polythene bag she had been holding at me. 'She's not done here yet. I need my trousers taking up.'

As Sal and David went laughing into the living room, Beth sidled up to me.

'Mum,' she said. 'I meant it when I said you look better than I've seen you in ages. I don't know what it is, but something is different. And it's brilliant. Give me some of it!'

It was true, I felt better in my own skin than I had in ages. It wasn't about my weight – I had no clue what that was any more. It wasn't about the size of my jeans, I just felt different. Although, I was eating fresher, healthier foods than before. If Greta had taught me anything, it was to love the skin I was in and be grateful for every day. Yet, despite the new me, David still hadn't been able to make love to me. There was just one trick left up my sleeve. Somehow, I had to have David again, at last. I owed it to myself to feel desired again. Besides, I couldn't stand another month without sex. Just that morning I had put on a low cut top and raced to the door to sign for a parcel, telling myself enough was enough – if the man even remotely flirted with me it was going to be his lucky day. One thing was for sure; I wasn't the sad, under-confident person David had married any more. However, when the toothless old codger had gone, I cursed myself for even thinking of being unfaithful. What was happening to me? Every little thing made me think about sex these days. I was going nuts! Ooh, nuts . . .

Later that evening when the girls had gone home, I turned to David, who was snoozing on the sofa as I watched TV.

'David,' I said, nudging him gently. 'I really fancy a brandy tonight. Would you nip out for some cola?'

He sighed loudly before lifting his head. 'For Pete's sake, what time is it?' he asked.

'Ten past eight.'

'Oh, Christ Bernice, I was just settling in for the evening. Do I have to?'

'Yes,' I said.

He sucked his teeth and sighed. 'Anything for a quiet life,' he said. 'I guess I could get a few beers myself. Pass me my wallet.'

There was little time to lose. The drive to the shop would take David all of ten minutes. That morning while he was at work I had spent two hours inflating a small paddling pool in the garage before filling it with twenty five large cartons of custard that I'd ordered from a local wholesaler. I knew he never put his car away until last thing at night and I'd hidden the remote to be sure. All I had to do now was leave the remote on the windowsill with a note, get on my bikini, down a large, neat brandy from a bottle I had stashed in there, dive in and wait.

The custard was gloopy, squelchy and freezing cold.

'This better be worth it,' I said to my second large glass of brandy, before downing it in one. He was taking a very long time to come back, but that was okay. I was funny, sassy and flirty again. If nothing else, at least we'd have a good giggle.

It was a good twenty minutes before I heard David's car pull up, just as a text alert on my mobile phone went off. No point in trying to read it now, my hands were immersed in custard.

The engine died and I heard the car door open, before footsteps and the sound of the back door banging shut. I held my breath, imagining David reading my note as I waited for him to join me:

Open the garage NOW! I have a surprise for you.

There was a second car coming up the drive. A second engine died and a second car door opened. Oh shit!

I dived out of the paddling pool and stood in front of it, custard-covered and freezing as the electronic garage door clicked and slowly rolled open.

'Bernice, is that you?'

It was Mr Taylor from next door, looking shocked. Just like Mrs Taylor, who was still sitting in the passenger seat of their car, staring at me, covering her mouth with her hand. Their teenage son, Mikey, broke the terrible silence.

'Bahahahahahaha!'

Behind Mr Taylor's car stood David, holding the remote control to the garage out.

'I . . . er . . . was just lending Tony my trolley jack,' he said.

'And I was just . . . er . . . making a trifle.'

With that, I took to my heels, racing past Tony without daring to look in the car at his wife and son, and dived inside the back door where I promptly lost my footing – what with all the slippery custard on my feet – and slid onto my arse with a slap.

Pushing the door shut with my feet, I took myself quickly upstairs and started the shower, knowing hot water wasn't going to be necessary. The heat from my face would do it. As I crept up to the bedroom window to watch the neighbours' car reverse away down the drive, I spied my mobile phone on the dressing room table. *Wait a minute. Didn't that just go off in the garage?*

I picked it up and examined it. Yep, it was definitely my phone. Before I had chance to think about it any further, David came into the room.

'What on earth were you doing?' he said with a grin, clearly knowing full well what I'd been doing. By now though, I had other things on my mind.

'Where is your phone?'

He put his hand in his jacket pocket and pulled it out. 'Here, why? You didn't send me any warning messages.'

Pulling on my robe from the back of the bedroom door, I walked past him and headed downstairs again.

'What's wrong?' he said, following me.

Wordlessly, I stepped over the custardy mess on the floor by the back door and headed back out to the garage with David at my heels all the way.

'What is it?' he said, sounding more and more anxious now. 'You look angry, Binnie. What's wrong?'

I walked over to the paddling pool, my eyes searching the shelves on the back wall. There was a phone there somewhere, I knew it.

'Binnie, what is wrong?'

'I heard something when I was in here earlier,' I told him.

'What were you doing in here anyway?' he asked, looking down at the pool full of custard.

'I think you can guess,' I said, turning my attention to the cupboard on the far wall that was filled with gardening chemicals. I opened it.

'Binnie,' David said, racing across to stand in front of it. 'Come on, let's get messy together.' He tried to kiss me but I pushed him away, feeling a growing revulsion in my stomach.

'Let me open that cupboard please,' I said.

'What for? There isn't anything in there but garden stuff.'

I pushed him aside and opened the cupboard door. There on the shelf was a small, cheap-looking mobile phone. And it was lit up with a message. I picked it up.

'Well,' I said. 'Will you look at this? It's a little phone and there's a message on it, too.'

David gulped and looked redder than I'd been in front of Tony Taylor a short while before. 'I wonder who that belongs to then?'

'Perhaps Sal or Beth left it here?' he said weakly.

I held it up and saw the first part of the message, highlighted in neon blue at the bottom of the screen underneath the day's date:

80210: Hi there David, JACINTA is soooo wet for you right now.

I didn't have to look at David's face to know he was in a cold panic, turning another series of great excuses over in his brain. Only this time he and I both knew I wasn't going to wait to hear them. Without a word, I took off out of the garage towards the back door.

'Binnie!' he shouted. 'Wait! I can explain.'

'How many times do I have to tell you, David?' I shouted over my shoulder. 'My name is Bernice!'

I opened the back door and headed indoors, without turning back.

Chapter Thirty-One

Girls, when life hands you melons . . . wahey!

'Well,' said Chris, turning to me from the driver's seat of his car. 'What happened?'

I turned to look at him, my heart heavy but my head full of hope, optimism and countless possibilities. Whatever happened now, I wasn't going to let myself be embarrassed to tell him the truth. Just like I wasn't going to be ashamed to tell everyone my ex-husband was addicted to porn – a virtual adulterer. I had set the boundaries about what constituted trust in our relationship and he had crossed them.

'I told him it was time for him to get off,' I said, ending my brief explanation for why I was no longer Mrs David Dando . . . 'But I did it with *meraki*.'

I waited for the look of surprise, the 'Aren't you the frigid one?' 'Is that it?' 'Is that all he did?' But the only thing Chris said was, 'Eh?'

'*Meraki*,' I repeated. 'With all of my soul and all of my

love. Because I do love him, honestly. And I don't owe anybody an explanation for the mistakes I make in my life except myself and my daughters. What they know is that their mother wasn't afraid to change direction in her life when the old way was sucking away all her happiness. I can pat myself on the back, proud not to have just told them that but to have showed them too.'

'And what about David?'

'It's not all his fault. I married in haste. All my life I've been getting into, and then trying to hold on to, impossible relationships. I thought I needed that one person to make me feel special because I felt unworthy of people who might actually value me. I was a product of my past, wrapped up in the dizzy, happy buzz of knowing that someone wanted to marry me. I based my own sense of self-worth on his being prepared to marry me. I'd been moulding myself to fit David and him to me, trying to force what I thought were the two final pieces in the jigsaw of my life together, to complete me. But they were the wrong pieces. David isn't all bad, but he's bad for me. I want to be myself again. When I'm with David, I'm so preoccupied with trying to change things I can't ever fix that I always forget to stop and dip my toes in the Aegean.'

'I think I get everything except that last bit.'

'You know, really stopping to watch, feel and be in my life. I mean, it's passing us all by, Chris. With him, I wasn't living authentically,' I said. 'I wasn't really experiencing every moment. And I need to do that, with every part of my being. I need to be me, Bernice Annabel Anderson. Not Mrs David Dando. I know that now. I don't need to be somebody's wife to consider myself somebody. I had to stop and make a promise to me to put my own happiness first. I have spent a lifetime believing I need that one person to save me. But it was me that needed to save me, all along.'

'And you're sure leaving someone you love is the right thing to do?'

I was surprised, and a little cheered to see him say nothing of the rights and wrongs of my leaving David because of his porn use. I hadn't expected this from the first man I explained it to.

'Chris, I had no job and no idea what I wanted to do with my life,' I went on. 'Yet the last time I left here I thought the world was full of possibilities again and I felt really good about myself. That all disappeared the minute we hit the tarmac at East Midlands Airport. I know now that this is where I want to be. Do you know, I spent seven years convincing myself I wanted everything David did? I don't want to do that anymore. Who knows what time I have left? All I know for sure is that from this day onwards I want to make my own choices, not someone else's.'

'Wow,' said Chris, scratching his head. 'That is profound. Where has all this come from?'

'It's come from me having a desire to get out and enjoy my own life, my own way for the first time in forty one years,' I said.

'Who gave you permission to do all that?' he joked.

I stared out the car window to the sea, blinking back tears. 'My dad,' I replied.

'Well,' he said. 'I never met the man, but he sounds a decent bloke.'

'He was,' I agreed.

'Good for you. I think – although I confess I do feel terrible for David. He's pretty cut up, poor guy.'

'Well, it's understandable you feel that way, he is your best friend,' I said.

'I hope you're right,' he replied. 'Because I feel like I am helping him lose his wife forever by giving you a place to stay.'

'No, you're not. This is all my doing and he's grateful I have a friend to go to.'

'He said that?'

'Yes, he did, in the end.'

'Although,' I went on, 'if I'm honest, it was you packing up your life and heading out here that inspired me to try it too.'

'Yes, but I was running away,' he said seriously.

'It turned out okay in the end though, didn't it?' I said. 'You seem happy now.'

His clear blue eyes fell and I knew he was looking at my mouth; maybe allowing himself to consider what might have been with us for a moment. A meeting at a different time, in a different place, before David and I had ever laid eyes on each other. But that time had been missed and was gone forever which was, in some ways, a great shame. I remembered the last time I'd been here and that last night of the party, just before I'd jumped on stage to meet David. Thanking Chris for his honesty in telling me he loved me and whispering in his ear the reason why I'd needed to know right at that moment, just before going back to my husband, whether he'd been having an affair with Ginger.

'I just wanted to know there are still some good men in the world.'

Chris was a good man and an attractive one, but he was David's best friend; I was still in love with David and had been, albeit briefly, his wife.

'Yes,' Chris replied finally. 'I'm happier now than I've ever been. Plus there is always the possibility of brighter things to come.'

'Certainly a lot of sunnier days,' I grinned.

'Yes, Greece has lots of those.'

'And I've got a lot of Blondie songs to sing with Adonis.'

'Nudeoke?'

'You know it. There's nothing like belting out, '*Your hair is beautiful*' to a man in the buff.'

He coughed, which I knew was to disguise a guilty chortle.

'And you have your kayaking,' I reminded him.

'Ah, yes,' he smiled. 'Maybe I'll even let you come with me again, if you promise to do as you're told this time. But what about your house in England?'

'I'm just going to let it every summer, and the girls are over the moon to have somewhere for holidays. It's only a couple of hours on the plane. I'll still see my mother and be around when she needs me. I'm not deserting my family. I'm daring to take a detour of personal discovery – just because I can.'

'Well,' he said. 'For what it's worth, I think you're doing the right thing.'

'Oh, yes. For once I think I am. I'm going to have to find work and look for something a bit bigger than your place though, no offence.'

He laughed and put the key in the ignition.

'Chris,' I continued. 'Can you drop me off at the stables instead of back at the apartment? I have a little business proposition to discuss with Michaela.'

He paused. 'You do?'

'Yes, I do,' I answered. 'I've been going over some plans for the new Meraki Equine Therapy Centre for Women.'

'I didn't know there was one of those here?'

'There isn't . . . yet,' I grinned.

'Don't you need some kind of qualification for therapy?' he asked.

'I guess so,' I said. 'The kind you can get online – unless you're a horse. They just seem to have the knack. On the other hand, maybe I'll be the singer I always secretly wanted to be. Don't stop me, Chris, I'm on a roll. Somehow, some way, I'm going to make this, or something like this, happen. I've told the girls and, okay, they're worried about me right now, but I told them I've never felt freer. They're happy if I'm happy. And do you know what? I know I'm going to be; I just need to take one day at a time.'

'That's a lot of big decisions in such a short time,' Chris replied, looking thoughtful. 'But you seemed so sorted when you left here. You were changed. Why did you go back?'

'I think it was because he'd made such a fuss in front of everyone, I felt I just had to give him another chance. The people-pleaser in me kicked back in again,' I replied truthfully. 'But I realised quite early on that I'm not that person any more. I think in my heart I always knew I would end up back here, I just had to take that one, last trip home to be absolutely sure.'

Chris started the engine.

No more looking back. Only onwards from now on. New beginnings.

I sighed. 'You know, I think I'm going to be enjoying my own company for a while. Sure, everyone craves love in their life but the first place it has to come from is within. If I can't love me, no-one can. If I can't be myself, I'm failing to do whatever it is I came to earth to do. Because there is only ever going to be one me.'

'Well, that is philosophical,' said Chris. 'Who wrote it?'

'That,' I told him with a satisfied smile, 'is a page from the journal of my life.'

'Oh, sure, I've read a few bits of that book,' he laughed. 'It's a page turner, for sure.'

'Chris,' I said, putting a hand on his arm. 'Could you wait here a minute?'

'Of course,' he said. 'Why? Did you forget something?'

'No,' I said. 'I just need to go dip my toes in the Aegean.'

He reached over to pat my hand and smiled. 'Sure, you go ahead,' he said. 'I'll wait for you.'

Dear Facebook friends and family. I'd like it to be known that I am no longer Mrs David Dando. I am no longer Mrs anything. I am Bernice Annabel Anderson. Free-spirited and horsing around daily in the Aegean with meraki – which means putting a bit of myself into it. *SPLASH*

Epilogue

Got a nude life in Greece, making lots of
nude friends. I feel like a nude woman! It's
Blondieoke this evening. Come on down!

'I keep having these recurring dreams. A sea of two
hundred, beautiful, smiling faces watch me take to the
stage. But wait! I'm not wearing any clothes!'

The sea of two hundred beautiful, smiling faces erupted
into a crashing wave of laughter. Of course I wasn't
wearing any clothes. Neither were they. Who needs pants
on a twinkling, balmy evening on the Aegean coast?

'It's true, you lovely, absurdly generous people, we are
living a common dream tonight. Only this time, it's for a
fantastic cause.'

I pointed to my team welcome of disciples; Greta,
Hughie, Linda, Michaela and Chris, walking amongst the
crowd shaking collecting tins, every one of them as naked
as the day they were born except for a pink ribbon on
their wrists, ankles – or, in Hughie's case – tied around
the family jewels.

'I've come bearing gifts, Bernice,' he'd chortled with his

now familiar wink, on arrival at the beach bar earlier that evening. Greta and Hughie were here for the concert and another adventure holiday. Linda had come out to join me six months earlier, moving into Michaela's home, before initiating a welcome move into Michaela's life. I hadn't seen that one coming.

Every islander, just-returned members of Gelle, breast cancer survivors, their friends and family members present were waving euros, all ready to pour in cash for the cause. In the centre of the crowd, I saw Linda greet Eydis and her new girlfriend with a hug. Everyone was so happy. Even Ginger, who was running about carrying cocktails to and from the bar with Edvard; except, she'd insisted on them both wearing aprons.

'Empty your pockets!'' I shouted to the cheering crowd. And then, 'Oops, you haven't got any pockets!'

'Ye'll be telling us to shake wur tits next!' Greta shouted, to more raucous laughter from the crowds.

'Amazing,' Adonis said into my ear. 'We should do this every year, pretty laydee.'

'Yes, let's,' I replied.

He nodded to the band, who started up with a familiar, Blondie riff. Looking back with pride, I smiled at my beautiful, multi-talented, butt-naked guitarist, Sal, before stepping up to the mike again.

'Uh huh, make me toniiiiiiiiiiiiiiiiight. Toniiiiiiiiiiiiiiiiight! Make it right!'

It was one year since my move to Greece. One year since The New Mrs Dando turned into the Not Mrs Anything. Life couldn't have felt better if I'd fallen in love with somebody new. But then, I had. I'd fallen in love with me.

To all the lovely ladies and the equally lovely men,

Put on that favourite album from your youth, march to
the kitchen henceforth, open the drawer – you know
the one – with the wooden spoon inside it! Pull out that
spoon-cum-microphone, turn up the music and sing your
heart out. Use nothing less than the power of the top of
your voice.
Now, be thankful.
You're a legend in your own lifetime.
And there will never be another you.

BC	5/15